Naughty

ALSO BY VELVET

The Black Door
Seduction
Betrayal

Naughty

A Black Door Novel

Velvet

ST. MARTIN'S GRIFFIN ⚹ NEW YORK

NAUGHTY. Copyright © 2009 by Velvet. All rights reserved. Printed in the United States of America. For information, address St. Martin's Press, 175 Fifth Avenue, New York, N.Y. 10010.

www.stmartins.com

Library of Congress Cataloging-in-Publication Data

Velvet.
   Naughty : a black door novel / Velvet.—1st ed.
       p. cm.
   ISBN-13: 978-0-312-37584-3
   ISBN-10: 0-312-37584-0
   1. African American women—Fiction.   2. Spouses—Fiction.   I. Title.
   PS3622.E555N38 2009
   813'.6—dc22

                                                        2008035894

10   9   8   7   6   5   4   3   2

Acknowledgments

Naughty is my fourth baby, and as with any birth there's a dedicated team assisting with the process. So, I'd like to thank the people who helped with the gestation of this book.

Monique Patterson, one of the best editors in the business! And the rest of the St. Martin's Press pros who helped bring this baby to life—Matthew Shear, John Murphy, Katy Hershberger, and the rest of the team. Though she's no longer at St. Martin's Press, I'd like to thank Kia DuPree for her assistance!

To my agent, Sara Camilli, who's been in the delivery room with me from book one!

To my family and friends, you guys know how to coach a sister along with encouraging words when she can't see the forest for the trees! Without all of you (too many to list), I would be in a private suite at Bellevue . . . LOL!

And to the readers, book clubs, booksellers, Web sites, and other media outlets, thanks for spreading the word about the Black Door series! Your help has truly been appreciated!

Now it's time to conceive another novel, so let me assume the position (fingers poised over the keyboard . . . LOL!) and get to work!

Much Love,

Velvet

Naughty

1

"PLEASE LET me just look at it," Jessica pleaded, tugging on Chad's arm.

Chad pulled away, and moved his body over to the edge of the sofa. "No," he said adamantly.

Jessica was a woman with determination, and wasn't about to take "no" for an answer, she wanted him badly, and would do and say anything to get her way, especially tonight. She hadn't seen Chad in months, since they had broken up, and was desperate for some much-needed sex. She had lured him over to her apartment under the guise of being a damsel in distress, telling him that there had been an attempted break-in, and that she needed her locks changed. He had insisted that she call a locksmith. She told him that she did, but couldn't get anybody to come out on a Sunday. She feigned tears, saying that she was afraid and pleaded with him to change her locks. Being the kindhearted guy that he was, he finally agreed. Before he got there, Jessica jimmied the locks with a screwdriver and cut the security chain. She then drank a few glasses of red wine to get in the mood, and waited for Chad to arrive. Now that he was there, her plan wasn't going as smoothly as she had hoped. During their relationship, their sex life was explosive and they fucked at least three times a day. Jessica missed Chad's dick, and wanted to relive old times. "Oh, baby, don't be like that. All I want to do is have a look and say hello," she purred, scooting closer to him and resting her hand on his thigh.

After Jessica had abruptly ended their relationship, Chad swore that he would never fall back into her arms. She had said at the time that she wanted her freedom, and didn't want to be committed anymore. He was deeply in love with her, and the breakup broke his heart, but he had walked away like a man. Now she was trying to lure him back, and he was confused. "Look, Jessica, you're the one who said that you didn't want a relationship, so what's with this attempted seduction?"

She ran her hand up to his crotch area and rested it on top of his full mound. "I was wrong," she began, gently massaging his package. "I want you back. We were so good together," she said, increasing her pace.

Chad couldn't deny their chemistry. She had one hell of a tight pussy, and he missed filling her up with his rod. He didn't want to give in to her so easily, but she was making his dick hard. He hadn't been laid in weeks, and was horny as hell. He unzipped his pants and took out the head of his penis. "Is this what you want to see?"

Jessica looked down and swallowed hard. The tip was big, and beautiful. Just looking at it made her mouth water. She didn't say a word, but leaned over and licked him. She flicked her tongue back and forth, the way he liked it.

Chad began rotating his hips. She was driving him crazy. He wanted to fuck now. He knew that she was manipulating him, but didn't care. All he cared about at the moment was getting laid. He took the shaft of his dick all the way out so that she could deep-throat him. She was an expert at giving head, and he missed her mouth. "Yeah, that's it, baby, don't stop," he moaned with pleasure.

She bobbed her head up and down, faster and faster. She could feel the tip of his dick hitting the back of her throat, but she didn't gag. She just continued sucking until she tasted his sweet pre-cum.

"Stop," he breathed. "I want to be inside of you," he said, laying her back on the sofa and pulling down her jeans.

Jessica wiggled out of her panties, kicked one leg over the back of the sofa, and gapped her legs wide open, inviting him in.

Chad quickly dropped his pants to the floor and eased in between her thick thighs—

The phone rang before Naomi could finish reading the spicy love scene. She dog-eared the page and picked up the receiver. "Hello," she said in a breathy voice.

"Were you exercising?" Kennedy asked, picking up on her friend's lack of oxygen.

"Girl, I was reading *Auld Lang Syne*, and the phone rang as soon as I got to the juicy part," she explained, sounding slightly upset.

"I see you're living vicariously through the pages of a book again," Kennedy teased. Naomi's husband, Jacob, usually worked late or was MIA on an overnight business trip, which translated to a love life that was also MIA.

"Unfortunately since my husband spends more time making money than making love, I gotta get my thrills where I can," she said with a chuckle, trying to make light of her loveless marriage. "But it's not like you're getting any either," she shot back defensively.

Kennedy hadn't been on a date in several months, not since she broke up with Lance the cop. They met one night when she was speeding down the Long Island Expressway. He pulled her over and instead of giving her a ticket, he gave her his telephone number and made her promise to call. Checking out his pecs through the blue, city-issued uniform, she thought, why not? Lance was five feet eight inches of solid muscle and his face wasn't bad to look at either. He was chocolate brown with ripe,

succulent lips. She was weak for a brother with a delectable, kissable mouth. After her first call a few days later, it didn't take long
for her to taste those lips. Their sexual chemistry was sizzling. On
her days off, Lance would come over at night and ignite a fire
within her that would last until the wee hours of the morning.
But the flame began to fizzle when she tried to move their relationship beyond the bedroom. Kennedy was an international
flight attendant who traveled the world for mere pennies. She had
companion passes and invited Lance on trips to Paris, Tahiti, and
even to a four-star resort in South Africa, all of which he declined,
saying the only place he was interested in traveling was south of
her navel. Kennedy wanted more than sex, but as usual she had
fucked him too soon, and now all he wanted to do was screw. Realizing that she was never going to get a commitment out of
Lance, she ended the relationship as quickly as it began and
vowed to reclaim her virginity until the proverbial Mr. Right
showed up with the key to her chastity belt.

"Have you started reading *Auld Lang Syne* yet?" Naomi
asked, referring to their current book club selection.

Kennedy hadn't even cracked the spine of the book. She
leaned over, picked up the novel from the nightstand, and
dusted the cover with the sleeve of her robe. The jacket looked
interesting enough; an attractive couple dressed in black tie was
locked in an intense embrace. The title was scrolled in gold foil.
In smaller script the words "SHALL OLD ACQUAINTANCES NEVER BE
FORGOTTEN" was written across their bodies. "I haven't had a
chance yet. I've been flying so much that when I do have extra
time, all I want to do is sleep."

"Speaking of flying, was Mr. Cutie Patootie on your flight tonight?"

Kennedy had completely put the Mystery Man out of her
mind. The first time she had seen him was a month ago when he
boarded a flight from New York to Johannesburg. He had sat in
first class, which was her station. With the pastel pink pages of

the *Financial Times* covering the lower half of his body, she barely caught a glimpse of his face as she asked his beverage preference before they took flight. Once the plane reached a cruising attitude of thirty thousand feet, she returned to ask whether he wanted veal with rosemary and chive risotto or salmon on a bed of field greens. When he looked up from the newspaper to answer, what greeted her was a pair of sexy, smokey hazel eyes on reddish-brown cinnamon skin and a goatee framing a pair of lips that were even more succulent than her last lover's. "Salmon, please," he answered in a deep voice. Her knees almost buckled. She knew it wasn't the air pocket they had just passed through but the sexy sound of his baritone voice. Giving no indication of attraction, she remained professional and returned with his meal. The rest of the flight was uneventful as he read one newspaper after the other and she serviced the other passengers. Kennedy had seen him once thereafter but he never even looked twice in her direction. Today's flight should have been his usual bimonthly trip, but he hadn't been on board.

"No," she answered with disappointment dripping off the one and only syllable.

"Did he ever say anything to you?"

"You mean besides, 'Excuse me, miss, may I have another pillow?'"

Naomi cracked up laughing. "You know what I mean," she said, after recovering from her laugh attack. "Did he ask for your number?"

"He probably thinks I'm a fixture of the plane. Most first-class passengers have that sense of entitlement."

"You're right, they are an elitist bunch," Naomi agreed. "But I'm sure he's checked out how you rock that uniform," she countered.

"Girl, I'm not thinking about that man," Kennedy said, picking up the *Boiler Room* DVD. The movie was old, but she didn't care. "I've got to go because I have a date with Mr. Diesel."

"Who's that? Did you meet him at work? Was he on your flight tonight?" Naomi quizzed, anxious to know who this new man was.

Kennedy chuckled, and then said, "Diesel as in Vin, the actor." She absolutely loved looking at the man.

"Oh. It's going to be another Blockbuster night, huh?" Naomi asked, finally catching on.

"Yep," she replied, sliding the disc into the player. "I'll talk to you tomorrow," Kennedy said before hanging up.

"Okay, enjoy your movie." After Naomi hung up, she looked at the clock on the nightstand, wondering where her husband might be.

IT WAS after ten o'clock and Jacob should have been home by now. Naomi started to call his cell number, but didn't. He had scolded her too many times about blowing up his phone. He told her that when he was out entertaining clients, it was embarrassing to have to keep answering calls from his wife, as if he were a little boy. Naomi knew Jacob was a workaholic when they first met. He was a man on a mission to succeed, and it was his tenacity and drive that had turned her on, but now his late nights were getting old. She missed having sex on a regular basis, like in the beginning of their relationship. She still desired her husband and remembered the day they met as if it were yesterday.

She had been a carefree flight attendant at the time. Jacob Reed usually sat in row two, seat C, the aisle seat. He was six feet four inches tall, so the extra leg room along the aisle was an added benefit. Naomi was attracted to him the moment she laid eyes on him. He had a sweet, schoolboy quality. His mahogany skin was always shaved to perfection with no hint of razor bumps. He wore rectangle, tortoiseshell glasses that rested across the keen bridge of his nose. He kept his hair closely cropped, showing only a whisper of a natural wave pattern. The stark white shirts he wore underneath his navy suits were usually monogrammed at the cuffs with the letters J. R. It was easy to surmise that he was some type of executive.

Initially they played that coy game of cat and mouse, but his incessant ringing of the flight attendant buzzer was a dead giveaway that he was interested in more than the customary in-flight service. Naomi would sashay over, swaying her hips through the narrow aisle, and suggestively ask if she could be of service. He would smile shyly, saying that he meant to press the overhead light. This went on for months, until he finally asked for her telephone number. They began to date and she learned that Jacob was a certified public accountant and partner with Kirschner Gross, one of New York's largest accounting firms. Not only was the brother handsome, he was making serious bank. He lived in a richly appointed duplex loft in Tribeca and drove a sleek Jaguar. She would often meet him in London after he tied up a business meeting. They would shop along Bond Street, and then stroll over to his suite at the Sanderson, one of Ian Schrager's five-star hotels. They would order champagne and oysters from room service, and then service each other the entire night. Exhausted from a lust-filled night, they would lounge in bed until noon, before repeating the previous evening, kiss for kiss. When Jacob proposed marriage with a four-carat diamond solitaire on a weekend jaunt to Napa Valley, Naomi was ecstatic and as bubbly as the sparkling wines they were sampling. They were truly in love. And not only was Jacob handsome, he was financially secure as well, so Naomi wouldn't have to worry about money ever again.

Naomi had grown up in a lower-middle-class family, and though they were not dirt poor, they didn't have frivolous luxuries either. She had always dreamed of making enough money to indulge herself, which she did from her modest salary. But marrying Jacob would put her in an entirely different income bracket. He wasn't a millionaire, but made enough money to spoil her with diamond trinkets and designer goods. She envisioned a life of skipping across the pond accompanying Jacob on business trips to London and stopping off in Paris to do some serious shopping. But the dream was just an illusion.

The second she became pregnant after their first year of marriage, Jacob insisted that Naomi quit flying, which she really didn't have a problem with. He made more than enough money to keep her in first class. Her plan was to resume traveling once the baby was old enough to fly. And when the baby went to preschool, she had planned on starting an interior design business. Naomi had a knack for decorating from studying endless house and garden magazines, and had planned on converting the library in the penthouse into the baby's room, but Jacob had other plans.

One Sunday, they fueled up the Jag and went on an early-morning drive on the Long Island Expressway. After nearly forty minutes, they exited and drove through an area of Long Island that Naomi had never seen. She couldn't help but admire the manicured lawns and spiraling driveways that led to majestic mansions, some with Corinthian columns, others inspired by modern architectural designs.

Jacob drove down a tree-lined road and pulled into the circular driveway of a stately-looking home.

"I didn't know you had friends on the island."

"I don't." He smiled slyly and parked.

Puzzled, she asked, "Then whose house is this?"

Jacob didn't say a word, just got out, walked over to her side of the car, and opened the door.

"What are you doing?" she asked as Jacob reached for her hand. Since Jacob didn't know the family who lived in the house, Naomi wasn't about to stretch her legs in some stranger's driveway.

"Come on. Don't you want to see the house?" There was that sly smile again.

"Stop playing, Jacob, I'm not in the mood for trespassing. Would you please tell me whose house this is, before someone calls the cops?"

"It's ours, Naomi. I closed on it last week. I wanted to surprise you," he said, nearly pulling her out of the car.

Surprised? She was shocked. The last thing Naomi wanted was a house in the 'burbs. She was a city girl, and the complacency of the suburbs had no appeal to her. "Jacob, why didn't you discuss this with me before making such a major purchase?"

"Like I said, I wanted to surprise you. What's the matter? Don't you like it?" he asked, waving his arms at the monstrosity of a house. "Come on inside. Let me show you around," he said, taking a set of keys from the breast pocket of his blazer.

As he unlocked the massive door, she stood there feeling as if her world had changed right before her eyes. Once Naomi walked into the marble foyer, she realized it had changed forever. Visions of strolling their baby along Madison Avenue and having high tea at the Peninsula with her girlfriends began to dissipate as they toured the mini-mansion. Though she had always wanted to live in a million-dollar home, she preferred to live in their million-dollar apartment in the city. At least in the city, she'd be in close proximity to her friends, and could easily get out and have dinner with them when Jacob was working late, but now she'd be another suburbanite who only came into Manhattan on special occasions.

"This can be the baby's room, since it's near the master suite," Jacob announced, walking into a room the size of a studio apartment. "It's large enough to set up a play area once he's old enough," Jacob said, pointing to a nook near the back of the room.

"It's nice," was all Naomi could say. She wasn't the baking-cookies-Stepford-Wife type. "Jacob, it's really a nice house, but . . ."

"Nice," he interrupted. "It's well over seven figures of *nice*!"

"Don't get upset. All I mean is that I never planned on living in the suburbs. I thought we would continue to live in the loft. There's more than enough room to add a nursery," she said, trying to plead her case.

"This is not the suburbs, Naomi. It's Old Westbury. There's a distinct difference. Anyway, the school system is superb here, and I have no intention of raising a child of mine in the middle of a busy metropolis," he said in no uncertain terms.

Realizing that this was a done deal, and there wasn't any sense in arguing the point since he had already bought the house, she walked over and hugged Jacob around the waist. "Thank you, honey." Naomi could feel the tension in his back as he stood stiffly in her embrace. To clear the air, she reached up and kissed him on the lips. *"Thank you, honey,"* she repeated, this time emphasizing every word.

Jacob looked down at her and said, "You're welcome."

She tried to hug him closer. "Honey, don't be upset." But her slightly protruding pregnant belly stood between them.

"I'm not upset. Just disappointed that you don't appreciate what a wonderful house this is. Do you know how many women would jump at the chance to live in this elite community? There was a time that our ancestors could only work in this type of neighborhood, and you're telling me that you'd rather live in the crowded city," he said with a tinge of sadness in his voice.

She stepped back and looked up into his sable brown eyes. "I appreciate this house and I appreciate you. This is more than I could have ever dreamed of. I would be honored to live here with you and our baby." She searched his eyes for any signs of doubt, and then asked, "You believe me, don't you?"

"Yes. Now let me show you the master suite." He turned and walked out the door.

The master suite was three times the size of the baby's room. The vaulted ceilings and ivory marble fireplace gave the room a romantic feeling. Naomi walked over by the French windows as the sun cast a radiant glow throughout the room. "This is where the bed should go," she said, becoming more comfortable with her new home.

Jacob looked at the nook by the window that she was pointing to and nodded. "That looks like a good place."

It must have been a combination of the pregnancy hormones, the room, and the warm sun, because suddenly her body began to heat up with an overwhelming sexual desire. She could feel her nipples harden beneath her turtleneck. She removed her sweater and tossed it on the window seat.

Jacob looked confused. "Why'd you take your top off?"

"Because I'm *hot*," she whispered in a naughty voice as she slipped out of her slacks. She patted the cushion of the window seat. "Come here."

Jacob began to walk slowly toward her. "Naomi, what are you doing?" he asked, looking at his wife clad only in her bra and panties.

"Come closer and you'll find out."

With Jacob within inches of her open legs, she reached out and began to unbuckle his belt. They always had enjoyed a steamy sex life, but ever since Jacob found out she was pregnant, he'd been treating her like a porcelain doll, afraid to touch her, as if she would shatter into a thousand pieces. It had been three weeks since they had last made love.

"Stop, Naomi." He pushed her hands away. "You're pregnant."

"I'm pregnant, not dead," she remarked and continued struggling with his belt until it was unbuckled. Pulling his hips forward, she unzipped his pants. "Jacob, I want to make love to you."

"I do too, but . . ."

Jacob stopped midsentence the moment her hand made contact with his sex. She began to massage him until she felt him grow beneath her touch. His pants dropped to the floor as she unleashed his member. Naomi lay back on the cushions of the window seat and removed her lace panties, then unhooked her matching bra. Jacob licked his lips at the sight of her luscious, enlarged nipples. He leaned over and began to suck her swollen breast like a newborn feasting at mealtime in the middle of the night. She arched her back as he slipped in between her naked thighs. Naomi let out a slight moan as Jacob slowly and gently entered her.

He stopped suddenly. "Am I hurting you?"

"No, baby. Please don't stop. Don't stop," she pleaded, grabbing his backside and pressing him deeper inside. With no further instruction needed, Jacob made love to her like never before.

THAT WAS NEARLY five years ago, she thought, and glanced over at the window seat where they had first christened the house. Naomi looked at the clock again. *Where the hell is he?* She picked up the cordless to call his cell phone, but put it down when she heard him walking up the stairs. Naomi threw back the covers, exposing her body in a sexy, black lace negligee. She folded her arms underneath her breasts for increased cleavage, hoping her husband wasn't too tired to notice her rack. The romance novel that she was reading had made her horny, and she wanted to experience the exact same passion as the characters in the book.

"You're still up?" Jacob asked nonchalantly as he entered the bedroom, totally ignoring Naomi.

"I was waiting up for you," she said in a low, sexy voice.

Her come-hither tone escaped him as he walked over to the closet without looking in her direction. "For what?"

She climbed out of bed, followed him to the large walk-in closet, and stood in the doorway, letting the light shine through the sheer silk fabric of the gown, exposing her naked body underneath. "So we could make love." Naomi put her hands on her hips and pouted. "Jacob, it's been weeks and we're *past* overdue."

He walked over to her and finally noticed her titties poking through the sheer negligee. He rubbed the back of his hand against her nipples, and then grabbed her by the waist. "You look great, baby." He gave her a quick peck on the cheek. "But I'm totally exhausted."

"What else is new?" She sighed heavily and crossed her arms in front of her chest. "It seems these days the only thing you have time for is work. I'm feeling neglected. Jacob, don't you find me attractive anymore?"

"Don't be silly, Naomi. I just said how great you look. I'm tired, that's all. Just give me a few hours of sleep." He pecked her on the cheek again. "I promise, by morning I'll be rested and ready to make up for lost times," he said, and walked past her into the bathroom to take a shower.

Realizing that she was beating a dead horse, Naomi relented and got back into bed. With the anticipation of morning love-making dancing through her mind, she finally fell asleep and dreamed about wild, uninhibited sex with her husband. But the dream turned into a nightmare when she awoke to an empty bed the next morning.

There on his pillow was a note saying, "Forgot about an early meeting. I'll make it up to you tonight. I promise. Love J.R."

She crumpled the note in one hand and tore the covers from around her body with the other. In an attempt to extinguish her lust-induced inferno, she stormed into the bathroom and turned on the shower. Naomi stepped into the icy-cold spray trying to cool her fire until Jacob could quench her desire.

3

"MR. REED, your wife is on line two," Jacob's assistant announced through the intercom.

"Charlotte, please tell her I'm heading to a meeting and I'll call her as soon as it's over," Jacob said into the speakerphone, gathering notes for his nine o'clock meeting.

"Yes, sir," his assistant said, before disconnecting the line.

The mere fact that Naomi was calling this early was a clear indication that she was beyond upset about the broken promise of early-morning loving. She hardly ever phoned before noon. She was usually too busy getting their four-year-old son, Noah, ready for preschool. He truly loved his wife, but his time these days was limited. Being a partner for Kirschner Gross, one of New York's leading accounting firms, was demanding. The firm had recently landed an important account. The client, Mira Rhone, CEO of FACEZ, a cosmetics conglomerate, was temperamental at best. She needed to be handled with kid gloves, so Jacob decided to oversee the account personally. Suddenly his regular ten-hour days increased to twelve, oftentimes fifteen, leaving the remaining nine to cram in quality time with his family, get in a little golf, some sleep, and little else. Jacob's strong work ethic was instilled into him by his parents. Though they were blue-collar workers, they worked hard and sacrificed to send their children to college. His parents wanted him and his sister to have opportunities in life that they never had. Jacob knew that he could've eased up on his work schedule, but he didn't. He had promised himself years ago that he would work hard until he had a few million dollars in the bank, so in the event anything ever happened to him, his family would always be secure. In the back of his mind he could still see his father working two jobs just to make ends meet, and he was determined never to struggle financially like his parents had done.

Charlotte buzzed again. "Mr. Reed, Ms. Rhone is here."

"Show her to the conference room. I'll be right there." Jacob retrieved the file on FACEZ from the credenza, gathered the remaining notes from his desk, and headed toward the door with the file tucked underneath his arm. Unbuttoning the suit jacket that was hanging on the back of the door, he put it on, smoothed down the front, and then adjusted his tie before leaving for the conference room. Mira was a sharp dresser, and he wanted to make sure that his appearance was up to par.

The offices of Kirschner Gross were state-of-the-art. Every workplace, from the executive offices to the five-by-six cubicles, was equipped with high-tech, flat-screen computer monitors. In contrast to the staunch, dimly lit atmosphere of the Old World accounting firms with their mahogany corridors and tucked leather furniture, Kirschner's environment was bright and airy with contemporary Scandinavian furnishings and precision track lighting. Located on an entire floor atop the Empire State Building, the office had commanding views of the city. The floor-to-ceiling windows of the conference room faced west and offered unobstructed panoramic views of New Jersey. Rivaling the commanding view was the room's focal point, an imported, twenty-foot, rectangular, teak conference table. Sleek swivel armchairs in butter-soft taupe leather complemented the table perfectly. Completing the look were numbered prints by renowned artist Romare Bearden hung throughout the room.

At the head of the table sat Mira Rhone, with her long legs crossed, talking on her sleek cellular phone. Mira's great-grandmother, Mirabella Rhone, the grande dame of the cosmetics industry, had transformed FACEZ from a cottage industry initially based in the UK into one of the world's premier manufacturers of makeup, skin care, hair care products, and fragrances.

In her late twenties, Mira epitomized the look of the industry. Her golden brown skin was a shade darker than her light brown eyes, which had only a hint of shadow on the lids. Her high cheekbones had only a dusting of blush and her pouty lips were brushed with just a touch of nude gloss. The "natural" look was flawless. Her coal black, wavy hair was tied back in a tight chignon at the nape of her neck. Dressed in a midnight blue, haute couture, pinstriped suit with the skirt cut right at the knee and a pair of navy sling backs, Mira was the perfect picture of sophistication.

"Yes, Oliver, I understand that production is on schedule for the adult line, but I want to be *ahead* of schedule," Mira stated unequivocally.

Jacob cleared his throat to indicate his presence, so that she would end her conversation, and they could begin their meeting.

Mira looked up in his direction and mouthed, "Just a moment."

He was irritated that she was sitting at the helm of the conference table, a spot reserved for partners. But based on her body language—reared back in the chair with her legs crossed—he could see that she had no intention of moving. Instead of making an issue out of the seating arrangement, he pulled out one of the side chairs, sat down, and waited for her to complete her call.

"Being ahead of schedule was GG's motto and I intend to keep up the tradition," Mira said, referring to her great-grandmother, who had passed away a year ago. "Oliver, we'll have to table this conversation until later," she said, looking over at Jacob, who was thumping his fingers on the table. Obviously he was getting impatient.

Jacob listened as she wrapped up her conversation and couldn't help but notice how poised and in control she was for a young woman, and her confidence turned him on. His dick began to twitch at the thought of fucking her. He had a secret crush on Ms. Rhone, but had yet to act on it. He had to play the "cool" card, and act professional. She gave no indication of interest in him outside of business, so he'd just have to bide his time until an opportunity presented itself.

"I apologize for the delay," Mira said, depressing the end button on her cell.

"Not a problem," he said, taking his mind out of the gutter and focusing back on business. He removed two copies of the company's balance sheet that offered a snapshot of FACEZ's financial state, and handed one to Mira.

"I wanted to meet with you this morning to discuss the financial health of the company," Mira said, taking the balance sheet. She paused for a few moments and glanced over the report.

"As you can see, the company's assets far outweigh the liabilities."

Mira nodded. "As I expected."

He continued. "The key revenue driver is the skin care line. Over the last two quarters, FACEZ has held a solid market position."

Mira nodded again, and then said, "When my great-grandmother moved from Jamaica to London in her twenties and started this company, with a single product, night cream for women, she had a clear vision to succeed, and I plan to take FACEZ further by expanding into the children's market with Baby FACEZ, a line of body products for kids."

"Well, the company is definitely on solid financial ground and is in an excellent position to expand." Jacob had to admire Mira's tenacity. She could have easily rested on the laurels of the company, sat back, and collected a fat check. But here she was forging ahead with a new product line, geared to a completely different market.

"That's exactly what I wanted to hear, because I already have our chemist working on new formulas," Mira said, recrossing her long, lean legs. "I'm planning a trip to our London office next Wednesday to speak with the board regarding increasing the start-up capital for Baby FACEZ." Since the company was founded in the U.K., the main office as well as the board was still located there. "I would like for you to go along to present the financial projections." Mira took a leather-bound agenda out of her briefcase. "That won't be a problem, will it?"

Actually, it was a major problem. Next Wednesday was Noah's fifth birthday, and Naomi was planning an all-out celebration with riding ponies, clowns from Circus World, and actors dressed like Tinky Winky, Dipsy, and the rest of the Teletubbies gang. Working late and leaving early she could understand, but missing their son's birthday party would be unforgivable. "Actually, Mira, next Wednesday is no good for me. Can we move the meeting to the following week?" Jacob wanted nothing more than to go on a business trip with Mira. Maybe then he could orchestrate a seduction plan, but as luck would have it, London was out of the picture—at least this time.

"That won't work for me." She thumbed through the calendar in her agenda. "I'm booked solid with meetings for the next month, so it'll have to be next week," she insisted.

He pondered the situation for a few seconds trying to come up with an amicable solution. Finally it hit him. "What if I have one of my senior associates accompany you and make the presentation?"

Mira sighed, as if frustrated. "I'd prefer it if you went instead.

It would make for a stronger case if a partner presented the financials."

"I assure you Nina James is more than qualified to make the presentation. Not only is she a CPA, but she's also a CVA and a CFE. Furthermore, I would not have someone on my team that was not capable of making a simple financial presentation," he stated adamantly.

Mira looked confused. "A what? What's a CVA?"

"A CVA is a certified valuation analyst and a CFE is a certified fraud examiner. So as you can see, her credentials are top-notch, and she's more than qualified."

"Well, I guess she'll do," she said, sounding unimpressed. "Have her call my office so we can review the agenda."

Relieved that he had won that round, Jacob offered, "You can meet Nina now. Her office is right down the hall."

Mira looked at her watch. "I can't. I have a ten o'clock and if I don't leave right now, I'll be late." Mira was a stickler for time and prided herself on rarely being tardy. She gathered her belongings and stood to leave.

Mira's height always took Jacob by surprise. She was at least five feet ten inches, and with heels on stood a little over six feet. She was beautiful, tall and lean, and could have easily been mistaken for a model, instead of the CEO of a major corporation. He reached out to shake her hand, and held it a little longer than he should have. Any skin-to-skin contact with Mira was better than none at all, and he got off on the cheap thrill. Finally, he dropped her hand and said, "I'll have Nina call your assistant this afternoon to hammer out the details."

"Thank you, Jacob." She smiled.

He followed closely behind as she walked to the door. "You are more than welcome." His eyes zeroed in on her petite ass. *I can't wait to get my dick inside of that pussy.*

Jacob had lost the lust that he once felt for his wife. Once he witnessed her pushing their son out of her vagina, his sexual desire for her faded as if it never existed. He had no idea that a pussy could stretch that far. Witnessing childbirth up close and personal had completely turned him off, and he didn't view his wife as a sex object anymore, now that she was a mother. He loved Naomi, but his dick went limp every time the picture of her outstretched vagina entered his mind. To quench his thirst for sex, Jacob had taken up fucking around on the side, but was careful not to have affairs under his wife's nose. He used his frequent business trips as an opportunity to get his rocks off.

"Mira, I look forward to accompanying you to London another time." He smiled slyly, thinking about his hidden agenda, and walked her to the bank of elevators.

MIRA HAD a ten o'clock meeting. It wasn't a typical business meeting, but was important nonetheless. She pulled her sleek silver 850 BMW into the parking garage of her building, parked in the designated slot, got out, and took the elevator up to her penthouse apartment. Mira raced through the door and made a beeline straight to the bedroom. She stripped off her suit, unraveled her tight bun, and hopped into the shower. Since she had showered only hours before, she did a quick run-through underneath the pulsating spray to refresh key areas. Mira toweled off, rubbed her body with one of FACEZ's scented oils, and went to her bureau. She pulled open her lingerie drawer, took out a white lace bodysuit, and put it on. She looked in the mirror and couldn't help but chuckle. *If my colleagues could see me now, they'd do a double take.*

Very few people knew about Mira's wild side. In public, she was the epitome of professionalism and class, but in private she was a raunchy slut. And to accompany the slutty look, she smeared her lips with a bright red lipstick—a color reserved strictly for the boudoir—slipped on a pair of six-inch white patent leather plat-forms, and then fluffed out her long hair, causing the waves to expand into an unruly mess. With her lioness look complete, Mira got into bed and positioned herself on top of the imported silk duvet. She propped her elbow up on one pillow and lay on her side. Mira's pose was that of a sex kitten waiting to be stroked.

She looked at the vintage timepiece on her wrist. It was ex-actly ten o'clock. Mira watched the second hand sweep down the dial, and thirty seconds past the hour, she heard the lock to the front door turn. Mira slid her legs open wide, and spread her lips into a come-hither grin, in anticipation of her visitor.

"My, my, don't you look like the picture of seduction, all dolled up like that?"

"Well"—Mira's smile broadened—"that is the plan." She patted the bed. "Come here. I've been craving you all morning."

"Is that a fact?"

"Yep." Mira nodded her head.

"Why? We were just together yesterday."

"I know, but I want more." She waved her hand and purred again, "Come here."

"Your appetite is insatiable."

"I know, and only you can quench it. Now get over here and give me a kiss," Mira demanded.

Sam slowly walked toward the bed and began removing arti-cles of clothing with each step.

Mira smiled, and couldn't help but remember the first time she had laid eyes on Sam. She was on her way home from a late-night meeting and got a flat on the LIE. Mira was versed in many things, but changing a tire wasn't one of them. She called AAA and waited for them to send out a tow truck. Forty minutes later, the truck pulled up and out stepped the most beautiful woman that Mira had ever seen. Samantha wore a pair of over-alls with a white wife-beater underneath. She had on a Yankees cap, with her long ponytail pulled through the hole in the back of the hat. Her appearance wasn't chic or fashionable. Just the opposite, but Mira found her sexy nonetheless. Sam's dark chocolate skin was as smooth as silk. Her features were exotic. Her eyes were slanted, her nose broad, and her lips were a combination of large and small—her top lip was thin, and the bottom one full. Mira later learned that Sam was half Polynesian and half Nigerian. She was statuesque with broad shoulders and thick legs.

Though Mira had had plenty of heterosexual relationships, she also enjoyed the company of women. She was bisexual, but didn't flaunt her sexual preferences, due in part to her great-grandmother. GG was from the old school, and would have never understood Mira's intimate relationships with women. GG thought the sun rose and set on her great-granddaughter, and Mira didn't want to dispel GG's illusion, so she kept her sexuality under wraps. Though GG had passed on, Mira still felt obligated to uphold her perfect image in public as homage to her great-grandmother.

That night, on the side of the road, Mira flirted nonstop with Sam to get a read on whether or not she was gay. Fortunately for her, Sam was a lesbian, and made no bones about it. The two exchanged numbers, and Mira promptly called the next day. At the time, Mira was engaged to be married to a successful businessman, but that didn't stop her from fucking Sam on the side. Her fiancé was too preoccupied with work to keep her happy in bed, so she found a replacement. Sam could lick pussy better than any man, and Mira quickly became addicted. She would call Sam at all hours of the day and night, begging her to come over and scratch her itch. Their lovemaking was so hot that Mira eventually called off her wedding—that was of course after GG had passed away—and began seeing Sam full-time.

Initially Sam loved pleasing Mira, but Mira's demands were becoming overwhelming. Mira expected Sam to drop everything to answer her booty calls, and as a result, Sam's business was beginning to suffer.

"You know, I can't keep rushing over here every time you call," Sam said, kissing Mira on the neck.

"And why not?" Mira asked, putting her arms around Sam's neck and pulling her down on the bed.

"Because I have a business to run. As a matter of fact, I had to decline a towing job in the Bronx to come over here," she said, sounding a little upset.

"If it's money you're worried about, I'll make up for your lost job," she said, planting a juicy kiss on Sam's lips.

Sam pulled away. "Mira, I don't want your money. I've worked long and hard to build my business. I've got three trucks now, and am working on buying a fourth one, so I need to service every job that comes in. Unfortunately, I didn't have my business handed down to me, and don't have the luxury of kicking back when I feel like it," she said, with a hint of disdain in her voice.

Mira didn't like the way Sam was talking to her, and wanted to set the record straight. "Look, Sam, I may have inherited my great-grandmother's company, but trust me, I don't 'kick back,'" she said, putting emphasis on the phrase, "whenever I feel like it. I work my ass off. GG left the company to me because she knew that I would take it to another level. I'm not fickle like my mother, who could care less about business. Fortunately, today my schedule is light, which is a rarity, and I thought maybe you'd be in the mood to come over and play, but I guess I was wrong." Mira sat up and crossed her arms in front of her chest, obviously upset.

"I do want to play. It's just that you can't expect me to drop everything whenever you call." She scooted closer and kissed Mira on the lips, trying to smooth things over. Sam truly enjoyed being with Mira and didn't want to ruin their morning lovemaking, especially after she'd blown off a client.

Mira was still pissed and didn't return Sam's kiss. She was used to being in control and didn't like being spoken to like *she* was the subordinate. All of her life, Mira had been in a leadership-type role. As a child she felt more like the parent than her mother, who was usually out partying or at home entertaining. Mira's mother Rose was wild and had Mira when she was only seventeen. Rose never acted like a mother, but an older sister, and treated her daughter like an adult, often leaving Mira to fend for herself. As a result Mira had to make grown-up decisions at an early age. Thus was born her controlling nature.

"Come on, baby, don't be mad," Sam said, picking up on Mira's sour disposition. Sam knew Mira's weak spot was her neck, and began slowly nibbling on her left earlobe, then trailed her tongue down to Mira's sweet spot. She started sucking, and didn't stop until she heard Mira's moans. Sam then slipped her hand in between Mira's legs, and unsnapped the crotch of her bodysuit. Unlike some men who had no clue how to find the clitoris, Sam knew exactly where it was and began rubbing Mira's.

"Oh, yeah, that's it, that's it!" Mira sang out. This was just what she had been waiting for, so she closed her eyes and gave in to Sam's touch.

Sam followed with her tongue, quickly brought Mira to a heated climax, and then started over again. She finger-fucked Mira and sucked on her clit until Mira squirted a light stream of cum in her face. Their lovemaking session went on for over an hour, until they were both exhausted and fell asleep.

Sam's beeper woke her up, and she looked at the time. It was late afternoon and she silently cursed herself for missing yet another tow. Although she had two other employees, she still had to drive to keep up with the demand. "I've got to be going," she said, picking up her clothes off the floor and putting them on.

"Oh, don't go. Now that I've had a nap, I'm ready for some more," Mira whined.

"Look, I've already missed two jobs. I'll call you later, but now I've got to run," Sam said, heading for the door.

"Well, if you get finished early, come by. You have the key, so if I'm not here, let yourself in," Mira said, still trying to get her way.

"I'll be working tonight. I've got to make up for this morning." Sam threw up her hand, waved good-bye, and was out the door before Mira could say another word.

Mira slumped back on her pillows and pouted. She didn't like being dismissed like yesterday's news. *I've got to get another lover. One who's at my beck and call. After all, I am Mira Rhone!*

KENNEDY BREEZED through the international terminal of Kennedy Airport with her company-issued, four-wheeled, navy blue carry-on keeping pace with her every step. She was scheduled for a two-day round-trip flight to Johannesburg. As she rolled past a newsstand, her eyes caught a peripheral glance of the pastel pages of the *Financial Times*, and she couldn't help but wonder whether or not her Mystery Man would be on board the flight today. Ever since her conversation with Naomi the other night, she couldn't stop thinking about him. He was handsome, sexy, and had an air of sophistication, all the qualities she admired in a man, but for all she knew he was already taken. Men like him usually were. As Kennedy continued to the gate, she began to run the preflight checklist through her mind. She'd rather think about work than a man she knew absolutely nothing about.

Kennedy had made that mistake one time too many. She had a knack for getting to know a man's favorite sexual position before she knew how he took his coffee. She attributed her hardy sexual appetite to her teen years. In high school the girls wouldn't let the boys penetrate them in order to keep their virginity, but would freely give out blow jobs. Kennedy was reluctant at first, but soon caved in to the peer pressure. Once she got the hang of it, she found herself getting off on the experience. And as she grew older, her libido grew stronger. She often had sex on the second date, if not the first. She thought about sex so much that she felt like a freak. Kennedy loved reaching an orgasm, and masturbated on a regular basis to satisfy herself. Most men she dated misunderstood her sexual desires and thought that she was just a quick lay when in actuality she wanted a committed relationship, and not just sex. But as soon as they fucked a few times, the men were history. Once they heard the "C" word, they couldn't get away from her fast enough. After a few heartbreaks, Kennedy vowed not to jump the gun and have sex too soon, so she kept a variety of vibrators on hand for those lonely nights.

Once on board, she put away her luggage, strapped on an apron, and began the perfunctory drudgery of preparing the cabin for the flight. Kennedy had been flying for nearly ten years and was getting bored with the job. Being a flight attendant was not even her first career choice. In high school it was Naomi who had always wanted to crisscross the globe, so after graduation she applied to all the major airlines and was finally hired by Pan-Afrika. After a year of hearing Naomi expounding the virtues of her glamorous lifestyle, flying to exotic destinations and meeting new people, Kennedy was intrigued, especially since the pre-law classes in college were a snore, so she put school on hold and filled out an application. After a series of interviews and basic exams, she was hired within a few months.

Passengers would often mistake Naomi and Kennedy for sisters, which was easy since they were both five feet seven inches tall and possessed curves that made the cheap polyester-blend blue uniform dresses look like designer originals. Together they were a lethal combination, partying on the coast of Casablanca one night and line dancing in Lagos the next. Even on their off days they would jet over to Paris to scout out the sales at the boutiques along the Left Bank. Those were the good old days before Naomi got married and quit. Now Kennedy was seriously thinking about returning to college. She was no longer interested in law and was thinking about changing her major to merchandising, and becoming a buyer for a clothing store. Over the years she had spent plenty of time in offshore boutiques and duty-free shops. Kennedy loved shopping and figured that she might as well get paid for it, but that plan was still a long way off since she would have to practically start from square one, and take all new classes.

When the details were taken care of, Kennedy checked the first-class seat roster. As hard as she tried, she couldn't get her mind off of the Mystery Man. Well, he wasn't exactly a mystery since she knew his identity. She ran her finger down the names, but there was no Nigel Charles listed. Her heart sank. She felt like a teenager whose latest crush hadn't made it to third-period English. She knew that his presence or lack thereof shouldn't have affected her one way or the other, but it did. From the very first time she laid eyes on Nigel, she had a strong attraction to him, and though he didn't give her a second look, she thought that if he was on board today, she might be able to catch his eye. Though it was a long shot, Kennedy thought that maybe Nigel would eventually ask her out on a date, but he wasn't on board, so that wasn't a possibility this trip. She tried to mask the feeling of disappointment with a phony smile when she greeted the passengers as they began to board.

"Not feeling well today?" That was Monica, her crewmate.

"What do you mean? I feel just fine." She smiled quickly, trying to brush off the comment. Kennedy wanted to keep her thoughts of Nigel to herself, so she pretended not to know what Monica was alluding to.

Monica gave her that "Mother Knows Best" look. "Ken, how long have I known you?"

"Girl, what are you getting at?" she asked, playing the dumb role.

Monica was the mother hen of the crew and insisted on knowing everyone's business. "Just answer the question."

"We've been flying together for over eight years," Kennedy answered, trying to put an end to this senseless inquisition.

"Exactly!" She nodded. "So I know when something's up with you and I can tell by that phony-baloney smile that something's bothering you."

What was Kennedy going to say? That she was pining over a man she didn't even know, that she was missing the presence of a virtual stranger? No, Kennedy wouldn't say anything of the sort. Monica was a hopeless romantic, and Kennedy knew that any mention of a possible attraction would just spur her on and Kennedy would have to spend the next forty-eight hours listening to how Monica met her husband at thirty thousand feet. Well, Kennedy had heard that story a gazillion times and wasn't in the mood for an instant replay, so she just said, "My sinuses are flaring up."

"Uh huh," Monica grunted, knowing full well that it was more than a sinus infection that was troubling her friend. But whatever it was, Kennedy didn't want to talk about it, so Monica didn't press the issue.

Once they were in flight and the passengers were fed and tucked into their private reclining seats with fluffy duvets and plump pillows for the overnight flight, Kennedy couldn't help but fantasize about the possibilities of meeting the perfect man. If Monica could find love among the clouds, why couldn't she? Maybe this Nigel guy was the one. Suddenly she felt a surge of panic jolt through her body. What if he never flew Pan-Afrika again? What if he was married with children? What if he was gay? Why was she panicking? She had no vested interest in this guy. He was just one of many random passengers whom she encountered on a regular basis. After all, Kennedy flew internationally and saw more than her share of "beautiful people." So even if he wasn't the one, it was just a matter of time until "the one" redeemed his frequent flyer miles and boarded her flight. With that comforting thought in the back of her mind, she finally drifted off to sleep, until the captain announced the preparation for landing a few hours later.

Johannesburg was balmy and in the mid-seventies when they landed. The crew was staying at the Park Hyatt, a short distance from the airport and within walking distance of several trendy boutiques and jewelry stores. Kennedy's plan was to check into the hotel, change, and then hit a few shops. She was in the market for a gold toggle bracelet and what better place to shop for gold than in the land of gold mines? But once she reached the room, the bed began to whisper her name, and before she knew what hit her, she was out for the count; so much for spending a few hundred rand.

And just like déjà vu, she was back on the plane for the return flight to New York. While Monica reviewed the first-class passenger log, Kennedy opened several bottles of wine for the preflight beverage service. Stepping out of the galley as the passengers began to board, she nearly fainted when she saw him walk down the breezeway and onto the plane. There in the flesh was Nigel Charles. He looked like a model gracing the runway, in his slate gray suit, lavender shirt, and matching tie. The suit was tailored and hugged his shoulders ever so slightly, showing off his physique. His bronze face was clean-shaven, exposing his perfectly square jawline. His eyes were intense, his nose was a straight slope, and his lips were full. He was even finer than she remembered. His good looks began to make her moist, and she wanted to go into the lavatory and masturbate.

"Good afternoon and welcome to Pan-Afrika." Kennedy smiled nervously, trying to mask her desire.

He looked at her and returned the smile. "Good afternoon."

She wanted to snatch off the stupid blue and white plaid

apron around her waist and expose her curves, so he could take notice. Instead, she quickly smoothed down the front pockets and casually ran her hand through her hair. He proceeded to his seat without looking back. His lack of attention made her wish she were also a first-class passenger instead of an in-flight waitress. She retreated back to the galley and discreetly watched as he settled into his seat, buckled up, and took out an assortment of newspapers. Kennedy inhaled and walked over to his seat, wondering if he would remember her from his last flight.

"Would you care for a beverage before we depart from the gate?"

"Yes, I would." He smiled. "I understand there are some outstanding vineyards in South Africa. What would you recommend?" he asked, looking up at her.

She searched his eyes for a hint of recognition, but there wasn't any, so she went into her spiel. "We have a rich, fruity-tasting Bouchard Finlayson Kaaimansgat Chardonnay."

"That's a mouthful," he interrupted.

She chuckled and continued. "We also have a mature oak-fermented Sauvignon Blanc. And, if you're into reds, we have an awesome Cabernet Sauvignon by Kleine Zalze, as well as a full-bodied Merlot."

"I'll have the Cabernet," he said, opening one of his newspapers.

"Excellent choice." She smiled weakly and retreated to the galley. *"Excellent choice,"* she silently mimicked herself. "What a lame response. Couldn't you—"

"Who the hell are you talking to?" Monica asked.

"Nobody." She reached for the bottle of wine. "Just talking."

"Well, you know what they say? It's okay to talk, as long as you don't answer yourself." Monica peeked her head out of the galley and looked down the aisle. "Girl, have you seen that handsome specimen in row two?"

"Yep." Kennedy nodded.

"Yep?" Monica looked puzzled. "Is that all you have to say? Girl, that man is fine with a ph, as in PHINE!" She put her index finger in her mouth and bit down, emphasizing the point.

"He ain't all that," Kennedy lied, not wanting to reveal her attraction.

"Girl, you must be blind. He looks like a cross between Gary Dourdan and Vin Diesel. I tell you, if I wasn't married, I'd be all over him. You're free and single. Go get the four-one-one." Monica nudged her with her elbow. "What are you waiting for?"

Little did Monica know that Kennedy could have walked right over and straddled him without an ounce of shame in her game. She had a tender spot for Vin Diesel, and since she couldn't have him, Nigel Charles would do just fine. But she had to maintain her composure. Any form of desperation on her part would be an instant turnoff. "If he's interested, let him approach me."

"Cool Ken." Monica rolled her eyes. "That's what I'm going to call you."

She surely didn't feel cool. Her panties were moist from the attraction she felt toward him. "Yeah, that's me," Kennedy mused, pouring the wine.

Putting the goblet of wine on a silver tray with the airline's signature single white rose in a bud vase in the center of the tray, Kennedy walked back over to his seat. "Here's your Cabernet. Enjoy."

"Thanks," he said, looking up, giving her direct eye contact.

Kennedy swallowed hard as their eyes locked. For a few seconds, they just stared at each other without saying a word. She could feel a hot sexual desire emanating inside of her, and her mouth began to water at the thought of tasting his dick. She loved giving head and couldn't help but wonder what type of cock he had—was it small, large, thick, or average size? Did it curve to the right or to the left—but it really didn't matter, as long as he was well versed at licking clits.

Nigel returned his gaze to the newspaper, ending their stare-down. Kennedy took the hint and walked away. She immediately went into the lavatory, pulled down her panty hose, put her foot on the tiny sink, and stroked her clit. She closed her eyes and imagined Nigel doing the job. The thought of him between her legs made her cum even faster, and after a few minutes, she had reached orgasm. *I'm going to fuck that man, sooner rather than later,* she thought, forgetting about her new self-imposed rule of waiting for the perfect relationship.

6

"OPEN THEM legs wider, so I can get all the way up in there."

"Okay, big daddy," she panted, and did as instructed.

He settled his naked body in between her thighs. "That's what I'm talking about. Now tell me how much you want this dick."

She could feel his erection pushing against her and wanted him inside of her badly. His sexual prowess had turned her on, and now she couldn't get enough of him. "Pleaseeee," she begged, putting emphasis on the last syllable. "You know I need it."

"You need it? How badly do you need it?" he whispered in her ear.

"I need it like a plant needs water. Like a junkie needs his daily fix." She bit her bottom lip. "Come on, baby, stop teasing and fuck me," she said, getting frustrated.

"Now you sound like a junkie. Are you a junkie, baby?"

She wrapped her legs tightly around his back, trying to pull him in closer. "You know I'm a junkie for your dick. Now stop playing around, and let's get down to business," she said, clenching her ankles together, tightening her vise grip.

He grabbed his shaft and rubbed the head of his penis against her pussy lips. Teasing her made his dick harder, and he loved prolonging their foreplay, since it made the sex hotter. He released his shaft and stuck two fingers into her wanting hole. She was oozing with wetness, and he couldn't wait to get inside, but he still had a little more teasing to do. He finger-fucked her repeatedly, until he felt her squirt a stream of cum. He then licked his fingers to savor her juices. "You taste like sweet cream."

Unable to wait any longer, she reached underneath him, found his rod, and guided it toward her pussy. "Fuck me. Please," she begged.

He was getting weaker by the second and couldn't prolong the foreplay any longer. He slid his cock into her wetness and went to work. He grabbed her ass and pulled her into him. They fucked in the missionary position for a few minutes, and then he flipped her over. "Get on your knees."

She got on all fours and arched her back so that he could penetrate her deeper. "Oh, yeah, that's it. *That's it!*" she screamed out in ecstasy as he pumped her doggy-style.

He grabbed her hips, increased his pace, and didn't stop fucking until he exploded deep within her pussy. After their heated climax, they collapsed facedown on the bed and drifted off into a comalike sleep.

ATLANTA WAS FRAGRANT and in full bloom, reminiscent of the antebellum South. Tyler Reed could picture Rhett and Miss Scarlett lounging underneath the soft, snowy white petals of the dogwood and magnolia trees that dotted the landscape of the city. Being a transplant from New York, Tyler was astounded every spring at the spectacular show Mother Nature put on in this region of the country. April in Paris was nothing more than a

mere song compared to April in Atlanta. The city was efflores-
cent. The overall effect was positively romantic.

Tyler hummed the melody to "April in Paris" as she sped
along Piedmont Avenue on her way home. She couldn't get
there fast enough, but first she had a few errands to run. She
had a special evening planned for her lover Liz, who'd been
working hard lately and desperately needed a dose of relaxation
coupled with the best stress reliever of all—SEX.

Not only was April dogwood season, it was also tax season,
and Liz, an accountant, was inundated with W-2s, 1040s, 1041s,
1120s, and schedules from A to Z. Tyler looked at the clock on
the dashboard; it was 2:45.

Liz didn't get home until after seven, so she had plenty of
time to run the three important errands that would complete tonight's tête-à-tête. The first stop was their favorite restaurant in
Little Five Points to pick up dinner, then the package store to
buy a nice bottle of Pinot Grigio, Liz's favorite wine. And finally,
the most important stop of all, the natural body shop to buy a
bottle of Patchouli scented oil, for a sensual full-body massage
after dinner.

As she drove through L5P, short for Little Five Points, it
occurred to her that the neighborhood was an eclectic cross
between New York's Greenwich Village and the French Quarter.
Looking at the artsy shops and boutiques that lined Euclid Avenue, it was hard to imagine that twenty years ago, this area was
considered seedy and undesirable. Back then, most of the store-
fronts and theaters were boarded up and in a serious state of
decay. Time had surely brought about a positive change. She
found a parking space near Ginger Grill, a restaurant that was
a taste of the Caribbean in the city. The menu was a hip tropi-
cal mix, from lobster fritters and curried crab cakes to jerk
chicken and barbecued ribs with honey-rum sauce. She walked
into the restaurant and was instantly transported to the islands.
Bob Marley and the Wailers were wailing *Rebel Music* through

surround-sound speakers. The ocher-colored walls of the restaurant were covered with photographs of the sandy beaches of Antigua, the Blue Mountains of Jamaica, and brown children splashing in the aqua waters of Barbados. A serene picture of a burnt orange orb dipping into a tranquil sea at sunset hung behind the hostess's podium. Tyler was lost in thought trying to decide if the picture was taken at Rick's Café in Negril or on the shores of St. Bart's.

"Excuse me, miss, how can I help you?" asked the dreadlock-wearing host, bringing her back to reality.

"I phoned in a take-out order of blackened salmon, coconut-curried shrimp, and a side of coco bread and calaloo."

"What name is the order under?"

"Tyler Reed," she replied.

"Just a minute. Let me check on your order," he said, and turned toward the kitchen.

Five minutes later, the host came back to the podium, balancing three large, white foam boxes in his arms. Tyler could see steam wafting through the side of each container and smelled the intoxicating aroma of Caribbean spices.

"That'll be $43.87," he said, carefully placing the boxes in a thick brown paper shopping bag.

Tyler handed over a crisp fifty-dollar bill. "Keep the change."

She had just completed an on-site graphics assignment and as a bonus for being ahead of schedule, the company paid her on the spot, instead of making her wait the customary thirty days.

Tyler's freelance career as a graphic artist was sketchy, with assignments coming in dribs and drabs. She suffered through the inconsistencies of a freelance lifestyle because she loved the flexibilily it offered. Deciding which projects to work on and making her own schedule gave her a true sense of freedom. But independence from the confines of the "Big House" came along with a price—giving up medical, dental, two weeks vacation, and a guaranteed paycheck twice a month. When the checks did roll in, she could usually count on a hefty sum.

Tyler and Liz had been together for five years, so Liz was used to the erratic cash flow. Unlike most couples who argued about money or, more importantly, the lack thereof, they rarely let finances interfere with their romance. Living with an accountant had its advantages as well as its disadvantages. On the upside, Liz outlined a budget for Tyler to follow, so that her funds would last between droughts when the projects were nonexistent. The downside was, if Tyler went over budget one iota, Liz would become irate and give her famous "You Ought to Get a Full-Time J.O.B." speech. Fortunately, there would be no speeches tonight, only the sweet sound of lovemaking.

Tyler walked down the street to the liquor store and bought not one but two bottles of wine, just in case their lovemaking lasted until the wee hours. She walked back to the car, put the bags in the backseat, then took out her cell and called Liz's office.

"Tyler Reed calling for Elizabeth Alexander."

"I'm sorry; she's gone for the day," announced the receptionist.

"Gone?" Tyler couldn't believe her ears. Liz rarely left before five o'clock, especially during the crunch time of tax season. "Are you sure?"

"Positive. Would you like to leave a message?"

"No thank you," she said before hanging up.

Tyler hit the end call button, then dialed Liz's cell, but after four rings, her voice mail answered. "You have reached the cellular phone of Elizabeth Alexander. Please leave a detailed message and I'll return your call at my earliest convenience. Thank you."

"Hey, babe, it's me. Where are you? Call me as soon as you get this message."

Maybe she's already at the house, Tyler thought, then hit the speed dial to their home number. Once again, she was greeted with an automated voice. "Hey, babe, pick up." Tyler waited for a moment. "Okay, call me on the cell." Her mind began to race, trying to think of where Liz could be. Maybe she was in her office behind closed doors, buried underneath tax returns, and gave explicit instructions not to be disturbed. Or maybe she was comforting a nervous client. People often panicked around the fifteenth of April, thinking Uncle Sam would swoop down and cart them off to jail if their returns were not postmarked by the deadline.

Tyler drove the short distance home and was surprised to see Liz's car parked in the driveway. *Maybe she's sick,* Tyler thought, pulling in. She parked and reached in the backseat for the food and wine. "Oh, shit," she said, realizing she'd forgotten to pick up the massage oil.

Tyler walked around to the side door that faced the driveway. She loved their little house on the hill, as she referred to the cozy bungalow, because the house sat atop a small incline.

She unlocked the door, walked into the kitchen, and set the bags on the counter. It was quiet inside. *I'll bet she's asleep, no doubt exhausted from working so hard,* she thought, unpacking the food. They had hardwood floors, so she took her shoes off before going into the dining room to clear the table. Tyler was more domestic than Liz. As a child Tyler helped her mother keep a tidy home. Her family wasn't rich, but her mother always said that cleanliness didn't have an income bracket. Tyler always wanted the American dream, but her dream included another woman, not a man. Once the table was set, she tiptoed down the hall to check on Liz. Tyler slowly opened the bedroom door.

Liz was lying on her stomach underneath the covers and didn't hear the door open. "Hey, babe, are you sick?" she asked, concerned.

"What are you doing home?" Liz spun around, alarmed.

"I finished the assignment ahead of schedule and left early. What are you doing home? Are you sick?" she asked again.

"I, uh, think I'm coming down with something," Liz said,

pulling the covers up around her bare shoulders. "Can you run to the drugstore and get me some Robitussin?" She coughed.

"Sure, no problem. Why don't you put on some pajamas," Tyler said, and walked over to the bureau to get a nightgown.

"I'll get the gown!" Liz shouted and sat up slightly. "Just go to the store," she insisted.

"Excuse me?" Tyler was taken aback at her urgent tone.

"I'm sorry for yelling. I just need that cough syrup." Liz coughed again.

"Okay, okay, I'm going." She walked back toward the bedroom door, but stopped dead in her tracks when she heard . . .

"Hey, babe, where're the towels?"

Tyler spun around, and standing in the bathroom doorway, wearing only a smile, was a strange man. Their eyes met as he tried in vain to cover his rather large manhood with both hands.

"Who the hell are you?!" she shouted.

"I'm Wayne," he said in a deep, husky voice, "and who are you?"

Tyler ignored his question and glared at Liz, who was clutching the covers tightly underneath her chin. "Who the hell is *he*?"

"Wayne is, uh, Wayne is . . ."

"I'm her boyfriend," he said, finishing her sentence.

"Her what?" Tyler asked, mouth agape. She then shouted, "That's impossible, because I'm her *girlfriend*!"

"You mean her roommate," he said, with an air of assurance in his voice.

"Is that what she told you?" Tyler moved closer to the bed. "Tell him, Liz," she demanded. "Tell him, damn it!"

"Tyler is, uh," Liz's voice began to tremble, "Tyler is . . ."

"I'm her LOVER!" Tyler screamed at the top of her lungs.

Wayne dropped his hands from his privates. "Her what?"

"You heard me. I'm her lover, damn it!"

He looked confused. "What?"

"Oh, Liz didn't tell you that she's a lesbian?" Tyler asked, dropping her voice to a low register and staring at her girlfriend, who had begun to cry.

He suddenly began to chuckle, and then said with a sly grin, "Apparently not anymore."

She swung around to give him a piece of her mind, but stopped midsentence. She couldn't believe her eyes. He was standing in the middle of the floor butt naked, stroking his dick and suggestively licking his lips. "Why don't you come on over here and get some of this," he said, massaging the tip of his now rock-hard penis.

"Wayne. Please!" Liz shouted.

"Aw, baby, let Daddy turn her out, like you know I can. The three of us can have a lot of fun. I've got more than enough to go around," he said, stroking his shaft.

Tyler thought she was going to throw up right on the spot. She could feel bile rising from the pit of her stomach. How could this be happening? She had no idea that Liz was bisexual. Liz never gave any indication that she was interested in men. Tyler felt like a stranger in her own house. She had to get out of there before she lost her lunch in the middle of the floor.

Looking at Liz, she could see the devastation in her eyes. Tyler opened her mouth to speak, but no words came. A lone tear fell to her cheek, followed by another, and then another. "Good-bye, Liz," she said in a soft whisper, and walked out with her head held high. There was no way she was going to completely lose her dignity in front of Liz and her *man!* So much for her American dream.

NAOMI WAS beyond pissed! It had been a few days since Jacob's promise of serious lovemaking, and once again he was up and out of the house before she had a chance to open her eyes. He had called when she was in the shower, and left a lame message about an important early-morning meeting. He then promised yet again to make it up to her. Jacob had reneged on his word so many times that she was hard-pressed to believe anything that came out of his mouth. She listened to the message one more time before erasing it. Naomi had to admit that Jacob did sound sincere in his apology, but she still wondered why he was being so neglectful. He always had had a healthy sexual appetite, and it was hard to believe that his libido had done a complete one-eighty. He was still a relatively young man, and should have been making love to his wife on a regular basis. Though Naomi didn't want to entertain the thought that her husband was screwing another woman, she couldn't help but ponder the obvious. He wasn't fucking her, so chances were he was fucking someone else. Naomi may have been a housewife, but she wasn't an airhead. She knew that most men—especially her man—lived for sex. The more she thought about the possibility of Jacob cheating, the angrier she became. Naomi picked up the phone to call his office, but quickly put it back down. She had no evidence to support her theory, and would sound like a lunatic if she began hurling accusations at Jacob.

I need proof, Naomi thought, sprang up from the side of the bed, and rushed into the closet. She started rifling through the pockets of his suit jackets and pants, hoping to find something— a book of matches, a hotel receipt, condoms—anything that would prove that he was having an affair. Her search proved futile. She found nothing. Naomi was relieved and frustrated at the same time. If Jacob wasn't having an affair, then she was apparently the problem. Maybe he wasn't attracted to her anymore. Naomi couldn't fathom that reasoning either. She went to the gym on a regular basis and ate healthy. Her body was tight and in better condition than it was before she got pregnant. She also made a point to keep her hair and nails done weekly. If her husband didn't desire her any longer, it was no fault of hers. She ran her hand across her taut midsection and rubbed her round ass. *Well, if he doesn't want all of this, I'm sure I can find someone who does.* Naomi's anger at being rejected by her husband was making her think irrationally. The thought of cheating had never entered her mind until now. She was tired of getting cheap thrills from a novel and wanted to feel a hard dick between her legs.

Naomi stormed out of the closet and plopped back down on the bed. *What the hell are you thinking?* she asked herself. There was no way she would ever have an affair. She wouldn't jeopardize losing her family over a quick fling. She picked up *Auld Lang Syne* and read the last few steamy pages. At least getting cheap thrills from a book was safe; that way she didn't have to worry about getting caught in the act.

After Naomi finished reading the novel, she went downstairs

to the solarium, her makeshift office, and began finalizing the details of her son's birthday party. She loved the ever-present sunlight of the room, and though it was designed for house plants, Naomi had put a desk, computer, printer, and fax machine in one of the corners, creating her own cozy workspace. She was extremely efficient, and had folders for every aspect of Noah's party. He was their only child and she indulged him in every way possible. She had taken him to see a Broadway show a year before, and he wanted the theme of the musical incorporated into his party, as well as a Zorro theme. Noah was infatuated with the swashbuckler and wanted masks and capes for all his friends. Naomi had secured the capes, but had yet to buy the masks.

She logged onto the Internet and began to search. She combed through several sites, but had yet to find an appropriate mask for children. Naomi couldn't find a local source on the net, so she reached for the old reliable—the neighborhood Yellow Pages. She thumbed through to the M's and found a section dedicated to masks. She earmarked a few companies and picked up the phone to call and find out more information. Instead of a dial tone, she was greeted by voices.

"Beth, I'm sure you have preconceived notions of what a sex club is, but trust me, you've never seen anything like this before."

"And what makes this place so special, Rhoda?"

"Well, for starters, it's extremely sophisticated."

"How so?"

"Instead of a run-of-the-mill champagne fountain, their fountain spews ice-cold Belvedere, and that's just for starters. Every stitch of the decor, from the chandelier to the drapes, is imported from Europe, not some tacky knockoff. You know that I don't give out compliments easily, but this place is exceptional."

Naomi didn't know what they were talking about, but was intrigued nonetheless. Obviously she had been patched into someone else's line by accident. She felt like the proverbial fly-on-the-wall, and continued to listen.

"Exceptional? That's a strong word," the other lady on the phone said, *sounding skeptical.*

"Well, I must give credit where credit is due, and the Black Door gets my vote hands down," Rhoda said.

"How long have you been a member?"

"Ever since my divorce I've been celibate. Not by choice, mind you. I needed a tune-up, if you know what I mean. I wasn't meeting any decent men, so Meri told me about this club that caters solely to the needs of women…"

Naomi's ears perked up. She desperately needed to be lubed up before she totally dried out, and this place seemed intriguing. She couldn't believe her timing. She'd picked up the phone right in the middle of a conversation meant for her ears.

"…men work there, but they can't be members. And to ensure anonymity, everyone wears a mask, so nobody knows your real identity."

"Hmm, that's interesting, but what about STDs?"

"Well, all the members as well as the servers go through a rigorous screening process, which includes background checks and medical exams. I'm telling you this place is totally safe."

"You're divorced, but I'm still married, and can't take the chance of my husband finding out about my involvement in any type of scandal."

"Trust me; the Black Door is above reproach. Meri told me that some of New York's wealthiest women are members, and she should know, since she's a seven-figure diva."

"Mmm, I've known Meri for years, and wonder why she has never mentioned the Black Door to me?" Beth said.

"She probably didn't think you needed its services, since you have a man at home, while on the other hand, my bed has been empty for months."

"I may be married, but having a man at home is an under-statement. Now that Doug has his own practice, he's been working at the firm around the clock. I hardly ever see him. Don't get me wrong, I love my husband... but a woman has needs."

Naomi nodded her head in agreement, even though the callers couldn't see her.

"Beth, I totally understand. What's ironic is that most men think that a woman will just sit around and wait until they have time to sex us up."

"Those days of waiting patiently are long over. Besides, it's not like I'd be having an ongoing affair, it's just a club; and I decide when, with who, and for how long."

"You're right; it's like going to the gym, except the muscles you're working out aren't visible to the naked eye."

They both laughed, and then Beth asked, "Okay, I'm in. How does the initial process go?"

"As far as I know, you have to be referred by a member. So let me call the club and give them your name and number, and some-one from the Black Door will contact you," Rhoda told her.

"Okay, just be sure to give them my cell number. I don't want some stranger calling the house in case Doug happens to be home."

"No problem. Oh, goody! I'm so happy you're going to join. Now we can really let our hair down!"

Naomi was anything but happy. She had gotten excited hearing about the Black Door, but unfortunately Rhoda—the woman who was a member—didn't divulge any pertinent in-formation, such as an address or telephone number. The only thing Naomi knew was that a club existed that took care of a woman's needs.

The women had changed the subject, and were now talking about finding a good hairstylist. Naomi already had the bomb stylist, and wasn't interested in hearing any more of their con-versation.

She clicked the phone off and began frantically thumbing

through the Yellow Pages. When she got to the B's, she ran her finger down the pages, looking for a listing for the Black Door, but found nothing. *I should have known it wouldn't be listed. I bet I'll find it on the Internet.* She typed "The Black Door" in Google's search box, and hit enter. Naomi read every listing, but nothing resembled the club. She then thought back and remembered that the woman had said membership was by referral only. The owner was clever enough to keep the club off the radar of the general public. Though Naomi didn't find what she was looking for, she admired the fact that the Black Door wasn't pedestrian, which really piqued her interest.

I wish I knew this Meri person, or someone who was a member. Now that she was aware of the club, she wanted to know more. If her husband was indeed having an affair, it would give her justification for the possibility of also having a lover on the side. Naomi had never thought about cheating before, and didn't know if she could actually carry out the deed, but one thing she knew for sure, and that was, she was tired of putting Jacob's desires before her own. Naomi had given in to Jacob and agreed to move to the suburbs, but she hadn't agreed to being neglected. Had she known that Jacob would be spending most of his time at the office, she would have started her interior design career years ago. At least then she would have something else to occupy her time with instead of just being a housewife and mother. She loved taking care of her son, but wanted more out of life than keeping a nice home, and waiting for her husband to pay her some attention. If she couldn't get the attention she needed at home, then maybe she would seek it out elsewhere.

TODAY WAS Noah's fifth birthday and Naomi was trying to break the bank. There were no ordinary helium balloons with streamers strung to the mailbox. Oh, no, there was nothing ordinary about this party. No puppet show, no petting zoo, no storytelling, and no magicians. Instead of the run-of-the-mill kiddy party with face painting and clumsy clowns, Naomi had chosen an *Into the Woods* theme. She had taken Noah to see the play and he fell in love with the characters. The Broadway musical by Stephen Sondheim was set in a mystical forest, combining various fairy tales. There were two twenty-foot-tall weeping willow prop trees on either side of the doorway, with drooping branches framing the entrance of the house. The overall effect simulated entering an enchanted forest.

Jacob unlocked the door and the moment he stepped inside of the foyer, he was instantly transported to the Broadway stage. It was as if a Tony award-winning set designer had come in and transformed the entire living room. The sofa, cocktail table, and two Maurice Villency chairs that usually sat in the center of the room were pushed against the far wall. In the space where the furniture once stood were two huge, adjoining, eight-foot-tall storyboards with a fairy-tale village of cobblestones and gingerbread cottages painted on the front. Covering the floor in place of their Moroccan area rug was emerald green indoor/outdoor carpeting. In addition to the play's theme, there were also Zorro masks decorating the walls, in honor of Noah's hero du jour.

Naomi had hired student actors from a local theater company to act out certain scenes from the play. Four actresses costumed as Cinderella, her stepmother, and wicked stepsisters, Florinda and Lucinda, whisked past Jacob as he entered the living room, followed by a masked actor, no doubt Zorro himself.

"Daddy, Daddy," Noah cried, running through one of the miniature doorways of the fake village, "goody, goody, you're home."

"Happy birthday to you. Happy birthday, dear Noah, happy birthday to you," Jacob sang, reaching down and swooping his son high in the air.

"Daddy, Daddy, put me down." He struggled. "You're going to wrinkle my costume." Noah was dressed as Jack from Jack and the Beanstalk, in brown tweed knickers, white knee socks, an emerald green vest, a white cotton shirt with billowy sleeves and an oversized collar and cuffs. Clenched in his right hand was a toy cow.

"What's that, Buddy?" Jacob asked, referring to the tiny animal.

Noah looked at him as if he had just asked the world's dumbest question. "Daddy, this is Milky White, Jack's best friend. Now let me down. Let me down."

The moment Jacob released him, Noah ran back through the miniature door. And from the sound of several petite voices beyond the village facade, Jacob assumed that's where the rest of the children were playing.

"Jacob, I'm so glad you're home. These kids are driving me crazy," Naomi complained, appearing from behind the facade.

"Wow, look at you!" he said, commenting on his wife's costume. She was dressed as the witch, the role played by the beautiful Vanessa Williams. In the first half of the play, Vanessa donned an ugly Wicked Witch of the West–type mask, with warts and all. But at the end of Act I, after losing her powers, she was transformed back into a stunning beauty dressed in a sexy, form-fitting, bloodred evening gown.

"You like it?" She spun around so he could get the full effect. The crimson gown plunged low in the front, just enough to give a glimpse of cleavage without revealing too much. The silky fabric hugged her hips and fishtailed out in the back. Her long brown hair was parted on the side and covered one eye like Jessica Rabbit, the sexy character from the movie *Who Framed Roger Rabbit.*

Jacob walked over and gave her a kiss on the forehead. "You look great, hon!"

"Now we have to get you into costume," she said, taking his hand and leading him toward the staircase.

"Me in costume?" Jacob stopped midstride. He had no intention of wearing a silly costume. "What are you talking about?"

Naomi tugged at his hand. "Come on, Jacob. You're going to be the Narrator. I already have the outfit laid out on the bed."

When they reached the bedroom, there, in the center of the bed, was a gray flannel, three-piece suit, a white French-cuffed shirt, horn-rimmed spectacles, and three leather-bound, over-sized storybooks. He breathed in a sigh of relief, glad that he didn't have to dress as some grotesque ogre with a hunchback and an exaggerated limp.

"What happened to Tinky Winky and the gang?" he asked, referring to the original party theme.

"Noah has outgrown the Teletubbies," Naomi said, picking up one of the volumes. "Now, Jacob, as the Narrator, all you have to do is read a fairy tale from each book." She handed him the scarlet, leather-bound book. "This one is 'Little Red Riding Hood.' The other two are 'Rapunzel' and 'Rumpelstiltskin.'"

Most people didn't realize that the German-born Grimm brothers wrote not of dreamy idyllic fairy tales, but of the often cruel and poverty-stricken life of Europe in the early 1800s. Over the centuries, their crude tales were softened into children-friendly stories. "I think I can manage that," Jacob said, and began to change into his costume.

"Don't be long. The natives are getting restless. After Zorro performs a few sword tricks, they'll be ready for a story." Naomi turned to leave, but stopped. "So"—she ran her hand up and down her midsection—"you like the dress?" she asked suggestively.

"Yeah, it really looks great on you."

"I bet it'll even look better on the floor, once I take it off tonight." Naomi had purposely chosen the sexy costume to make her husband drool with desire.

Jacob cast his eyes to the costume on the bed. He had forgotten about his earlier promise to make love to his wife, but obviously she hadn't. "Yep, I bet so," he said lamely.

"Once the parents pick up their kids, and I put Noah to bed, *we are* going to bed, and I don't mean to sleep." Naomi walked over to her husband, grabbed him around the neck, and gave him a juicy kiss. "Don't disappoint me tonight, Jacob. We're long overdue, and I'm horny as hell."

"I promise, honey, tonight is our night." He unwrapped her arms from around his neck and said, "Now go on downstairs, before Noah starts looking for you."

As soon as she left, Jacob began taking off his clothes and dressing the part of the Narrator. He looked at the books and wished that he could read every single last page in order to prolong putting off the dreaded lovemaking.

He was buttoning the last button on the vest when his cell

phone rang. He walked over to the dresser and picked it up. "Jacob Reed speaking."

"Jacob, I'm so glad I caught you. I just called your office and Charlotte said you had left for the day."

"Hello, Mira." He looked at his watch. "Aren't you supposed to be in the meeting with the board?"

"Exactly!" she shouted in a muffled hush, as if trying not to be overheard.

By the tone of her voice, he detected something was amiss. "Mira, what's going on? Why aren't you in the meeting?"

"Because I'm in the lobby waiting for your 'more than qualified' associate," Mira spat out, quoting his description of Nina.

"Calm down, Mira. She's only a few minutes late. I'm sure there's a logical explanation. She's probably lost, or in a traffic jam," he suggested.

Mira exhaled loudly. "Jacob, you know I despise tardiness." She then continued. "I should have insisted that you come, instead of some lame-brained associate who can't even find her way around London."

Mira Rhone was the epitome of the unyielding client who demanded nothing but absolute perfection. She expected everyone to perform like androids. And heaven forbid if someone should slip up and reveal a human trait like an honest mistake. "Mira, go on up to the meeting and I'll locate Nina. I'm sure—"

Before he could finish his sentence, Mira interrupted, "Don't bother. She's here." Click.

"What? No good-bye," he mused to himself. "I'm sure Mira will give me an earful on the virtues of time management at our next meeting." Though Mira was a tyrant, he still found her sexy and imagined how she would look wearing Naomi's dress. The thought of Mira in that ruby red gown clinging to her every curve was making his dick hard. *Calm down, boy. You'll have her soon enough.*

He clicked the phone shut and put it back on the dresser, then continued with his transition into the Narrator. Jacob put on the blazer and smoothed the fabric with the palm of his hand. He put the glasses on and adjusted them on the tip of his nose. As he tucked the books underneath his arm and headed toward the doorway, the phone rang again. He assumed it was Mira calling back and smiled. He crossed the room, cleared his throat, and dropped his voice another register in an attempt to sound sexy. "Jacob Reed speaking; how may I help you?"

"J . . ."

All he heard were the sounds of someone sniffling. "Hello? Who is this?" he asked, changing back into his regular voice.

"J . . . it's . . . it's . . . me."

"Tyler, is that you?" He was immediately alarmed. Jacob had never heard his sister sound so despondent. "What's wrong? Are you alright?"

"Everything's wrong . . . I don't . . . know what . . . I'm going to do," Tyler said in between sobs.

"Calm down, Tyler, and tell me what happened."

Tyler was eight years his junior and his only sibling. They had grown up in a tight-knit family in Queens. Their parents were in their mid-forties when Tyler was born; his mother would often say that Tyler was a change-of-life baby. Working eight hours a day as a file clerk and maintaining a household, their mother had little energy to spare for a toddler, and their father usually worked overtime as a train operator, and also had a part-time job on the weekend, so Jacob took Tyler under his wing. She went with him everywhere, to football practice, to Yankee games with him and his buddies, and even on dates to the drive-in. In some ways, she was the little brother he never had. Jacob wasn't too surprised when, at the age of twelve, Tyler told him she liked girls and had a crush on his girlfriend. Jacob told her the attraction was just a phase and that she would outgrow it, but she never did.

"Liz and I broke up."

She went on to tell him the sordid details. He was shocked. Liz was so reserved and seemed totally committed to their relationship. "Who is this guy and how long has she been seeing him?" Jacob asked.

"After I calmed down, I went back home and she told me that he's a former client of hers and they've been seeing each other since last March." Tyler blew her nose. "Can you believe that? She's been cheating on me for over a year."

"Did you know she was bisexual?" he asked, trying to find some type of justification for Liz's actions.

"No. She never expressed any interest in men. I guess that explains why she always wanted me to use the strap-on." She chuckled lightly.

Jacob coughed to clear his throat. He and Tyler were close, but he really wasn't interested in hearing the intimate details of her sex life. "What are you going to do?" he asked, switching gears.

She began to sniffle again. "I don't know. Liz wants me to stay. She had the gall to say that she wants to date us both."

"Is that what you want?" Jacob knew his sister would never go for that arrangement. Tyler wasn't the player type, she only dated one person at a time, and expected the same from her partner, but he asked just the same.

"No. I want to move out, but I can't afford to right now. My funds are tight. I just finished a big project, but who knows when I'll land another assignment, and the money from my last project isn't going to last forever."

"Don't worry, T. I'll wire some funds to your bank. What's your account number?"

"No, Jacob. I don't want to take money away from your family. I'll be alright. I just have to figure out my next move." Tyler tried to put on a good game face, but inside, she felt totally helpless.

Jacob had always been the protector of his little sister, especially after their parents passed away some years ago and he promised to look after her. He could hear the pain in her voice. And if she wouldn't take his money, he had another solution. "Why don't you come to New York and move in with us?" he offered.

"I don't want to impose, J."

"What do you mean impose? You're family, and besides, we have more than enough room in this big old house."

She stopped sniffling. "Are you sure?"

"Positive."

"What about Naomi?" she asked, with concern in her voice. Tyler knew that she wasn't her sister-in-law's favorite person. Naomi had a problem with Tyler's sexuality, and had made her opinion known on several occasions. "Don't you have to run this past your wife first?"

"Don't worry about Naomi. She'll be fine with you moving in. You just worry about packing up your things and getting on the next thing smoking."

She began to cry again. "I love you so much, J. Thank you."

"What are big brothers for? Now get to packing and I'll see you soon."

They both hung up. He had solved one problem and created another. He knew Naomi would be anything but fine with his sister moving into their home. Naomi was repulsed by his sister's homosexual lifestyle. But she would just have to get over the shock. After all, Tyler was his one and only sibling and her welfare came before his wife's prudish paranoia.

A smile began to spread across Jacob's face. He knew that once he told Naomi about Tyler's relocation that her sex drive would plummet. His wife would be totally turned off at the thought of a lesbian living under their roof. Yes, the situation would work to his advantage, giving him a pass on making love to his wife—at least for a while.

MERI RENICK hadn't been inside the Black Door in nearly a year. She had been too busy entertaining a stable of young men who satisfied her libido day and night. In her mid-forties, Meri was an extremely wealthy woman. Having been twice married, she was now a widow with a substantial bank account. In addition to her late husband's estate, she had also made a killing with real estate investments. With no kids to send to an Ivy League institution, Meri used her means for cosmetic procedures, including vaginal enhancement, until once again her twat was as tight as a virgin's. She also spent a considerable amount of cash on the young studs who kept her clit satisfied. Money well spent, in her opinion. Everyone had a vice, and hers happened to be sex.

Although Meri hadn't graced the club with her presence, her red, patent-leather mask hadn't gone to waste. She had loaned it to her best friend Ariel, who used it to take the edge off. The mask—or better yet, what she did behind the mask—had cost Ariel her marriage, but that's another story altogether.

Meri was meeting her friend Beth Lacquer at the club. Beth was a newly minted member, and Meri was giving her an unofficial tour. Beth had received the official tour when she joined.

"As you can see, this is one of the parlors, which I'm sure you saw during your initial walk-through." Meri strolled over to the champagne fountain in the middle of the floor. "However, did you happen to taste the delicious liquid flowing out of the spigots?" She reached for two flutes that were resting on a silver tray next to the fountain, filled them, and handed one to her friend.

"No, I didn't sample the champagne." Beth took a sip. "Oh! This is not champagne." She had totally forgotten that Rhoda had mentioned the vodka fountain in the center of the room.

"I know. It's Belvedere. They use vodka for those who need more than champagne to get their courage up," Meri explained, taking a sip.

"Courage for what?" Beth asked.

"To venture upstairs. Didn't you get the grand tour?" Meri asked.

"No. I only saw the main level. I had to rush off to dinner that day, so I didn't get a chance to see the entire club." Beth took a sip of vodka. "So . . . what's upstairs?"

"Behind those curtains"—Meri nodded in the direction of a beautiful pair of plush crimson drapes—"is the entrance to decadence." She grinned.

"Hmm, sounds intriguing." She took another sip, this one a little bigger than the one before.

"Trust me, daarling, it is. Now drink up. We have some exploring to do."

The women polished off their drinks, crossed the room, parted the curtains, and made their way up the narrow staircase.

"Wow, this area is totally different from downstairs," Beth said, squinting, trying to adjust her eyes to the deep indigo lighting.

"You haven't seen anything yet." Though Meri hadn't been

to the club in months, she still remembered the layout and the dens of debauchery. "Come on this way," she said, walking down the long corridor.

Beth followed without question. Her senses were now aroused, and she wanted to see more. "Wait a minute." She stopped in front of a two-way mirror, and stared. "Am I seeing what I think I'm seeing? Or is this one of those holograms?"

"No, daarling, it's not a hologram." Meri walked closer to the window and looked. "It's the real deal."

They watched as a woman dressed in a dominatrix outfit—complete with leather bustier, gloves, thigh-high spike-heel boots, and a black leather face mask—whipped a pair of undernourished-looking servers with a riding crop. "Looks like S and M to me, and if I'm not mistaken, they should be downstairs."

"What's downstairs?" Beth asked, stepping closer to the glass, nearly pressing the tip of her mask against the window.

"The Dungeon is in the basement, and it's where the whips, chains, and other pain-provoking apparatus are located."

"Well, it appears that they brought the whips upstairs tonight." Beth winced as the woman cracked one of the servers on the ass. "Now, that's gotta hurt!"

"I'm sure," Meri said, turning her head away from the consensual assault. "Come on, I've seen enough. I love sex, but I can't take pain. The S and M scene is not for *moi*. Let's find something more enticing."

As they continued along the corridor, Meri said, "When Rhoda told me that you were interested in the Black Door, I was surprised. Are you and Douglas having problems in the bedroom?" she asked point-blank.

"I swear, Meri, you are the most direct person I've ever known. My other girlfriends wouldn't dare ask that question." Beth had known Meri for years, but it still surprised her how brazen Meri could be.

"Daarling, I'm not like your other girlfriends. Now stop stalling and answer the question."

"No, we're not having problems in the bedroom." Unlike Meri, who talked about every sexual exploit that she'd ever had, Beth was more reserved, and kept her answer short, preferring not to elaborate.

"If you're not having problems between the sheets, then what are you doing at the Black Door?"

"Don't get me wrong, Doug is an excellent lover, but he's hardly ever around. And I need the 'Peninsula' more than two or three times a month," she said.

"The Peninsula?"

"That's my pet name for the male anatomy." She chuckled.

"That's cute. I like it." Meri had called a dick many things before, but never a peninsula. "I think I'm going to have to use that one."

"It is clever. Anyway, when Rhoda told me about this club, I thought it would be the perfect solution to my drought. And from what I've seen thus far, it is."

"Speaking of Rhoda, where is she? I thought she was coming with you tonight."

"Yes, that was the plan, but believe it or not, she has a date!" It was common knowledge that Rhoda hadn't been out with a man since her divorce nine months ago.

"A date with whom?"

"One of Doug's coworkers, who recently relocated from New Orleans. He didn't know anybody in town, so I arranged a blind date."

"Aren't you the little matchmaker? Let's hope it works out," she said, without an ounce of confidence that it would. Meri knew from experience that most blind dates turned out to be disasters.

"Well, if it doesn't, I'm sure she'll be back at the Black Door with a quickness."

Both women laughed in agreement.

"What's so funny?"

They turned around to the sound of the voice. Standing practically on their heels was a towering figure of a man. He must have been at least six feet seven inches in height. He was tall enough to be a basketball player, but the loincloth covering his genitalia was the uniform of a server, not a point guard.

Meri stopped laughing and expertly surveyed his body, from the burnt orange mask shielding his eyes, to his hairy chest, to the hefty package protruding from beneath the Tarzan-like cloth. His hair was coiled in long dreads that hung down his back. The bottom half of his face was covered with stubble. There was a wildness about him, as if he'd stepped right out of the Amazon. She reached out and ran her hand up and down his bare chest. "Daarling," she purred, "there's nothing funny about your sculpted pecs"—she reached down and boldly lifted up the loincloth—"and beautiful cock."

Beth stared in disbelief as Meri uncovered the man's privates. He didn't protest. He reared back with a smile of confidence on his face while she inspected his goodies.

"Like what you see?"

Meri licked her bottom lip. "I do." She turned to her friend. "Beth, come closer and take a look."

Beth seemed to be frozen. Her feet wouldn't move. She hadn't seen another man's penis since she'd said her wedding vows seven years ago. Though she had come to the Black Door to frolic, something inside was preventing her from indulging. That something was a serious case of guilt. Suddenly Beth was filled with an overwhelming feeling of unfaithfulness.

Meri stroked the server's long dong. "Not only does it look good, but it feels marvelous." She noticed that Beth wasn't saying *or* doing anything, just standing there like a statue. "What's wrong with you?"

"Uh, uh," she stammered, "I've gotta go."

"Go?" Meri seemed alarmed. "We haven't even been here an hour. Besides, the fun is only beginning," she said, rubbing the head of the server's dick.

"I'm sorry, but I can't stay. I thought that I could cheat on Doug, but all of a sudden, my conscience is getting the best of me. I'll talk to you later. Have fun." Beth fled down the hallway as if she were being chased by demons.

Meri hunched her shoulders. "Oh, well, looks like it's just the three of us," she said, making a reference to his cock and putting a firm grip on it at the same time.

"That works for me. Now tell me what you're in the mood for," he wanted to know.

"Take me to one of the private chambers. Once inside, lay me down and lick my clit until I cum. And then I want you to masturbate until you're really, really hard, because if there's one thing I can't stand, that's a soft cock. When you're ready to pop, I want you to ease that big dick inside of me and fuck me until my toes curl. Can you do that?"

"That'll be just for starters. I hope you're not in a hurry, 'cause I'ma fuck you all night," he said in a southern drawl.

"Daarling, that sounds absolutely perfect." Unlike Beth, Meri didn't have a husband to rush home to, and her boy toy de jour was busy tonight, so she had nothing but time.

He took hold of her hand, led her to a private room, and did exactly as she had instructed. For the next few hours, they fucked, licked, sucked, and fucked some more. Now that Meri was reacquainted with the Black Door, she promised herself that she would be back to sample another server before the month was over.

10

JACOB ARRIVED at the restaurant twenty-five minutes ahead of Mira. They were having lunch at Kaminsky's, an upscale restaurant in Midtown.

"Table for one?" asked the hostess as he approached the ornate mahogany podium.

Jacob straightened his tie. "No. There will be two of us."

"Would you care to wait for your party at the bar?" she offered.

"No, I prefer to be seated." He looked around at the richly appointed dining room with its ocher walls and lemon pastel chintz-covered furnishings, and marveled at the sophistication of the interior. Artwork reminiscent of Renoir and Degas, but with brown faces, adorned the walls in gilded frames. The tables were draped in starched pastel-colored linens, with fresh-cut roses in crystal vases as a centerpiece. Lining the far wall were several Art Deco, high-back settees facing each other, serving as cozy booths. "I'd like a booth if possible," he answered. Knowing how particular Mira could be, she would no doubt prefer a choice booth instead of one of the tables in the middle of the floor.

"Sure, no problem," the hostess said, walking into the dining room.

Once seated, Jacob took out the debriefing reports from the London board meeting that his associate Nina had prepared. From her written as well as oral report, things had gone according to plan, all except for her tardiness due to an unforeseen traffic jam. Mira would surely belabor the incident, with a lecture on the virtues of time management. Jacob looked at his watch; it was twenty minutes to twelve. He knew from past lunch meetings with Mira that she always arrived fifteen minutes before the scheduled time. He began to fidget, but realized it wasn't because of the impending lecture, but from the thought of seeing Ms. Rhone. Though she was nearly half his age, he found her extremely attractive. Being married with a child, Jacob realized that he shouldn't have such thoughts. Naomi had been pressuring him lately to make love to her, but every time he tried, all he could picture was her legs in stirrups and their son coming out of her womb. In his mind, her role had changed, from lover to mother. It had been over a month since they had had sex, and over the past few weeks, he couldn't stop fantasizing about Mira and those long, lean legs of hers. He often imagined those legs wrapped tightly around his back, while he fucked her over and over again. He could feel the beginning of an erection at the thought of being in between those luscious limbs. Jacob didn't want to greet Mira with a woody, so he shifted his thoughts back to business. And as if on cue, Mira appeared in the doorway at exactly eleven forty-five. Jacob discreetly watched as she approached the table.

She wore a tailored, chocolate brown blazer that cinched her tiny waist, a brown silk blouse, and a brown tweed skirt that stopped just above the knee, emphasizing her well-defined calves. A pair of brown and black stilettos completed the outfit. Her hair was tied back in her signature chignon, giving her the perfect couture executive look.

"Good afternoon, Mira." He stood up and greeted her, extending his right hand.

She firmly returned the handshake. "Good afternoon, Jacob."

He motioned the waitress to the table so they could order quickly. Knowing his overscheduled client, she probably only had forty minutes to spare for lunch before dashing off to yet another appointment.

Mira sat down and, to Jacob's delight, took off her blazer. He couldn't help but gaze at her lacy, low-cut bra and ample cleavage exposed through the sheer fabric of the blouse.

She fanned her slender hand across her face. "Is it me, or is it warm in here?"

"Now that you mention it, it is a tad warm," he lied, and unbuttoned his suit jacket. Actually, the temperature in the restaurant was quite comfortable, but Jacob didn't want Mira to put her blazer back on and deprive him of a few cheap thrills.

"Would you care for a drink before lunch?" asked the waitress, appearing at their table.

"No, just the menu please," Mira said as she continued to fan her face.

The waitress handed over a set of menus and began to explain the specials. "This afternoon, we're serving poached skate, which is a mildly sweet, fleshy fish, topped with a pesto aioli and served with a medley of vegetables. We also have pan-seared tuna served with a creamy asparagus and white cheddar risotto."

Without pondering the menu, Mira said, "I'll have the tuna."

"How would you like that prepared?"

"Medium rare, please."

The waitress then turned her attention toward Jacob. "And you, sir?"

"I'll try the skate."

"Should I bring a bottle of water for the table, or would you prefer tap water?"

Before he could respond, Mira said, "Evian, please."

After the waitress disappeared toward the kitchen, Mira started in, "Jacob, I must say that I was extremely disappointed by Nina's performance. Her tardiness was——"

"From her reports, the meeting went well," he cut in, stopping her short, and then continued, "and the board has approved the additional funding for the children's line, so I don't see how you could be disappointed."

"Listen closely, Jacob. I need more than someone who can wield a pointer at a pie chart. I need the complete package." Her eyes shot him a piercing look. "And frankly, Nina doesn't possess that quality. She may be smart, but frankly, she's a bit on the frumpy side. Not that I'm judging, but she could benefit from using some of the products from the FACEZ makeup line, and . . ." She paused for a second, as if trying to decide to keep going with her laundry list of faults. "And her clothes are—how should I say—dated."

"Don't you think you're being a tad harsh on her?" he asked, leaning in within inches of her face. "After all, Mira, she was only a few minutes late and the tardiness had no bearing on the outcome of the meeting. I'll admit she's not a fashion plate, but she's one of my best accountants," he said in defense of Nina.

"Jacob, I realize that clothes don't make the person, but they do make a formidable impression. And besides, you know that punctuality is high on my list of attributes." Mira was a stickler for time. Her mother Rose was always running late. Most mornings Rose would be laid out in bed from a hangover and wouldn't get Mira to school on time. By the time Mira arrived, the morning would be nearly over, and she would have to play catch-up. Mira hated being tardy. She vowed once she became an adult that she would never be late again in life.

Mira then reached into her briefcase and took out a black appointment book. She flipped through the pages and said, "I suggest you mark your calendar. An emergency board meeting has been scheduled in two weeks, and I expect you to attend. I'm not going through another episode with your lame associate," she said in no uncertain terms.

Jacob felt like a fifth grader being chastised by an overbearing librarian for returning an overdue book. But at the same time, her directness gave him a sexual charge. He could just envision her barking orders in the bedroom—"Jacob, don't stop. Jacob, deeper. Jacob, harder. Jacob, fuck me again. Jacob . . ."

"Jacob," she nearly shouted, pulling him out of his trance, "did you hear what I said?"

Looking directly into her beautiful brown eyes, he responded, "I'll be at the next meeting." He eagerly took out an appointment book from his briefcase and marked the date in his calendar. Little did Mira know that Jacob was champing at the bit and couldn't wait to get her on another continent. London was far enough away that he could put the moves on Mira without the chance of being caught by his wife.

"Good." She put down her appointment book and took a manila file folder from her briefcase. "Now that we're guaranteed the funding to expand into the children's market, I want to earmark every single penny, so we'll need to schedule another meeting for next week before going to London."

Mira went down a laundry list of products for the new line. "After we complete the production on Baby FACEZ, I want to focus my attention on updating the adult line."

"Absolutely." He nodded in agreement.

They spent the remainder of the lunch discussing the financial projections for the next twelve months. Jacob admired her tenacity. She hadn't even completed the children's line, and here she was talking about revamping the adult line. "You should think about expanding into Australia," he suggested.

Mira put her water glass down. "I think that's a great idea; we could"—she stopped in midsentence, as if having an epiphany—"develop a line of high-end sunscreen products especially designed for the people down under."

"Exactly," he agreed. They were on the same wavelength, and he enjoyed brainstorming with such a sharp and sexy woman.

"As well as a specially designed sunblock for children. Our advertising agency can do a model search and find an unknown Aussie as our spokesperson." Mira's face was radiant as she began to tick off one idea after the other, until the complete campaign was fleshed out.

"Would you care for dessert?" asked the waitress, interrupting their conversation.

"No, thank you. Just the check, please," Mira said. "Jacob, this has been a very productive meeting." She stood to gather her belongings.

"Indeed it has," he said, watching her put on her blazer. She didn't button it, so he was able to steal another peek at her enticing cleavage.

Before the waitress came back with the check, Mira had her purse on her shoulder and briefcase in hand. "Thanks for lunch, Jacob. I hate to run, but I have another meeting in an hour."

"The pleasure was all mine." He smiled, standing up to get one last glimpse.

"I'll have my assistant call yours to schedule our next meeting." And with that said, Mira strutted toward the exit.

Jacob sat back down and watched her disappear out the door. Before settling the bill, he called the waitress over and ordered a slice of boysenberry cheesecake along with a demitasse cup of espresso. Over dessert, he could feel his erection returning as he envisioned unbuttoning Mira's blouse and unhooking her bra to expose her succulent breast. Smearing cheesecake over her nipples, he would feast on them, as if they were a decadent dessert. "Mira Rhone, I'm going to fuck you three ways to Sunday." He smiled to himself and slid a forkful of cheesecake into his expectant mouth, all the while fantasizing about Ms. Rhone.

11

"PERFECT," NAOMI commented to herself as she put the last French tulip in the vase, completing the exquisite floral arrangement of tulips, lilies, and freesias. She looked around the solarium, taking a visual inventory, making sure everything was perfect for today's book club meeting. The sun was beaming through the leaded triple pane windows, bouncing off the crystal vase and casting a kaleidoscope of color throughout the room. Identical celery-colored chaise lounges were the perfect complement to the ferns and philodendrons that lined the perimeter of the sun-drenched room. She went to the kitchen and retrieved a silver tray filled with crab, tuna, and chicken salads on water crackers. Returning, she placed the tray on the beveled glass cocktail table, then went upstairs to get dressed before the book club members arrived. The minute she stepped into the bedroom, she got an immediate flashback from the night before. Contrary to his usual late hours, her absentee husband had left the office at a decent hour.

*   *   *

"JACOB," NAOMI LOOKED up from the novel she was reading, "you're home early."

He walked over to the bed without saying a word, then sat on the edge among the myriad of books that were spread across the duvet, and placed a white foam box on the nightstand.

"What's that?" she asked, referring to the box.

"Cheesecake." He unbuttoned his shirt and loosened his tie.

"Since when did you start eating dessert during the week?" she asked, knowing Jacob was weight conscious and rarely indulged in sweets unless it was a special occasion.

Unbuckling his belt, he said in a strange, faraway voice, "It's not for me."

Naomi had a confused look on her face. Before she could ask why he had brought the dessert upstairs instead of putting it in the refrigerator, he stood up, slipped out of his pants, and said, "It's for us." Then, totally out of character, Jacob straddled her, closed his eyes, and began to massage her breasts, all in one swift move.

Naomi's nipples hardened beneath the sheer fabric of the nightgown. She was confused and excited at the same time. She couldn't remember the last time that her husband had initiated sex. She wanted to ask what had gotten him all riled up, but didn't want to destroy the mood, so she sank back into the down-filled pillows and enjoyed the sensation. Jacob began to suck her nipples through the sheer fabric of the gown.

Suddenly he stopped. "Take that off."

Naomi quickly slipped the gown over her head and Jacob stared at her breasts like he was seeing them for the first time. He then reached over to the nightstand and picked up the foam box. He took out the cheesecake and smeared the rich creamy dessert all over her breasts. "Jacob, what are you doing?" Naomi was caught totally off guard. He'd never done anything this imaginative before. She was instantly transported to the movie *9 1/2 Weeks*, when Mickey Rourke and Kim Basinger were sitting on the kitchen floor in front of an open refrigerator feasting off of each other's bodies, like love-starved animals.

He didn't say a word; with his eyes closed, he began sucking her breasts like they were the most delicious thing he had ever tasted. After hungrily devouring the cheesecake from her bare skin, he licked remnants of cheesecake from the corners of his mouth.

Now that they had finished dessert, Naomi was ready for the main course. She was completely moist and wanted to feel the length of her husband's penis inside of her wet canal. Reaching down, she found the rim of his underwear and began to massage the tip of his manhood.

Suddenly his eyes popped opened, as if he were coming out of a trance. He looked at her and said, "Stop, Naomi."

But she didn't stop until her hand was completely inside of his shorts and she had a firm grip on his cock. Instead of his dick growing at her touch, it began to slowly deflate, which didn't make sense to her. She could remember a time when she could make him ejaculate from one of her famous hand jobs; now her hand wasn't even close to doing the job.

He pulled away, and slightly raised his voice. "Naomi. Please. Stop."

"Stop!" she shouted. "You've got to be kidding me. You come in here, smear cheesecake all over my titties, and suck on my nipples like a newborn starving for breast milk. Now you want to stop! You've got to be kidding me!" she said again, totally sexually frustrated at this point.

"Calm down, Naomi," he said, lowering his voice, trying to defuse the situation.

"I'll calm down, after you fuck me!" she demanded. "And don't give me that 'I'm tired' bullshit, 'cause it's getting old."

"Come here." He pulled her close to his chest. "It's not that I don't want to make love to you; just let me relax a minute and let the blood flow back down where it belongs. Licking your breasts made me so excited that I nearly came. Now I'm going to need some time to regroup," he said. Jacob's explanation was just another excuse not to make love to his wife. The truth was that he was envisioning feasting on Mira's titties, but the moment he opened his eyes and saw Naomi's face, his libido plummeted like a fighter pilot going down in flames.

Naomi wanted more than a warm embrace, but she reluctantly leaned back into him anyway, hoping that the spark that lit his fire when he walked into the room would reignite so that they could make love.

Jacob seemed to feel the frustration coursing through his wife's body and began rocking her back and forth until her shoulders relaxed. Before long, she drifted off to sleep. When she awoke the next morning, the tenseness in her body was gone and so was Jacob. Once again, he had escaped like Houdini.

THE BELL RANG, bringing Naomi back to the present. She tried to hook the clasp on her pearl necklace, but couldn't find the catch. The doorbell rang again, and she put the necklace back in the jewelry box instead of tackling the tiny clasp. She quickly brushed her hair and rushed downstairs to answer the door.

"So, you are home? What took you so long? I was just about to leave," said an irritated Kennedy.

"Sorry. I was trying to fasten my pearl necklace, but the clasp is so intricate that I couldn't hook it by myself."

Kennedy stepped into the foyer. "Yeah, those things can be tricky. I bought a necklace in Nigeria that has a tiny clasp, so I just slip it over my head. Am I the first one here?" she asked.

"Yep, Susan isn't here yet," Naomi said, leading the way to the solarium.

"When is she ever on time?" Kennedy hissed.

Susan was a single mom whom Naomi had met at parents' night at Noah's school. As they each waited their turn to speak with the teacher, Naomi noticed she and Susan were reading the same novel. After striking up a conversation, she discovered that Susan was an avid reader, as well as the mother of Noah's friend Simon. At that time, the book club was down to two people, so Naomi invited her to join. Initially, Susan was the ideal member, recommending bestsellers and sparking engaging commentary. But lately, her commitment had begun to wane.

"Give her a break, Ken. She just started a new job. Susan used to be the first one here and the last one to leave." Switching gears, Naomi asked, "Do you want a Bellini?"

"I'd love one."

"Come on in the kitchen while I mix up a batch."

Naomi opened the refrigerator, took out a bottle of champagne and a bottle of fresh peach nectar. "So, tell me. Did you see your mystery guy on your last trip?"

"Yeah, I saw him." Kennedy plopped her body onto one of the bar stools at the counter island.

Taking a pitcher out of the cabinet, Naomi asked, "What's his name again?"

"Nigel Charles," Kennedy answered unenthusiastically.

Pouring the champagne and nectar into the pitcher, she asked, "So you gonna keep me in suspense or tell me what happened on the flight?"

"There's nothing to tell." Kennedy looked down at her nails.

"Well, did he at least say anything personal this time?" Naomi asked, stirring the champagne and nectar together to make Bellinis.

"No." She shifted uncomfortably on the stool. "He didn't even look in my direction after I served dinner. So suffice it to say, the rest of the flight was uneventful." Kennedy omitted the part about her getting so turned on by Nigel that she masturbated in the lavatory. Some business was just too personal to discuss, even with close friends.

Naomi poured the Bellini into a champagne flute and handed it to Kennedy. "Do you think he's gay?"

"I doubt it. He just isn't interested," she uttered, with a hint of rejection in her voice.

Naomi looked over at Kennedy, and suddenly felt a wave of relief rush over her. Though she was married to a workaholic, it was still better than being on the front line of the dating scene. The ratio of men to women was so disproportionate, with women outweighing men by at least five to one, which translated to multiple women sharing one man. And if the man did decide to commit, he'd do so in his own sweet time. Men had too many options—translation, too many women to choose from—which was probably why this Nigel Charles guy didn't feel the need to frantically pursue Kennedy.

"Don't be silly," Naomi said, trying to cheer her up. "Why wouldn't he be interested? You're gorgeous, and have a great sense of style."

Kennedy was, by all accounts, *Jet* centerfold fine, with warm, caramel-macchiato skin highlighting half-moon eyes, and a warm personality that could thaw the coldest iceberg. She ran her hand through her hair, which she wore cropped closely, reminiscent of a Halle Berry–style cut. "Thanks, Naomi."

They were silent for a moment, as if lost in thought. Kennedy sipped the champagne cocktail, put the glass on the counter, and then spoke in a quiet tone, almost a whisper. "Be grateful you have a husband who loves you, and that you don't have to be out there anymore. It's rough trying to find a man. The competition is fierce, and men know that they have the upper hand."

She must have been reading Naomi's thoughts. "Trust me, I am. The thought of being back on the dating scene makes me cringe. The only competition I have to deal with is Jacob's job," she said matter-of-factly, trying to hide her disappointment.

"So, I take it Jacob hasn't cut back on his hours?" she asked.

"No, but he came in early last night and almost rocked my world."

"Almost? What does that mean?"

Naomi told Kennedy how Jacob came into the room horny and heated up, painting her breasts with cheesecake, and how excited she was to be getting laid, but before he delivered on his overdue promise, his fire was snuffed out.

"Why do you think he stopped?" Kennedy had never experienced anything like that, and wondered what would make a man go cold in the middle of foreplay.

"I have no idea. Your guess is as good as mine," Naomi said, sounding totally exasperated.

As they were pondering the reasons for Jacob's sudden change of heart, the telephone rang. "Hello?" Naomi answered. "Hey, Susan, where are you? . . . That's a bummer . . . Well, if your hours change, we'd love to have you back."

"I take it Susan isn't coming," Kennedy said, once Naomi hung up the phone.

"No, she's working the night shift over at Memorial."

"Is she a nurse?"

"Yeah, and since she's the new person at the bottom of the totem pole, she's stuck with overnights." Naomi poured herself a cocktail and clinked Kennedy's glass. "Looks like it's just gonna be the two of us."

"What happened to Caroline?" Kennedy asked, referring to the fourth member of their book club.

"Girl, didn't I tell you?"

"Tell me what?" Kennedy looked perplexed.

"Caroline and her family moved a week ago. Her husband's firm relocated to Denver."

"We're losing members faster than a leper colony," Kennedy teased.

"You're right. Maybe we should place a classified on Craigslist that reads: Book club in desperate need of members," Naomi joked back. "Do you know anybody who'd be interested in join-ing?"

Kennedy hesitated for a minute. "No, not really."

"What about Monica?"

"Between flying and babysitting her husband, I'm sure she would not be interested in reading books with us. Besides, I see her enough at work."

Naomi had thought about giving up on the whole book club idea, but it was such a great social outlet for her. Aside from vol-unteering at the Museum of Urban Art a few times a month, she was the basic suburban housewife. Though she had dreams of one day becoming an interior designer, she'd yet to start making that dream a reality. "Do you want to postpone the meetings un-til we have a full house?" Naomi asked anyway, in case Kennedy wanted to spend her free time elsewhere.

"No. It's not like my social calendar is overflowing. Besides, we'll find more victims soon." Kennedy laughed. "Now, pour me another drink and let's discuss this cheesy love story."

"It's not cheesy," Naomi said in mock defense of the book she had chosen. "It's romantic."

"Cheesy? Romantic? What's the difference? The next book, I get to choose, and you can best believe it won't have a Fabio look-alike on the cover."

"Let's forget about the book. I've got something juicier to talk about," Naomi said with a gleam in her eyes and sat on one of the stools across from Kennedy.

"What's that look for?"

"I think I've found the solution to both of our problems."

"And what problem is that?"

"Kennedy, you're not getting any dick, and neither am I. Correct?" Naomi said, more as a statement than a question.

"Unfortunately, that is correct. So what's the solution? Hire a pair of gigolos?" She laughed.

"You're laughing, but I'm serious."

Kennedy stopped laughing, and looked at Naomi like she had lost her mind. "Serious about hiring a gigolo?"

"No, no! Well . . . not exactly."

"Not exactly? Naomi, what are you talking about?"

"The other day, I picked up the phone and instead of a dial tone, I was patched into another line. I was going to hang up, but these women started talking about this place called the Black Door. Have you ever heard of it?"

"No, I haven't. Is it a new restaurant?"

Naomi slowly shook her head. "Girrl, it's an erotica club exclusively for women. Men work there, but they can't be members."

Kennedy put her elbows on the counter and placed her hands underneath her chin. She was intrigued. "Really? Tell me more."

"From what I heard, this place sounds like the bomb. For starters, everyone wears a mask."

"Sounds like the movie *Eyes Wide Shut*."

"I know, but it gets better. There's a champagne fountain that spews ice-cold vodka, and the furnishings are imported from Europe," Naomi said excitedly, as if she'd seen the club with her own eyes.

"Where is it located?"

"I don't know. The woman never said. She didn't even mention whether it was on the East or West Side. I looked on the Internet and in the Yellow Pages, but couldn't find any information."

"I'm sure a club like that is totally under the radar. Now the big question is, how can we find out more? As horny as I've been lately, the Black Door sounds like exactly what I need. If nothing more than to just have a drink and look at some fine men in tight shorts. I'm sure they only hire model-looking types." Kennedy could envision an array of buffed hunks parading around in their skivvies, showing off their cocks.

"I've never paid for sex before, but I'm feeling desperate.

The woman also said that everyone is tested for STDs, so the club is safe."

"This place is sounding better and better. Since the Black Door is not listed on the Internet, how are we going to find out where it is?" Kennedy asked, again.

"I don't know. All I know is if I don't get some sex soon, I'm going to lose my mind."

"Me too," Kennedy agreed.

"I know I should be concentrating on getting my interior design business off the ground instead of focusing so much on sex, but I can't help it," Naomi said, taking a sip of her drink.

"You haven't talked about starting your business for so long that I thought you had forgotten about it."

"I've been putting it off and putting it off, but now that Noah is in school and Jacob is at work most of the time, I figured I might as well do something for myself."

"I know what you mean. I've actually been thinking about going back to school," Kennedy said.

"Law school?"

"No. I'm not interested in being an attorney anymore. Buying unique clothes and pieces of jewelry on my travels has gotten me interested in becoming a buyer, or maybe starting my own import/export business."

"Wow, Ken! That sounds perfect for you. You have such great taste."

"Thanks. I'm getting tired of flying. I don't want to be an old hag still trying to maneuver those tiny aisles in my blue polyester uniform," she said, chuckling.

"You're far from being a hag. So when are you planning on quitting?"

"I don't know yet. I've only begun to think about this buying thing. I need to save more money before I leave the airline, so that I can have a cushion."

"That's wise. Speaking of saving, I need to talk to Jacob

about investing in my business. He's been so busy lately that I haven't had a chance to tell him my plan."

"You think he'll have a problem with it?"

"I don't think so. It's not like we're hurting financially, and he can see from the way I decorated our home that I have the talent. Knowing Jacob, he'll want to do a budget projection and map out the next five years on paper, before I even have a company name."

"That's the accountant in him. Good luck with your plan." Kennedy raised her glass. The two friends toasted to their impending businesses, and chatted the evening away.

12

"GIRL, YOU won't believe this shit!" The remote speaker clipped onto the sun visor magnified every syllable. "I'm so upset!" Naomi yelled.

"Stop screaming and tell me what's wrong," Kennedy said calmly. She was surprised at Naomi's erratic tone. The night before at their pseudo book club meeting, Naomi was relaxed and jovial; now she was shouting at the top of her lungs.

Naomi was darting in and out of traffic like Mario Andretti in the Indy 500, speeding along the LIE on the way to the Museum of Urban Art. Twice a month, she volunteered in the curator's office cataloging artwork. "Jacob is about two seconds from getting a divorce petition from my attorney!" She screamed, honked the horn, and then yelled at the car in front of her, *"Pick a lane!"*

"You have a divorce attorney?" Kennedy asked, sounding surprised. She knew Naomi's relationship was far from perfect, but she had no idea that divorce was on her friend's mind.

"What?" Beeepppp. *"Pick a fucking lane!!"*

"Nothing," Kennedy said, thinking twice about quizzing Naomi while she was experiencing road rage. *Beep, beep, beep.* Kennedy could hear the blare of the car horn through the phone.

"You no-driving..."

Kennedy cut her off, "Naomi!"

"Son of a..."

"Naomi, pull over right now!" Kennedy yelled into the receiver, trying to get her friend off the road before she had an accident.

Naomi pulled over on the shoulder and exhaled hard. "Alright, I'm off the road with all of those no-driving assholes," she said, still fuming.

"Good. Now, tell me why you're so upset. Are you seriously thinking about divorcing Jacob?" Kennedy asked hesitantly.

"I should divorce him for letting Tyler move in without even consulting me!" Naomi spat out.

"Tyler who?"

"Jacob's sister."

"Oh, yeah. I thought she lived in Atlanta. When is ... hold on, my other line is ringing." After a few seconds, Kennedy came back on the line. "Sorry about that. It was an annoying telemarketer. Now, tell me, when is she moving in? But I guess the question should be, why is she moving in?"

"She broke up with her girlfriend and moved out of the house with no place to go." Naomi recounted the story that Jacob told her over the phone. "But the kicker is that he didn't even ask me before he invited her to move in with us. He basically *told* me after the fact."

"What! You've got to be kidding. It's your house too, and that should've been a joint decision."

"That's exactly what I think, but obviously Jacob thinks totally differently. Evidently she played the defenseless little sister, damsel in distress role with her gay ass."

"Now, now, no name-calling."

"To each his own as far as I'm concerned, but this is a little too close to home. I mean, Tyler is okay. I just don't want her bringing that homo mess into my house," Naomi said, hitting the steering wheel with her fist out of frustration.

Naomi was homophobic. When she was a teenager, Naomi's favorite cousin, Roselyn, moved in with her family. Naomi and Roselyn were as thick as thieves and did everything together, until Roselyn started hanging out with the girl next door. Naomi tried to include herself on their trips to the mall and to the movies, but Roselyn would always have an excuse as to why Naomi couldn't come along. Naomi became jealous and resentful. She wanted desperately to be a part of their two-person clique, but was kicked to the curb and didn't understand why, until one day she came home early from school and caught Roselyn in bed with the girl next door. Naomi stood in the doorway in horror as she watched them suck each other's breasts. Naomi nearly threw up. She couldn't understand how two people of the same sex could be attracted to each other. Even as a teenager, she felt it was unnatural for two women to be intimately involved. Naomi never told Roselyn what she saw that day, she just distanced herself from her cousin and had carried around her prejudice ever since.

"Naomi, you're being paranoid. She probably just needs a little support. After all, she did catch her girlfriend in the mix with a *man*," Kennedy said, commenting on the thirdhand information filtered down from Tyler, to Jacob, to Naomi, and now to her. "How devastating must that have been?" she asked, trying to see Tyler's point of view.

"Well, let her move in with you, since you're so damn liberal." Naomi couldn't believe Kennedy. She was fuming mad, on the verge of rupturing a vessel, and Kennedy was sounding so damn calm and cavalier. "I thought you were on my side."

"I didn't know there were sides," she shot back.

"You know what I mean." Naomi exhaled loudly. "I just don't

need the extra stress. With Jacob putting in 140 hours a week, who do you think will have to deal with her on a daily basis? Certainly not Mr. Workaholic." She banged the steering wheel again.

"Naomi, I'm sure it's not going to be that bad. With her living in Atlanta all these years, you guys haven't had the opportunity to get to know each other. Give her a chance. She's probably really a cool person." Kennedy thought back to Naomi and Jacob's rehearsal dinner and remembered the heart-warming speech Tyler gave. From her tender words everyone could see how much she loved her brother. She wasn't hard-core like some gay women. She was artsy and stylish.

Naomi wouldn't relent. "Cool or not, I don't want to live with a lesbian."

"Well, it's not like she's going to be sleeping in the same bed with you."

"Ugh, don't be lewd." Naomi looked at the clock on the dash. She had fifteen minutes to make it to SoHo. She put the car in gear and pulled back into traffic.

"Just give the girl a break. After all, she is your sister-in-law," Kennedy said, trying to be the voice of reason.

"You sound like Jacob. Anyway, it doesn't matter what I think, since she's moving in as we speak. I'm so glad I'm out of the house this afternoon, because I don't feel like rolling out the welcome runner and pretending like everything is hunky-dory."

"Play nice." Kennedy laughed.

"Are you laughing at me?"

"I'm not laughing at you. I'm laughing with you."

"But I'm not laughing." She was dead serious. "I'll talk to you later." Naomi expected more support from her best friend and since she wasn't getting it, she didn't have time to be Kennedy's source of amusement for the afternoon.

"Are you mad, Naomi?" Kennedy asked, sensing her mood.

"No, but I'm hanging up now because I'm running late and need to concentrate on driving."

"Okay. Call me tonight and let me know how the move went."

"Yeah, okay. Talk to you later," she said, disconnecting the line.

Naomi was still fuming, and began to babble. "I called her for support and she's talking about 'give the girl a break.' I know what I'm going to give her and that's a month of free room and board. After that, girlfriend is on her own. Since Jacob was bold enough to *tell* me his sister is moving in, I'm going to be bold enough to *tell* him that she only has four weeks to figure it out."

"Jacob. Work," she spoke into the speaker. A second later, the automatic dial had connected her to his office.

"Good afternoon. Mr. Reed's office," answered his secretary.

"Hi, Charlotte. Is he in?"

"Hello, Mrs. Reed. Actually, he's in a meeting. Do you want me to interrupt him?"

She thought about it for a second, but decided not to disturb him. *Since he didn't have the decency to consult me before he made a decision that affected us both, why should I consult him now? I'll tell Tyler myself that she has a month to find a place, and if Jacob doesn't like it, then too bad.* "No, Charlotte, don't interrupt his meeting. I'll speak to him later."

After hanging up, she turned the radio to the easy jazz station and sang along with Celine Dion. Now that Naomi had regained her power, she immediately felt better. And would feel even better once she let Tyler know that *her* home wasn't some damn Motel 6!

13

MIRA COULDN'T get Sam's words out of her head. *It's over* kept ringing in her ears as if it were on rewind. Mira had called Sam earlier that day for one of their afternoon lovemaking sessions. She expected Sam to drop everything like she had done so many times before, but Sam dropped a bomb on her instead, and abruptly ended their relationship. She said that Mira was too clingy and demanding. Sam also said that she, too, had a business to run, and couldn't afford to drop her clients at a moment's notice for a booty call. Mira was hurt. She had grown accustomed to Sam being at her beck and call. Mira was used to getting her way. Midway through her adolescence, GG stepped in and moved Mira in with her. Rose gladly gave up her daughter. She preferred spending time partying to taking care of a child. Trying to make up for the neglect, GG spoiled Mira to death, giving her anything she wanted. Now as an adult Mira still expected people to give in to her whims. But Sam had had enough.

Not being the sulking or begging type, Mira didn't skip a

beat. She was a realist, and knew there was no sense in trying to talk someone into being with you when they obviously didn't want to. However, she was still horny, and determined to have sex. Since Sam was now history, she dusted off her custom-made Venetian mask, put on a gold thong and gold stilettos, wrapped herself in a black satin evening coat, and headed out the door.

Mira had been a member of the Black Door since they first opened. She wasn't a regular, but kept her membership active in case of a sexual emergency, and tonight definitely qualified as urgent.

The cab ride up the West Side Highway was smooth sailing. It was late at night, and traffic was light. Mira paid the driver once he pulled up in front of the club, but before exiting, she strapped on her mask, adjusted the belt around her coat, and stepped out. Mira sauntered toward the black shiny door and tapped lightly.

A tiny window slid open, and all she could see was a pair of piercing, coal black eyes. "Password, please," the keeper of the gate demanded in a deep, baritone voice.

"Powerbroker Pussy," Mira replied. She noticed his eyes glancing down, as if he were looking at some type of list. A few seconds later, she heard a bolt slide, and then he opened the door.

"I don't need tweaking," she said to him before he asked. Having been to the club a few times before, Mira knew that the doorman digitally stimulated the members once they stepped inside. Her pussy was already moist, therefore she didn't need his fingers roaming across her clit. Mira walked into the main parlor, but bypassed the vodka fountain. She didn't need any liquid encouragement either. The only thing she needed was to get laid, and that's exactly what she intended to do, so she headed directly to the second level looking for lust.

Once upstairs, Mira untied her belt. As she walked down the hallway, her coat flowed open, exposing her bare breasts, tight torso, and tiny thong. The club was lively, and Mira slowed her pace to get an eyeful of the activities that were taking place. Her peripheral vision caught sight of a server nailing a member against the wall. The woman's legs were wrapped around his waist, and he was gripping her naked ass as he rammed his rod deep into her hot box. Mira heard the woman moan out in ecstasy. *Get that dick, girl,* Mira mused as she passed them.

Mira decided to go into the Pink Room, which was where most of the lesbians hung out. Everything in the room was pink, from the furniture to the carpeting to the cocktails. Mira removed her coat and settled herself on one of the vacant sofas.

"Hmm, don't you look tasty?"

Mira looked up and standing before her was a member wearing a white wife-beater, a pair of tight jeans, and a tangerine mask. The woman bore a striking resemblance to Sam. Mira couldn't see her entire face, but her muscular body was a dead ringer. Suddenly Sam's words, *It's over,* started ringing in her ears again. Mira thought she wanted her clit licked by a chick, but the pain of Sam's rejection was too fresh. And after seeing the couple fucking in the hallway, she decided that she wanted some dick instead. "Excuse me," she said to the member as she got up to leave.

"Where're you going?" the woman asked.

"To get laid. Now if you'll excuse me," she said again.

Mira made her way to the Leopard Lounge, sat at the bar, and perused the room. It was too dark to make out much of anything, so she ordered a Cumtini and waited to get propositioned. With her firm breasts exposed, it didn't take long for a server to approach.

"Hey, sexy."

"Hey, yourself." Mira swiveled around on the bar stool to get a better look. She couldn't see the bottom half of his face clearly, but his neck was thick, like a linebacker's. *I wonder if his dick is as thick.* Her eyes continued down his body, stopping at his muscular chest and continuing onto his taut midsection, then traveled south beyond the waistband of his jeans. Even though it was dark, she could see the bulge protruding from his jeans. She swallowed hard. Mira hadn't had a real penis inside of her body since her engagement, and up until now, she hadn't missed it.

"You up for some fun?" he asked, glaring at her boobs.

Mira crossed her legs and poked her chest out farther. "What did you have in mind?"

He stepped closer, so that his cock brushed against her thigh. "I'm thinking first you might want to find out what I'm packing."

She could feel him admiring her assets, and it made her feel like a woman. Not that being with another female made her feel any less feminine, but somehow a man's appreciation of her body was more gratifying. Mira equated the feeling to her being more bisexual than homosexual, but at the moment she was feeling totally heterosexual. At his invitation, she began caressing his package. It was warm and hard. She slowly unzipped his jeans, careful not to catch his peter in the process. She then reached inside and pulled out what he had to offer. His offering was more than substantial. Not only was he long, but the circumference of his penis was thicker than two silver dollars wielded together. "Nice," Mira heard herself say.

"You like what you see?"

She rubbed the round tip. "Yes, I do."

"You want what you see?"

Their verbal foreplay was making her hotter. "Yes."

He leaned down and lightly kissed the soft skin in between her breasts, and then trailed his tongue from one nipple to the next, until he heard her gasp. "Come on," he whispered in her ear.

Mira stepped off the stool and followed him to the back of the lounge where the private booths were. He sat down and pulled her on top of him. She straddled him until she could feel his girth grow beneath her moistness. "Fuck me," she hissed in his ear.

"Slow down, little lady," he said, resting his hands on her hips.

Mira was accustomed to being in control and didn't like taking a backseat. "What's the problem? Can't you keep it up?"

He lifted his hips and poked his penis deeper against her vulva. "Does this feel up to you?"

Mira couldn't help but smile. His dick was harder than earlier, and the tip was wedging its way past the thin thong into her waiting canal. She opened her legs wider to allow him easier access. "Now that it's up, why don't you follow through and complete the task?" she said, sounding like the CEO that she was.

He didn't say another word. He grabbed her ass cheeks with both hands, spreading them apart. He then rammed her once with his weapon, stopped, waited a few seconds, and rammed her again. His rhythm was erratic, and it was driving her crazy trying to anticipate his next thrust. "Come on. Give it to me!"

"I see you're one of them control freaks." He gave her another hard thrust. "But you ain't controlling shit tonight!" He slapped her ass.

Mira flinched, not only at his touch, but also from his words. She wasn't accustomed to anyone speaking to her harshly. As much as she didn't want to admit it, being manhandled felt good, so she decided to go with his program. After all, he was the professional and she was going to let him do his job.

Once she submitted, he pushed his penis deep inside of her, fucking her with such force that he nearly bounced her off of his lap. "Is this what you want? To get fucked?" he asked between clinched teeth as he grabbed her waist and pressed her farther down onto his shaft.

He was penetrating Mira so deeply that she could barely talk. "Yeess," was the only word that she was able to utter.

His random ramming became a succinct rhythm. Mira wrapped her arms around his neck and rode him like a prized steer. They fucked hard for what seemed like hours, when in actuality it was only minutes, but in those few minutes, Mira came harder than she had ever come in her life. She had to admit, getting fucked by a man was much better than getting fucked with a strap-on. However she still enjoyed the softness of a woman's lips on her pussy. When they finished, her V-spot was aching, and her thighs were sore—a sure sign of hard-core fornication. He had punished her pussy, and his assault was just what she needed to forget about her lost love.

"YOU'RE QUIET this trip."

As usual, Monica had her finger on the pulse of Kennedy's feelings. Kennedy was in a sulky mood because Nigel Charles was on board, focusing his attention on a stack of papers spread out on the pullout table in front of his seat, instead of focusing on her. Not that she expected him to bow at her feet, but it would've been nice if he took notice. He barely looked in her direction when she served him dinner. "I'm not in a talkative mood," she responded, arranging the miniature bottles of port on the liquor shelf.

"You need to change your mood and mosey on over and talk to Mr. Man," Monica said, referring to Nigel.

"Thank you, but no. I'm not interested in making a fool out of myself. He doesn't even know I exist," she sulked, sounding like a jilted ex-girlfriend.

Monica peeked her head out of the galley to see what Nigel was doing. "Maybe you're right. He does seem to be preoccupied with work," she commented, noticing the menagerie of documents spread out before him. "He's busy with paperwork *and* talking on the phone."

"What could be so important that he has to waste money on an in-flight call? Those international rates are astronomical," Kennedy added, secretly wishing that he was talking to her instead of whoever was on the other end of the line.

"He's probably not paying for the call out of pocket anyway. I bet he's some type of bigwig with a hefty expense account," Monica surmised.

"I'm sure you're right, even though he looks more like a model than a businessman," Kennedy said, finally acknowledging his appearance. His wavy hair was cropped close and lined perfectly as if he had just gotten a fresh haircut. His eyes were tiny slits, with an Asian look to them, and his bronzy complexion was flawless. The one feature on his face that had her captivated was his luscious-looking lips. His bottom lip was fuller than the top one, and she could just picture herself sucking on it. Kennedy could feel her desire for him heating up. Even though she didn't know Nigel, it didn't stop her from wanting to fuck him. Kennedy's sexuality had been awakened at an early age, and it just kept growing. Now, as an adult, she didn't have a problem with expressing herself sexually, but she realized that acting on her every impulse wasn't wise. Kennedy couldn't help but think about the conversation she had with Naomi regarding finding the Black Door. The club would relieve her sexual tension, which she needed desperately, before she became impulsive and sexed up a stranger. Kennedy's panties were getting moist at the thought, and she quickly changed the subject before she began drooling. "Anyway, enough about him, we need to start the turn-down service," she said abruptly.

They were on an overnight flight from South Africa to New York, and had another twelve hours before touching down in the Big Apple. Kennedy went through the cabin and took one last check before dimming the lights for the evening.

"Okay, we'll continue this conversation once I get stateside," Nigel said, finishing his call and putting the phone back in the cradle.

"Would you care for a nightcap, maybe a port or some brandy?" Kennedy offered, approaching his seat.

He looked up into her eyes and stared as if seeing her for the first time tonight, then said, "Excuse me?"

She was shocked into silence by his piercing stare, a stare that seemed to penetrate her soul. For a moment, Kennedy felt a cosmic connection with him, but quickly shook it off. It was probably the altitude—coupled with lust—that had her head swimming in the clouds. "Would you care for a nightcap?" she repeated.

"No, thank you, but I would like another pillow if you have one available."

"Sure, no problem." She walked to the utility closet in front of the plane and took out a small, square, down pillow. When she returned, he had his head turned toward the window with his eyes shut. Not wanting to disturb him, she tipped away and checked on the rest of the passengers.

Once everyone was tucked in for the night, Kennedy went back to her compartment and settled in with her book club selection of the month, *A Few Dollars and a Dream*, which was actually quite good; the main plot focused on an ex-con who was trying to finance his dream of opening a youth center. Because of the misdemeanors he had committed in his youth, banks wouldn't give him the time of day. His only alternative to raise the money for the center was to do a "favor" for a local street pharmacist. All he had to do was drop off a "package" and he would get paid. He carefully weighed the pros and cons, then decided against his better judgment to make the drop. The first delivery went as smooth as silk without incident, which led to a second and third drop, until he was back in the business full-time, making more money in ten minutes than most people made in ten hours. Realizing that he didn't want to land back in the clink, he decided to make one last delivery. But just when he thought he was home free, an attractive female undercover detective nabbed him after he completed the drop. After interrogating him and learning that he wasn't the average drug dealer, but a man who was trying to keep kids from following in his tainted footsteps, she called in a few favors to keep him out of jail. Soon her attraction to the sexy ex-con heated up and they began a torrid affair.

"If she can find romance on the streets, why can't I find it in the sky?" Kennedy mused, and turned off the light in her compartment for a little shut-eye. A full bladder and a few air pockets later, she was up and on her way to the lavatory. The two restrooms in first class were occupied, so she made her way back through coach. The cabin was quiet except for the soft sounds of sleeping passengers.

"I could've stayed in first," she mumbled, looking at the red occupied signs on both lavatories. Kennedy crossed and recrossed her legs as she waited impatiently. Thinking that the restrooms in first were probably now available, she turned to walk away.

"Hey, where are you going?"

Kennedy swung around, and her mouth fell open as she stood there in shock like Bambi caught in the crosshairs. Standing in the doorway of the lavatory was Nigel Charles.

"Come here," he whispered, crooking his finger back and forth, gesturing it toward her.

Kennedy looked around the cabin for prying eyes, but everyone seemed to be sound asleep. She took a step forward, and when she got within arm's distance of Nigel, he pulled her into the lavatory and quickly closed the door. Standing there face-to-face inside the tiny confines of the restroom, she could feel heat emanating from his body. Kennedy opened her mouth to speak, but the words were caught somewhere between her mind and her larynx. Their eyes seemed to say what their mouths could not. His eyes searched her face, as if memorizing every minute detail.

"What are you do . . . " she attempted to say.

He put his finger to her lips before she could complete the sentence, then slowly removed his index finger and replaced it with his lips. He kissed Kennedy softly, introducing his lips to hers. Once the introduction was made, he wrapped his arms around her waist and pulled her into him so close that their bodies seemed to mesh into one. Their tongues did a sensuous duet, moving to a silent, seductive rhythm, until she suddenly pulled back. Though she desired him, she didn't want to jeopardize her job by making out in the bathroom. "What are you doing?" Kennedy asked, this time completing the question.

He took half a step back, but held firm to her waist. "I'm sorry. I know this must seem as if it's coming out of the blue, but I've been wanting to kiss you for a long time. You're so beautiful, and I just couldn't help myself. Please forgive me if I've offended you."

"I thought you were disinterested. You never seem to notice me," she said, sounding slightly annoyed that he hadn't said anything until now.

"Notice you?" He chuckled. "How could I miss you? You're a knockout. I was smitten the very first time I saw your face."

"You never said anything. As a matter of fact you never even looked twice in my direction."

"Trust me, I looked," he said, licking his lips. "You just never caught me staring."

"Then why didn't you say something before now?" She wanted to know.

He looked away for a moment, and then turned back to her. "To be honest, I've been burned in the past and I'm a little gun-shy."

"Well, pulling me into the restroom surely wasn't a shy move."

He blushed and then said, "I apologize again if I offended you. I didn't plan to pounce on you like that, but when the opportunity presented itself, I thought fate was telling me to take a chance, so I went for it."

"I'm glad you did." She blushed back.

He extended his hand. "I'm Nigel Charles," he said, making a formal introduction.

"Kennedy Bryant." She shook his hand.

"Well, Ms. Bryant, if it's alright with you, I'd like to start from square one and take you out to dinner."

"How do you know that I'm not married?" she teased.

"Well, I didn't see any rings. And if you have a boyfriend, that's just a minor detail that we'll deal with later," he said with an air of confidence.

She couldn't help but laugh. This guy was so full of himself. Usually arrogance was a serious turnoff, but his cockiness oozed a certain sex appeal that she found attractive. "I guess I could say the same thing about your girlfriend."

"I don't have a wife, girlfriend, or significant other," he said, looking directly into her eyes.

"Neither do I," she admitted.

"Well, I'm glad you don't have a wife or girlfriend, because you never know these days," he said matter-of-factly.

"I'm as straight as they come. Don't get me wrong; I'm not homophobic. It's just that I like men too much to go to the other side."

He smiled. "Good. Now that we've established our sexual preferences and availability, when can I take you to dinner?"

Kennedy couldn't believe the sudden turn of events. Just a short while ago, she was living vicariously through a character in a novel, and now she was talking to the man of her desires. She reached into the pocket of her smock and took out a pen, then tore off a piece of paper towel and jotted down her home number.

"Call me." She handed him the paper. She tried to turn around in the small space. "I need to get out of here and get back to work." The need to use the bathroom had vanished for now, besides she couldn't possibly go with Nigel in such close proximity.

He folded the number, put it in his pocket, and then stepped aside. As she squeezed past, he kissed the back of her neck.

Kennedy's knees buckled as he nuzzled close behind. She could feel the bulge in his pants pressing against her ass, and it felt good. For a scant moment, she thought about joining the Mile High Club, but it was too risky. Without turning around, she said, "Just so you know, I'm not into casual sex. Been there, done that, and frankly, I don't like the empty feeling afterward." She said it more for her benefit than for his. Kennedy needed to remind herself of her promise to wait and get to know a man before screwing him.

"Good, because I'm not a casual type of brother."

"We'll see." She had dated men who agreed to refrain from having casual sex just to appease her, when in actuality they had no intention of waiting. She turned the latch on the door. "I think you should stay in here for a few seconds just in case one of my nosy coworkers is lurking about," she said, referring to Monica.

"Okay. Talk to you soon, Kennedy," he said softly.

He spoke her name with a familiarity that usually comes from years of togetherness. The sound of his voice was comforting and reassuring, a feeling that she hadn't felt in a long time. Maybe Nigel Charles was *The One*. For a minute, Kennedy was lost in the romantic fantasy of waltzing down the aisle to Mendelssohn's "Wedding March"; then she snapped back to reality and thought, *Don't call Vera Wang just yet. For all I know, he's the one alright, the one that'll break my heart.*

As she walked down the aisle, back to the lavatory up front, her thoughts returned to the Black Door again. *Instead of sleeping with Nigel on the first date, I'll get my freak on at the club and still keep my promise. That is, if we can find the place.*

15

SETTLING INTO her new environment was proving to be more of a challenge than Tyler had anticipated. Although she had only seen glimpses of Jacob, due to his hectic work schedule, it was good being around her big brother again, but his wife was another story altogether. Naomi had relegated Tyler to the servants' quarters above the kitchen, which wasn't necessarily a bad arrangement since the accommodations in their Tudor-style home were more than adequate. Exquisite Tiffany stained-glass windows were spaced above the oriels, and the baroque woodwork throughout the room was striking. The furnishings were a throwback to another era. An antique fainting couch upholstered in ecru raw silk sat angled in one corner; a rolltop desk sat in the opposite corner. A queen-sized, oak sleigh bed covered with an ivory French lace duvet with matching pillows was the focal point of the room. The only piece of furniture out of place was Tyler's old rickety drafting table, which she placed in front of the bay window. The table obstructed the window seat, but giving up the quaint seating area was a small price to pay for a great view while she worked. The window looked out onto the meticulously manicured back lawn complete with a rose garden and small reflecting pool.

She walked over and hung her artist smock in the armoire, then headed downstairs to the kitchen. The cherry-paneled back staircase was characteristic of the English Tudor style. Tyler stopped midstride and ran her hand along the raised wooden carving and thought it resembled folds of cloth. The house, with its ornate details and vaulted ceilings, was magnificent. Jacob's childhood dream had been to one day own what he called a "Robin Leach" home. And from the looks of things, he was definitely living the *Lifestyles of the Rich and Famous.*

The kitchen was quiet, with no signs of Naomi. *Good. She's gone,* Tyler thought. She was starving and just wanted to fix a sandwich and go back to the drafting table. She had a lead on a freelance assignment and wanted to get cracking on the drawings for her upcoming interview. Furthermore, she wasn't in the mood for another one of Naomi's snide remarks. Naomi had been snippy with her since she moved in nearly a week ago. Tyler didn't know what her sister-in-law's problem was. It seemed as if Naomi had something to say, but didn't quite know how to speak her mind.

Tyler opened the refrigerator and took out packages of smoked turkey, Swiss cheese, mayo, lettuce, and tomatoes. Turning around to put the ingredients on the counter, she ran smack-dab into Naomi.

"Excuse me, I didn't hear you come in," Tyler said, startled.

"It's a little early for lunch, isn't it?" Naomi commented in a snotty tone.

Tyler looked at her and wanted to say, *It's nearly eleven-thirty. Besides, what's it to you?* But instead she said, "It's never too early for a turkey and Swiss sandwich with chips." She smiled halfheartedly, trying to make nice.

Naomi didn't respond. She just rolled her eyes, walked over to the cabinet, and took out a glass. "Excuse me," she muttered, reaching around Tyler to get a bottle of water out of the refrigerator.

"You want a turkey sandwich?" Tyler offered.

Naomi shot her a look that read, *If I want a sandwich in my house, then I'll make it myself.* "No, I do not." She rolled her eyes again.

"Listen, Naomi," Tyler spoke, but hesitated. She didn't want to get into a confrontation with her sister-in-law, but if there was something on Naomi's mind, Tyler wanted to know what it was. "Do you have a problem with me living here?"

Naomi's back was facing Tyler, but as soon as those words filled the air, Naomi swung her head around. "Living here? Tyler, let's get one thing straight." She put her hand on her hip. "You're not living here as in a long-term arrangement. You're here strictly on a temporary basis, like a *guest*," she said, putting emphasis on the word.

Tyler nearly dropped the mayonnaise on the floor. Naomi spoke with such venom that the tone rattled her. Tyler was stunned by Naomi's rudeness. Naomi was speaking to her like she was some person off the street, instead of a family member. She stood there with her mouth agape, watching as Naomi flailed the bottle of water in midair.

"Look"—she forcefully put the glass on the counter—"Jacob probably didn't tell you this, but you cannot live here permanently. Is that understood?"

Coming out of her trance, Tyler said, "I don't intend on living here permanently. I'm only here until I get back on my feet."

"Well, I hope you land like a cat." Naomi twisted the cap on the bottle, put the water to her lips, and took a quick swig. "Because I don't want any gay mess in my home."

Tyler looked shocked, but she finally understood why Naomi had been treating her so badly. Naomi obviously didn't approve of

Tyler's sexual preference. "Gay mess? What are you talking about?"

"I don't want you bringing no chicks up in my house and do whatever it is that you do, that's what I'm talking about," she said, finally airing her true feelings.

"Naomi, I wouldn't dare do anything like that. I'm gay, not a slut. I don't whore around. I've always had meaningful relationships, and when I'm not in one, I don't have random sex," she said, setting the record straight.

Naomi rolled her eyes. "Whatever. All I know is that you only have one month of free room and board." Naomi had been waiting for the perfect moment to tell Tyler about her master plan, and now that she had gotten it off her chest, she felt better.

Tyler couldn't believe her gall. Not only had Naomi just insulted her, her sister-in-law was living a life of leisure at the expense of her brother. While Jacob was working like a Hebrew slave, Naomi had the nerve to stand in the house that *his* hard-earned money was paying for and say that her stay had an expiration date. "You're right. Jacob didn't tell me anything of the sort." Tyler put the mayonnaise on the counter. "What he told me was that his home is my home. How about that?" she spat out, unable to control her anger any longer.

"Well, this is *our* home, Jacob's and mine. Not a family retreat! How about that?!" Naomi shouted back.

They stood there a few seconds glaring at each other like a matador and a raging bull, Naomi the aggressor, waiting for Tyler to charge ahead without a strategy. Tyler counted to ten and thought she'd better talk to Jacob before waging war with his irate wife.

"Look, Naomi, I don't want to argue with you. Actually, I was hoping we could be friends," she offered, extending the proverbial olive branch.

"I have enough friends, thank you very much," Naomi said,

flipping her long ponytail from one side to the other, like Marcia Brady.

What a bitch! How could Jacob have married such a spoiled, selfish woman? When she looked into Naomi's face, the answer was obvious. She was gorgeous. Her milk chocolate skin was flawless. She had deep, Debbi Morgan–type dimples and her hair had a soft, flowing wave pattern. She wore a soft pink, Baby Phat velour jogging suit, probably going to the gym, which explained how even after bearing a child her hips were as slender as a teenager's. She looked more like a model than a mom. She definitely had a face and body that was easy to love. "Well, if that's how you want it, then so be it," Tyler finally conceded.

Naomi didn't say another word. She just swung her ponytail again and strutted out of the kitchen, leaving Tyler standing there in her wake.

Tyler watched Naomi until she was completely out of sight. Standing at the counter, Tyler pondered the situation. Either she could match Naomi's contempt and verbally spar on a daily basis or she could try and befriend her sister-in-law, so that Naomi could see that she was no different than any straight person. To keep peace in the house, Tyler decided to choose the latter.

Getting on her good side is going to be a J.O.B., she thought. But Tyler had plenty of time to devote to winning Naomi over, because she wasn't going anywhere—not in thirty days or anytime soon—no matter what Naomi said.

16

KENNEDY COULDN'T get the feeling of Nigel's dick pressing against her ass off of her mind. She had returned home from an exhausting international flight and wanted nothing more than to crawl into bed and sleep for eight hours, or until her eyes popped open the next morning. But sleep eluded her as she tossed and turned thinking of Nigel. Kennedy was glad that she didn't have his telephone number, which prevented her from ringing him up for a booty call. *I need to get Nigel off of my mind.* She sat up, turned on the light, picked up the phone, and called Naomi. It was late, but she knew that her friend was probably still awake.

"Hey, Ken," Naomi answered on the first ring.

As often as Naomi greeted her in that manner, it still irked Kennedy. "Can't you ever just say hello?"

"Why should I pretend like I don't know who's calling? Those days of anonymous calls are long over. Get with the program."

"Whatever," Kennedy responded lamely, now regretting that she had called.

"Anyway, I'm sure you didn't call for a lesson on caller ID. What's up?"

"Can you talk?" Kennedy asked, making sure Naomi was alone before she got into the details of her sexual dilemma.

"Yes, I can talk. Jacob is still at the office as usual, and Tyler is holed up in her room, or should I say, *my* guest quarters. Girl, let me tell you what that heifer said. We got into a verbal sparring match. I told her ass that this is not her house, and she can't live here forever! She then had the nerve to tell me that Jacob said that our home is her home!! Can you believe that shit?" Naomi was talking so fast that she didn't leave enough dead air for Kennedy to respond. She went on, "After going toe-to-toe for a few rounds, Ms. Thang had the nerve to ask if we could be friends. Well, I promptly told her NO. I told her I have enough friends and don't need any more!" Naomi finally took a breath.

"Isn't that a little harsh? After all, she is family."

"*She ain't my family!*" Naomi shouted into the receiver. "Even if she was related to me by blood, that don't mean a thing. I remember when my cousin Roselyn moved in with us when I was a kid. Well, she and I were buddy-buddy until she started screwing the girl next door, and——"

Kennedy cut her off. "What? You never told me that story before."

"I know. I try not to think about it. We were tight, until Roselyn kicked me to the curb for some pussy. I'll never forget the way she treated me," she said, still sounding hurt.

"Is that why you're so hard on Tyler?" Kennedy asked, finally realizing where Naomi's hostility was coming from.

"*Hard? I ain't hardly hard on her,*" she yelled, her rage returning.

"Whoa, calm down. Don't you think you're overreacting? You're acting like the girl committed a crime."

"Well, as far as I'm concerned, sleeping with another woman should be a crime. What's wrong with her? I can't understand how a woman could not like the comfort of a man." Naomi shook her head in disgust.

"Obviously she doesn't find men comforting," Kennedy stated.

"Why are you always taking her side?" Naomi asked, raising her voice.

Kennedy had called to talk about her problems. Instead, she was listening to Naomi's rant, and now Naomi was yelling at her. "Wait a minute, don't scream at me. I didn't call for a tongue-lashing. All I'm saying is that Tyler shouldn't be condemned for what your cousin did to you, or because she has a different sexual preference. Just because you and I like dick, doesn't mean that every chick in the world wants to ride the joystick." Now it was Kennedy's turn to go off on a tirade. "Look, Naomi, I'm tired and am going to bed. I'll talk to you later." Kennedy was no longer in the mood to discuss her dilemma. She wanted a solid relationship with Nigel, but on the other hand she wanted to fuck him until her toes curled. Kennedy knew that if they slept together too fast, it would probably kill any chances of getting to know him outside of the bedroom. Initially, she wanted to hear Naomi's thoughts on the matter, but now she just wanted to get off the phone. She wasn't in the mood to hear any more of Naomi's rantings.

"Oh. Okay." Naomi sounded a little put off that Kennedy was ending their conversation so soon. She wasn't done talking about Tyler. "Talk to you later."

Once Kennedy hung up, she got out of bed and went into the kitchen. Naomi had rattled her nerves, and she wanted a drink to calm down. She poured herself a glass of Cabernet and went back to her bedroom. She dug *A Few Dollars and a Dream* out of her purse, settled back in bed, and continued the story that she was reading on the plane. The book was quite good, and before she knew it, she had read four chapters. The love scenes were written with explicit detail, so detailed in fact that Kennedy started sali-vating. Her body was heating up with each erotic word, and she threw the covers back in an effort to cool down, but it didn't help. The more she read, the hornier she became. Kennedy envisioned the main characters as herself and Nigel intertwined in a tight embrace. She closed the book out of frustration. Kennedy was on the verge of combusting and needed some release.

She opened the drawer to her nightstand and took out a twelve-inch vibrator. She switched on the power and the rubber dildo started gyrating. Kennedy planted her feet on the mattress, spread her legs, lifted up her gown, and started tickling her clit with the tip of the vibrator.

"Ohh, that feels so good," she said aloud.

The combination of the wine and the steamy sex sequences had Kennedy so fired up that she started plunging the fake dick in and out of her wet hole. She closed her eyes and imagined that Nigel was on top of her fucking her brains out. "That's it, baby, take your pussy," she moaned, turning her head from side to side as she plunged the vibrator deeper and deeper inside of her V-spot.

Kennedy kept working the mechanical organ until she came, but she still wasn't satisfied and wanted more. She reached into the open nightstand drawer and took out a tube of lubricant. She smeared the gel along the shaft of the rubber member. Kennedy then turned over on her stomach, got on her knees and started easing the tip of the dick into her crack. Once the head was in, she began anally masturbating. Her sphincter greeted the dildo with a tight grip. *"Oh, shit!"* she screamed as she maneuvered the wand slowly into her anus. The pain was so good that she bit into a pillow. Kennedy clenched the pillow with her teeth as she wiggled the wand up inside her. She kept working it until she climaxed. She then removed the magic stick, got up, washed it, and got back into bed. She stared up at the ceiling.

Nigel, if you can make me come like that, then I'll be in love for sure! With that delicious thought in her head, she curled up in a fetal position and drifted off to sleep.

WITH TWO women in the house, estrogen was permeating the air so much that Jacob could have sworn that his voice had gone up an octave or two. And to make matters even worse, Naomi and Tyler were at odds. He received Tyler's call before he had a chance to settle into work. She was calling to tell him that Naomi had given her her walking papers. Jacob couldn't believe his ears. How could Naomi tell his one and only sibling that she had thirty days to vacate? He knew that Naomi had a problem with Tyler's sexual preference but that wasn't the true crux of her problem. Naomi was obviously taking her sexual frustrations with Jacob out on his sister. He reassured Tyler that she could stay indefinitely, and not to worry about Naomi, that he would handle her.

No time like the present, Jacob thought, reaching for the phone to call his wife, but before he could complete dialing his home number, Charlotte was buzzing the intercom. Jacob released line one and picked up the direct line to his secretary. "Yes, Charlotte."

"Your wife is on line two, Mr. Reed."

"Thank you, Charlotte," he said, depressing line two. Jacob held the receiver to his shoulder, exhaled, and then said in a cheery voice, "Hey, hon, I was just about to call you."

She started right in without preamble, "Look, Jacob, I don't know what you told Tyler, but I'm telling you like I told her, she has thirty days to stay with us and then she has to find another place to live. Period!"

Spoken like a bona fide sexually frustrated wife. If she were a man, she'd have a serious case of blue balls. Jacob's last failed attempt at seducing Naomi only seemed to make the situation worse. The time had definitely come for him to make good on a long overdue promise; maybe then she would give his sister a break and stop that nonsense about her moving out in a month. He had just the plan. "Calm down, Naomi. I assure you Tyler's situation is only temporary. As soon as she's reacclimated to New York, she'll be out on her own in no time."

Naomi spat out, "And exactly how long is no time, *Jacob*?"

By the way his name rolled off her tongue, Jacob knew that Naomi was beyond pissed. He needed to put his plan into action posthaste, so he immediately changed subjects. "Sounds to me like you need a break from the day-to-day routine." Before she had time to lament any further, he began talking faster than the auctioneer at Sotheby's. "Why don't you meet me in the city at the Sofitel around six-thirty?"

"What? Where?" She sounded put off. "Jacob, what are you talking about?"

"The Sofitel is a fabulous French hotel in Midtown, with a romantic restaurant. We'll have drinks in the lobby bar, then a nice relaxing dinner." There was a moment of complete silence, and he knew Naomi was stunned. It had been a long time since they had gone out for a romantic evening. "I'm not taking no for an answer," he added, to seal the date.

"Jacob, I don't—"

He cut her off. "Look, Naomi, I know I haven't been the

most attentive husband lately, but I promise you that's going to change." He lowered his voice, adding a little baritone, trying to sound seductive, "Starting tonight."

"What am I supposed to do about a babysitter at the last minute?" she asked, in protest.

"I'm sure Tyler would be delighted to babysit Noah, just—" Before he could continue, Charlotte was buzzing again.

"Wait a minute, Naomi," he said, putting her on hold and depressing the intercom button. "Yes, Charlotte."

"Ms. Rhone is here for your two o'clock. She's waiting for you in the conference room."

"Tell her I'll be there momentarily." He looked at the desk clock. It was one forty-five; true to form, Mira was fifteen minutes early. Jacob clicked back over to Naomi. "Look, hon, I've got to run, but I'll see you at six-thirty, right?"

"I, uh, don't . . ."

"Look, Naomi, ask Tyler to babysit and meet me at the Sofitel. Don't disappoint me. Love you," he said, hanging up before she could continue her protest.

Confident that he had put out one fire, Jacob straightened his tie and smoothed the front of his shirt. Playing mediator between Tyler and Naomi had gotten Jacob totally distracted and he had forgotten about his meeting with Mira. This afternoon's meeting was twofold. The first order of business was to hammer out the outsourcing details of the FACEZ children's line. The second order of business was to fuse the divide between Mira and Nina, since they had gotten off to a rocky start. And quiet as kept, Jacob had his own hidden agenda. He walked over to the door, removed his navy suit jacket from the wooden hanger, and put it on. Before heading to the conference room, he walked back to his desk and retrieved the FACEZ file.

"Charlotte, buzz Nina's office in about ten minutes and have her join us in the conference room," he instructed before going into the meeting.

Trepidation mounting with each step, Jacob knew exactly why he was feeling uneasy about today's meeting. Well, it wasn't exactly the meeting that was making him anxious. He had client meetings on a regular basis. The source of his sweaty palms, glistening brow, and accelerated heart rate was none other than Mira Rhone. Jacob didn't want to overstep his position by acting unprofessionally and possibly lose an account, but he needed to know if Mira's interest extended beyond balance sheets, and he had ten scant minutes—before Nina joined them—to find out if she was interested in him personally.

Tightly clenching the knob of the conference room door, he turned it and slipped inside the room. Mira didn't hear him enter. She was on the cell phone, standing at the window with her back to the door. She seemed to be admiring the view, and so was he. She had a runner's ass, high and tight.

If her butt looks this good through a dress, I can imagine how it looks and feels in the flesh, he thought as he licked his lips. The thought of pressing up against her ripe ass was making Jacob hot. He wanted to rip her dress off and fuck her right at the window.

"Down, boy," he whispered to his swollen sex. It was now or never, time to reveal his hidden agenda before Nina joined the meeting. Like a stealth bomber on a covert mission, Jacob walked quietly toward Mira. The plan was simple; if she let him get within touching distance without flinching, then she was obviously attracted to him as well, and it was just a matter of time until he was riding that ample rear of hers. On the other hand, if she spun around in reproach, then he could forget about being her jockey of love.

Just as he was zeroing in on his target, the conference room door opened.

"Jacob, I'm here for the two o'clock." It was Nina arriving five minutes early.

DAMN, he wanted to scream, *can't you see I'm trying to get my freak on,* but instead said, "Have a seat. As soon as Mira's finished with her conversation, we'll begin." Forced to retreat, Jacob took a seat at the head of the conference table, opened the file folder, and shifted his focus back to business.

Mira didn't turn around to face them. She just continued to talk as if she were alone in the room. "I know it's unorthodox, but this is my decision." She nodded her head as if having a face-to-face conversation. "I'm at Kirschner now getting the paperwork set up. Yes . . . I know . . . okay . . . okay . . . Oliver, goodbye." And with that, she clicked off the cell phone and joined them at the conference table.

Mira took the helm without hesitation, but not before cutting her eyes at Nina. She looked at Nina's outdated gray suit and slightly rolled her eyes. *Somebody should tell the poor girl that huge shoulder pads haven't been in style since the eighties.*

Jacob had informed Mira in advance that Nina would be sitting in on the meeting. Initially she had protested, but her objections were unfounded, based on a one-time occurrence. Mira finally agreed to overlook the London incident, but from her menacing glance, she obviously still wasn't ready to embrace Nina's presence.

"As you know, I've decided to appoint Kirschner Gross custodians of the Baby FACEZ account. I know it's unconventional for an accounting firm to oversee the funds of its clients, but the accountants at FACEZ are overwhelmed preparing for the firm's year-end audit," she said, directing her conversation to Jacob, and completely ignoring Nina.

Jacob nodded in agreement. "You're right; it's extremely unorthodox, but as CEO, it's your call." He wanted to tell her that for a hefty fee, accounting firms will do just about anything. Theoretically, it would be a conflict of interest for Kirschner to audit the books of an account that it was overseeing, but Jacob had a ready solution. "Considering that Baby FACEZ is a special project, it's going to require individual, hands-on attention. That's why I'm appointing Nina as senior accountant. She'll oversee departmental cost variances as well as cash flow distributions, but not the auditing of the account, so there won't be any conflicts," he said, glancing over at Mira, half expecting her to reject Nina's appointment. But she didn't bat an eyelash, so he continued. "This will be Nina's sole account and she'll report directly to me."

Nina spoke up, "The first order of business should be to earmark production funds, since the projected launch date for the new line is fourth quarter."

"My thoughts exactly," Mira said, scribbling notes in her black leather-bound planner. "I'm confident that we'll come in on schedule and under budget, and—" Her ringing phone stopped her thought. Mira fished the tiny phone out of her Berkin bag. "Mira Rhone speaking. Yes, hello, Nigel," she spoke into the phone.

"What's the problem?" she asked, and listened closely.

"So, you're saying the shea pods you earmarked didn't test well? Maybe the karite trees that yield those pods were diseased. I know you just came back from Uganda, but you need to go back pronto, because we need those pods. Uh huh . . . and how did you find that out? Look, Nigel, we'll discuss that later. Right now I'm in a meeting." And with that, she clicked off the phone. "Sorry about the interruption."

"No problem. Is everything okay?" Jacob asked.

"The shea pods that we plan to use as the base ingredient for the children's line didn't test well. Also, my head chemist just found out that one of FACEZ's major competitors is in the research and development phase of a children's line as well. Therefore, we need to accelerate the R & D on Baby FACEZ to beat them to market," she said, sounding frustrated.

"How did he find that out? Isn't R & D considered proprietary information?" Nina asked.

"Some underpaid employees sell insider information to the highest bidder. That's why a hefty compensation package is key.

Luckily, I have a close-knit group of employees that are well paid. Therefore, I don't have to worry about leakage." She closed the planner and put it back into her bag. "I hate to rush off, but I have another meeting," she said, standing to leave. "I'll expect a costs breakdown by next week."

"Not a problem," Nina said.

Jacob watched Mira gather her belongings. Her fluid movements were quietly seducing him. Smiling to himself, he mused, *If she's this smooth performing a rudimentary task in the boardroom, I can just imagine how she moves in the bedroom.* His thoughts had returned again to his hidden agenda. He hadn't gotten a chance to carry out his plan, but the London trip was coming up soon, and Jacob would finally find out if Mira was interested in balance *under* the sheets.

NAOMI HAD ambivalent feelings. On the one hand, she wanted nothing more than to enjoy a romantic evening with her husband, but on the other hand, she wasn't thrilled about asking her sister-in-law to babysit. She picked up the cordless to call Kennedy, but hung up when she remembered Kennedy was preparing for a trip. She sat on the edge of the bed flipping through her phone book, perusing names from A to Z looking for a suitable sitter. Either they were school moms with children of their own to watch, or distant relatives too distant to come over at the spur of the moment and sit for Noah. The thought of asking Tyler for a favor was making Naomi nauseous. She'd done a successful job of avoiding Tyler since their last encounter, when she had ripped into her like a rabid dog. Now she was supposed to have a civil conversation and ask for help, after practically kicking the girl out? *Well, Noah is her one and only nephew; besides, she needs to start pulling her weight around here,* Naomi reasoned. Now that she had justification for groveling, she set out to find Tyler.

She went to the kitchen, since that was Tyler's favorite room in the house. The girl ate like a man and seemed to live off smoked turkey on cracked wheat with Swiss, mayonnaise, lettuce, and tomatoes. When Naomi reached the kitchen, there were no signs of turkey sandwiches or Tyler. *She's probably upstairs drawing*, she thought and headed up the back staircase.

At the top of the stairs, Naomi could hear music coming from Tyler's room. Standing outside the door, she listened to James Blunt belt out lyrics of a lover gone astray and thought about her own dysfunctional marriage. Well, it wasn't exactly dysfunctional, unless having sex once a quarter was considered abnormal.

Maybe tonight's date will put us back on track. Naomi raised her hand to knock on the door when the music stopped, and she heard Tyler talking. She put her ear to the door to hear what Tyler was saying.

"I've already put together a series of designs. When does he want to meet?"

Naomi surmised that Tyler was having a conversation about a potential job. She pressed her ear closer, but didn't hear anything. Tyler was obviously listening to the other person on the line. After a few minutes, the music came back on. Naomi took the cue that the conversation was over, and knocked.

"Come in," Tyler yelled over the music.

Tyler was sitting at the drafting table drawing. Naomi couldn't believe that she had obstructed the quaint window seat with that old broken-down excuse for a workspace. She cringed, but didn't want to make a federal case out of it and blow her chances for a babysitter. Forcing out a phony smile, Naomi asked in a chipper voice, "Hey, Tyler, whatcha up to?"

Tyler spun around on the swivel stool with a look of astonishment on her face and sat there for a millisecond. Naomi's chipper tone took her totally off guard. The last time they spoke, Naomi was anything but cheerful. "Uh . . . I'm working on a series of designs for a potential job. What's up?"

Naomi hated like hell to ask, but she didn't have a choice. "Are you busy tonight?"

"Uh . . . no. What's up?" she asked again. This was the first civil conversation that she and Naomi had had since she moved in, and she was curious as to why her sister-in-law was being so nice all of a sudden.

Thinking Tyler might be more receptive if the request came from her brother, Naomi asked, "Jacob wants to know if you'll babysit for us tonight?" she asked, faking a smile.

Tyler chuckled, as if seeing clearly through Naomi's facade. She should have known that Naomi had an ulterior motive. "Sure, Naomi, keeping my nephew won't be a problem." Tyler started to turn back toward the drafting table, but didn't. "So where are you guys going?"

"Out to dinner," Naomi simply said.

"Is this a special occasion?" Tyler asked, pressing for more details, trying to use the opportunity to strike up a real conversation.

Now that she had gotten what she came for, Naomi didn't want to stand there and entertain another question, so she was brief. "No special occasion, just going out to dinner." Then, switching the subject, she said, "Noah usually has dinner around six-thirty. There's ravioli and broccoli in the refrigerator. He can have ice cream for dessert, but he has to be in bed no later than eight-thirty." Not giving Tyler a chance to ask another question, she said, "Thanks. I have to get dressed now," and walked out.

That wasn't too bad, Naomi thought, once back in her room. Tyler seemed agreeable enough, but Naomi still wanted her out in thirty days. She walked over to the closet to pick out an outfit. It had been awhile since she and Jacob had gone out on the town and she wanted to look irresistible. Thumbing through the rack of dresses, she finally decided on a magenta jersey wrap dress, a pair of matching sling backs, and a silver chain necklace.

Naomi went into the bathroom, turned on the water in the

Jacuzzi tub, and poured in an aromatic bath salt. Once the tub was brimming with foaming bubbles, she slipped in, leaned her head back on the headrest, and closed her eyes. As the warm water caressed her body, her mind began to drift. *Maybe tonight Jacob will put work aside for once and focus on us.* Naomi smiled at the possibility. But her smile didn't last long; it began to dissipate as quickly as the delicate bubbles, as her mind drifted back to reality. *Jacob's probably going to have a quick dinner with me, rush back to the office, and work on some project that can't possibly wait until tomorrow.* Her body felt heavy with despair as she stepped out of the tub. Naomi sighed and willed herself to dress.

The traffic on the LIE was light, and within thirty-five minutes, she was pulling into the circular driveway in front of the Sofitel. The valet immediately appeared at the driver's side door. "Good evening, miss. Are you checking in with us this evening?" he asked as she stepped out of the car.

"No, I'm just here for dinner," Naomi said, looking up at the white, asymmetrical structure. She marveled at the glass-infused architecture; it resembled a museum housing modern art instead of a hotel housing weary travelers.

She walked through the glass doors into the lobby. The black marble flooring had recessed lighting that changed from lime, to teal, to lavender. Naomi walked past the cozy sofas into the bar area, which was to the right of the lobby. She looked around for Jacob, but didn't see him among the men smoking cigars and drinking cognac and martinis at the bar.

"Excuse me." Naomi caught the attention of the waitress. "Where's the restaurant?"

"Café Des Architectes is to the left of the entrance," she said, pointing toward the front of the hotel.

How apropos; they probably named the restaurant to pay homage to the architects that designed the hotel, Naomi thought.

"Do you have a reservation for dinner?" asked the maître d', once she stepped inside of the uniquely designed restaurant.

The decor was a whimsical color combination of red, white, and black, with touches of silver.

"Yes. I'm meeting my husband. The name is Reed, party of two," she said, looking over the maître d's shoulder into the dining room.

He scanned his clipboard. "I'm sorry. I don't have a reservation for Reed. Could it be under another name?"

"No." *What the hell is going on? Don't tell me Jacob forgot to make the reservation*, Naomi fumed silently.

"Would you care to put your name on the wait list?" he asked, running his finger down several names. "I have an eight-thirty reservation."

"No, thank you." She smiled faintly, feeling totally embarrassed. Naomi slunk back to the lobby and wearily sat on the sofa. She had half a mind to go over to Jacob's office and rip him a new opening.

How dare he have me come all the way into the city and not have the decency to show up? She looked at her watch; it was six-fifty. "I'll give him until seven, and then I'm out of here."

Seven o'clock came and went, and she was still sitting on the sofa, feeling too dejected to move. She heard a faint ringing, but it stopped, only to start again. Naomi opened her purse, realizing that the source of the ringing was her cell phone. *It's probably Jacob calling after the fact, to say he's running late,* she thought. But when she looked at the caller ID, she didn't recognize the number. "Hello?"

"Naomi," said a husky male voice.

She hesitated a moment, trying to recognize the caller. "Yes? Who is this?"

"It's me."

"Jacob?" she asked, surprised at his tone. "Is that you?"

"Yes, don't you recognize my voice?" he asked in a hushed tone.

"Why are you whispering?" She was annoyed. "And where

are you? I've been sitting in this lobby for over thirty minutes and I'm not waiting another second longer. You can have dinner by your *damn* self. I'm going home." Naomi's voice raised a few decibels. Not wanting to cause a scene, she immediately lowered her tone.

"Whoa, whoa. Calm down, Naomi, I'm—"

She cut him off. "I know, you're still at work. Yeah, Jacob, I know the routine by now. Good-bye." Naomi pulled the phone away from her ear, searching for the end button, but she could hear him yelling through the mini earpiece.

"Naomi, Naomi, don't hang up!" he shouted.

"What is it, Jacob?" she asked, putting the phone back to her ear.

"I'm not in the office; I'm—"

"Then where the hell are you?" she asked in a tight voice.

"If you stop cutting me off, I'll tell you."

She held the phone. "I'm listening."

"I'm at the hotel."

Naomi looked around the lobby. "Don't play with me, Jacob. You're not at the hotel. I've been here since six-thirty and if you were here, I would have seen you by now. Jacob, you're such a liar. You lure me out of the house with a false promise of a romantic evening; now you're—"

This time he cut her off. "Naomi, please be quiet and listen closely."

She didn't say one word. Because whatever he had to say, she wasn't interested in hearing. She held the phone as he continued to talk.

"Take the elevator to the sixth floor and come to six-ten. I've booked a suite for us."

Naomi was shocked and nearly dropped the phone. She couldn't believe her ears. Jacob had taken the initiative to seduce his wife.

"Hello, are you still there?"

"I'm here," she finally said, finding her voice.

"Well, come upstairs, so I can make good on my promise," he said with a smile in his voice.

"I'm on my way," she answered with renewed hope, and bounced off the sofa and headed to the bank of elevators.

In the elevator, Naomi's mind was racing faster than Flo Jo in the hundred-meter dash. She was still having a hard time believing that Jacob had finally taken the initiative to resurrect their love life without her prodding him. She was giddy with excitement. The elevator stopped on six and she stepped out. The corridor was just as spectacular as the lobby, with whimsical colored carpeting in bright geometric shapes, and ornate prints hung on mustard-colored walls. Naomi followed the arrow pointing the way to room six-ten. When she reached the room, the door was ajar.

"Hello? Jacob?" She gently pushed the door farther open.

"Follow the trail," was all he said.

Naomi stepped into the suite and shut the door. The room was aglow with flickering candlelight, with Norah Jones singing softly in the background. She followed the trail of white tulip petals down a brief marble hallway leading into the bedroom. Unlike most boutique hotels, this bedroom was huge. A king-sized bed with a stark white down comforter didn't begin to fill up the space. There was a chaise lounge in one corner and a teak leather-top vanity in the other. The room was also bathed in candlelight. Naomi looked around but didn't see Jacob.

"Hello, sweetheart," he said, approaching her from behind. He slipped his arms around her waist. "I keep my promises," he whispered in her ear, and then began kissing the back of her neck. He stepped in closer and Naomi could feel his naked erection on her backside.

Naomi was flabbergasted. Her workaholic husband had turned into Don Juan.

As he began grinding against her rear, she could feel herself getting moist. In one smooth motion, Jacob reached underneath her dress, removed her panties, and began to tease her clitoris. "Oh, Jacob," she moaned. "Don't stop."

"Take your dress off," he whispered.

Naomi fumbled with the ties of the dress as Jacob brought her close to a digital orgasm. "Yes, that's it!" she moaned as he hit her G-spot.

"I want to fuck you by the window," he whispered.

Her mind was reeling, "What?"

Standing there in only her bra, he walked her over toward the floor-to-ceiling window, unhooked her bra from the back, and began massaging her nipples. He then bent Naomi over the vanity, spread her cheeks apart, and inserted his rock-hard penis.

"Yes, yes, baby," she cried out, on the brink of orgasm.

"Mir . . . Naomi, you feel so good," he moaned in a low, nearly inaudible voice, almost calling his wife Mira.

"What?" She couldn't make out exactly what he was saying. And she didn't care, because he was speaking volumes with each deep thrust.

He made love to Naomi in front of the floor-to-ceiling window like a man possessed. He usually treated her with kid gloves, but not tonight. And she wasn't complaining. It had been a long time since she'd had multiple orgasms. Maybe he was guilt-ridden about working long hours and moving his sister in with them without consulting her. Guilt-ridden or not, he was inspired. She didn't care to know who or what was the reason behind his inspiration as long as it signaled the end of their sexual drought.

"DO YOU need for me to bring anything?" Kennedy asked. She was having dinner at Nigel's apartment, and didn't know what to bring. Usually men brought women flowers or candy, but she didn't know what a woman brought to a man's apartment for the first time.

"Yeah," Nigel said, chuckling, "you can bring something for me."

"Sure, what do you need?"

"You," he said, in a seriously seductive voice.

Nigel and Kennedy had been dating for two weeks, six days, and eighteen hours, but who was counting? "In that case, I'd better get a move on. See you in a bit," she said, smiling. It had been years since a man had been head over heels for Kennedy, and she was elated. The thought of having a fifty/fifty relationship, not seventy/thirty, with her on the losing end of the percentage, made her happy.

"Don't worry about a parking space. I know how crazy parking can be in this neighborhood. I'll have the building attendant park your car." Not only was Nigel handsome, he was also extremely accommodating and thoughtful.

"Okay." She hung up the phone and raced to the bathroom to shower. Warm water pulsated from the dual showerheads onto her body, instantly relaxing her muscles. Standing underneath the pulsating spray, she was transported back to the evening of their first date.

Usually reserved for momentous occasions, Tru was one of New York's premier five-star restaurants. That's why Kennedy was taken aback when Nigel said he had made an eight o'clock reservation for their first date. The instant they walked through the black, cloaklike drapes into the restaurant, the outside world seemed to vanish like a magician's sleight of hand trick. The focal point of the bar area, an exquisite cobalt sculpture of a woman's torso, was breathtaking. They were immediately whisked away to the dining room, where original pieces of artwork adorned stark white walls. A velvet cube was placed next to Kennedy's chair the moment she sat down. Initially she thought it was a footstool, but surmised that it was too tall to fit comfortably underneath the table to rest her feet on. Then one of the many well-versed waiters said, "For your purse, madame."

Kennedy was impressed. She had dined throughout the world, but never had she been offered a stool for her purse. And that was just the beginning. The wait staff was synchronized in their service. When one disappeared into the kitchen, another would appear at their table with an edible masterpiece. The French-influenced haute cuisine was presented with dramatic fanfare, from the caviar staircase tier to the tuna, salmon, and yellowtail tartars served on an oblong mirror. Over entrées of black bass with cannellini beans and milk-fed veal with a porcini mushroom sauce, Kennedy learned that Nigel was the premier chemist at FACEZ, the cosmetics conglomerate. The entire dining experience was long and drawn out, which was perfect for the dreaded "getting to know you" phase of their date. Over dessert, Nigel gave her the abridged version of how he had been jilted by his bride-to-be three days before their wedding.

"And you know what the funny thing is?" he asked rhetorically. "I didn't even see it coming," he said, stirring raw sugar into his cappuccino with a faraway look in his eyes.

Kennedy saw the sad expression on his face and wanted to kiss his pain away, but instead asked, "What was her excuse for calling off the wedding?"

"She said that she felt like a fraud marrying me and couldn't go through with the wedding."

"A fraud?" Kennedy crinkled her nose. "What did she mean by that?"

"It's a long story, and I don't want to bore you with all the details," he said, without any emotion.

Kennedy couldn't believe how matter-of-fact his voice was, like being jilted was no big deal. If she had been dumped days before her wedding, she would probably still be devastated. "You sound so calm and collected about the entire ordeal."

"Well, that was a year ago. Trust me, I've had more than a few private pity parties. Life goes on no matter what you're going through, so either you get with the program or drown in your misery. Besides"—he stared directly into her eyes—"I'm looking toward the future, which is looking quite good"—he winked—"not the past."

The word *future* resonated within Kennedy's soul; she could definitely envision a future with Nigel Charles. He was gorgeous, intelligent, and successful. In an instant, her mind fast-forwarded to their engagement, wedding day, and the birth of their first child. Within sixty seconds, she'd planned out their entire life, like most women do when they meet "the one."

Then he turned the tables and started peppering her with questions about her past. "As beautiful as you are, I'm surprised you're not married with children," he said, glancing down at her ring finger.

Without sounding like the walking wounded, she told him about a few failed relationships, sans the gory details of how she fucked them too soon, bringing the end to a potential long-term union.

"Their loss is my gain," he said, with a sly smile spreading across his handsome face.

He knows just what to say, Kennedy thought. This was going way too smoothly, when it suddenly occurred to her that he might have the usual ulterior motives in mind. "I hope you don't think I'm sleeping with you tonight," she blurted out. Though she had fantasized that her trusty vibrator was his dick, plunging in and out of her multiple orifices, Kennedy didn't want to go back on her self-imposed rule. And if she put him on notice, then the chances of them sleeping together too soon were nil.

"Excuse me?" he asked, with a perplexed expression.

The moment the words flew out of her mouth, she regretted every single syllable and clumsy consonant. *Now he probably thinks I'm a paranoid schizophrenic off of my meds,* she thought, and then said, "I don't have casual sex anymore," trying to explain her sudden outburst.

"I think we already established that fact on the plane. Relax." He reached across the table and patted the top of her hand. "I'm not looking for random sex. You're much more than a random booty call. I'm also looking for more than just sex. I've been ready to settle down for a while, and thought that I had found my future wife, but she turned out to be . . ." he stopped himself.

"She turned out to be what?" Kennedy wanted to know.

"Never mind, I really don't want to talk about her. I'd much rather talk about you," he said with a smile. "So tell me, how long have you been flying?" he asked, changing the subject.

"For too long. It's getting to be a bore. Initially flying off to different countries was fascinating, but now it's become routine."

"Are you thinking about leaving the airline?"

"Actually I have. Lately I've been thinking about either going back to school, or starting my own import/export business. If I start my own business, I won't necessarily need a degree in merchandising. I'll probably just take a few business classes instead. I've shopped all over the world and have a pretty good eye for unique finds, so I'm leaning toward import/export. I like the idea of running my own little company, instead of answering to someone else."

"I know what you mean. There's nothing like your own business, and being in control of your own destiny." He then reached over and lightly touched her necklace. "Where did you buy that? It's quite unique."

"Thank you," she blushed. "I bought it in Nigeria. It's handmade from eighteen-karat gold, and the diamonds are rough cut, which gives the necklace an ornate look. I'm surprised you noticed. Most men don't pay attention to detail."

"Well, I'm not like most men. And I notice everything about you, Kennedy Bryant," he said, and then winked.

Kennedy felt her cheeks getting rosy. She was enjoying his attention. Nigel was a great conversationalist, and she was feeling comfortable in his presence, as if they had known each other for years.

Their conversation eased the apprehension that had begun to build within her, leading up to the obligatory good-night kiss, which usually led to sex on the first date. Reassured that he wasn't going to connive his way into her panties—which, feeling the way she did about Nigel, she would have let him—she leaned back and enjoyed the rest of what was truly a memorable evening at Tru.

NIGEL LIVED ON the tony East Side. The twenty-six-story, twin apartment buildings were reminiscent of the "Glass Houses" designed by famed architect Ludwig Mies van der Rohe. The parking attendant must have been on the lookout for Kennedy.

The moment she pulled in front of the building, he magically appeared at the driver's side.

"Are you here for Mr. Charles?" he asked knowingly.

"Yes," she said, stepping out of the car.

"I'll park your car. Call down when you're ready to leave," he said, sliding into the driver's seat.

"Kennedy Bryant, for Nigel Charles," she announced to the doorman. Based on the waiting attendant, she was sure that the doorman also knew who she was, but followed protocol just the same.

"You can go up, Ms. Bryant, he's expecting you. It's apartment 2510. The elevators are straight ahead," he said, pointing the way.

"Thanks."

Alone in the elevator, Kennedy began to fidget with her skirt. Suddenly it seemed too tight. The minute she pulled the right side down, the left side rose up an inch. She looked down at her blouse and it, too, seemed too tight. She could see the imprint of her nipples against the silk fabric, even though she wore a bra, and the sight of them was making her hot. She and Nigel had gone out several times since their dinner at Tru, but had yet to make love, only juicy good-night kisses. This would be their first time alone without a hovering wait staff. Kennedy was extremely attracted to Nigel. She was getting bored with her vibrator and wanted the real thing, but it was still too early to consummate their relationship.

An anxiety that she hadn't expected crept into her body as the elevator neared his floor. She needed to take the edge off before entering his apartment and spontaneously jumping his bone. She pushed the stop button, hiked up her skirt, and stuck her hand into her panties. Kennedy immediately located her clit, and started flicking it with her index finger. The rapid back-and-forth motion was making her come faster than she normally did, and she spread her legs farther apart to get better access.

She was working her finger so fast that she had to hold onto the railing with her free hand in order to keep her balance. Kennedy had been masturbating since high school, and was an expert at pleasuring herself.

"Excuse me, miss, is everything okay?"

The voice booming through the speaker jolted Kennedy out of her state of masturbation back to reality. She quickly removed her hand and silently prayed that there were no hidden cameras in the ceiling. "Yes, everything is fine," she spoke into the air, and pressed stop again to restart the elevator.

The doors slid open on the twenty-fifth floor, and Kennedy stepped out of the car a little calmer, now that she had released some tension. She walked toward Nigel's apartment and rang the doorbell.

"Hey there"—he swung open the door—"what took you so long? I was getting ready to call out the bloodhounds." Stepping forward, he enveloped Kennedy in a tight bear hug. "You feel so good," he whispered in her ear. Releasing her, he took a half step back. "And you look good too," he said, zeroing in on her too-tight blouse and stepping aside. "Come on in."

Walking beyond the gray slate foyer into the living room, Kennedy was struck by the dazzling view of the Brooklyn and Manhattan Bridges. The white lights that adorned the perimeter of the bridges glimmered in the night like facets on a diamond. "Wow!" she said, walking over to the floor-to-ceiling windows for a closer look. "Great view."

"Actually, that was a major selling point for me. This view at night is so romantic." He snuggled up close behind, slipped his arms around her waist, and kissed the back of her neck. "But watching the sunrise above the river in the morning is priceless."

She wanted to ask if that was an invitation to spend the night, but didn't want to tempt herself. Nestled in his arms, she said softly, "I'm sure watching the sunrise is amazing. I would love to see it sometime." The moment she made that last statement, she realized that it sounded suggestive.

Nigel turned her toward him and began kissing her passionately. "You're more than welcome to stay over tonight and watch the sun come up," he said, coming up for air.

"Can I have a rain check?" As much as she wanted to fuck Nigel, she was determined not to sabotage their relationship by jumping into bed with him too soon.

Sensing her hesitation, he kissed her on the forehead and said, "Whatever you want, Kennedy; there's no rush. Like I told you before, I'm not looking for a random booty call. I really like your company, and getting to know you outside of the bedroom is important to me. Now don't get me wrong, I am a hot-blooded male, and I hope you don't make me wait too long." He smiled.

She reached up and kissed him again. "Don't worry, Nigel, I won't."

"Good. Now, I hope you're hungry," he said, switching gears. He grabbed her hand. "Come on into the kitchen and keep me company while I finish dinner."

"What's on the menu?" she asked, sitting at the stainless-steel counter, glad to have the counter as a barrier between them. She felt safe and sexy in his arms, and didn't trust herself when their bodies touched. On one hand, she was ready to throw her casual sex rule right out of his floor-to-ceiling window, but on the other hand, she knew waiting was the right thing to do.

"Grilled snapper, asparagus, and new potatoes sprinkled with fresh parsley," he said, uncorking a bottle of Chardonnay.

"Yum. Sounds good. Who knew you were a chef?" she teased.

Handing her a glass of wine, he smiled. "I'm no Emeril, but I got skills." He winked.

"I just love his show. Do you watch it?"

"I'll never tell." He chuckled.

"I bet you TiVo every episode, Chef Boyardee." She laughed.

"How'd you guess?" He winked. "I may not be Emeril, but my snapper recipe is finger-licking good."

"I'll be the judge of that. I'm starv—" Before she could finish her sentence, the phone rang.

He picked up the cordless that sat on the counter, looked at the caller ID display, and put the phone back on the counter without answering the call. The phone rang three more times before going into voice mail. "Work." He looked over at her. "My boss doesn't seem to understand the concept of private time."

"Some people need to get a life."

"Exactly." He turned his attention to the bunch of fresh asparagus on the cutting board and began slicing off the ends. "Dinner'll be ready in a few."

Relaxing on the high-backed bar stool, she watched Nigel take command of the kitchen like a pro. He lit the stovetop grill, took the fish out of a bowl of marinade, and placed the filets on the rack once it was piping hot. After brushing the asparagus with olive oil and a sprinkling of garlic powder, he placed the spears alongside the fish. A few turns later, he was plating up their dinner.

"How many potatoes do you want?" he asked, reaching for a pot filled with petite new potatoes.

"Just one. I'm trying to cut back on the carbs." She inhaled the enticing aroma of the fish. "Dinner surely smells good."

"Let's hope it tastes good," he said, placing plates on the counter.

They chatted over dinner with Sade playing softly in the background. Kennedy had to admit that Nigel could throw down. The snapper was grilled to perfection, not overcooked, but succulent and flaky.

"Well, what's the verdict, Emeril Lagasse?" he joked.

"I've got to give it to you, Nigel, you got skills," she said, polishing off the last asparagus spear.

"Thank you, thank you." He bowed his head in a mock subservient gesture. "Everything I learned, I learned from Julia Child. She was my culinary guru. Would you care for seconds?"

Kennedy rubbed her stomach. "No thank you. I'm full as a drum."

"Not too full for dessert I hope," he said, clearing the dishes. "Like Bill Cosby says," he changed his voice and facial expression to impersonate Mr. Cosby, "there's always room for J.E.L.L.O."

She cracked up laughing. "You sound just like him. And yes, I would love a little Je . . ."

Ring. It was the phone again. And once again, he looked at the caller ID and let the call go into voice mail.

Kennedy wanted to tell him to just answer the damn thing. Obviously his boss wasn't going to let up. But she didn't want to get in his business. She knew how territorial men could be about their work, so she decided to excuse herself. "Where's your bathroom?"

Nigel stared at the phone in his hand. He barely looked at her when he said, "Down the hall, first door on the left."

Kennedy got up and proceeded in that direction. Stopping her in her tracks was a series of Jacob Lawrence paintings mounted on the wall that led to the bathroom. The paintings were similar to his famous Migration series. She couldn't tell if they were originals or prints. She quickly surmised that they must be prints, because originals would cost a fortune. After admiring the paintings, she continued on to the bathroom. As she was primping in the mirror, the phone rang again, except this time Nigel picked up. Kennedy clicked off the bathroom light and opened the door. Walking down the hall, she heard him saying:

"I told you earlier that I don't have that information here. I'll get it to you first thing in the morning. Yes, I know time is of the essence." He turned around, startled to see Kennedy standing in the doorway. "Look, I've got to run." He hung up abruptly, without saying good-bye, and simply said, "Work."

Over bowls of raspberry Jell-O and cream, he didn't say much. Kennedy tried to make a lame joke about him pureeing the raspberries by hand, but he didn't return her quip with one of his wisecracks. His mood had completely changed. He was no longer joking around, but seemed preoccupied with his thoughts.

"Are you okay?" she asked, picking up on his attitude shift.

"I'm fine. It's just some issues going on at work that's starting to get to me."

"Anything you want to talk about?" she asked with concern.

"Not really. I don't want to bore you," he said, looking down, and then began twirling his spoon in the Jell-O mixture.

They sat silent for a few minutes. Obviously Nigel was lost in thought, and Kennedy began to feel as if it were time to go. "Thanks for dinner, Nigel," she said, and stood to leave.

"My pleasure. Do you have to leave already?"

Kennedy didn't really want to leave, but she didn't want to wear out her welcome either. "Yeah, it's getting late, and I should let you get some sleep."

He walked around the counter, took her chin in his hand, leaned down, and kissed her lips. "I'd much rather cuddle on the couch with you and sip an after-dinner drink," he said, his romantic mood returning.

The thought of snuggling up with Nigel and drinking a nice port or cognac was enticing. Too enticing. Kennedy didn't trust herself. "No, I think we better call it a night."

"You're right, because I don't think I would be able to just stop at kissing. Let me call down for your car." He walked her to the door and lightly kissed her again. "I'll call you tomorrow."

"Okay. Good night."

On the way home, Kennedy couldn't help but think how the mood of the evening suddenly shifted once Nigel answered the phone. Pre-call, he was the quick-witted, easygoing guy that she had come to know, but post-call, his mood was cold and dark. Even though he tried to shift back and become romantic again, his Dr. Jekyll transformation made her wonder what could possibly be that intense at work that would make him tense up so quickly.

20

TYLER'S REP Simon had called her a few days ago with a lead to a freelance assignment. Simon had an old friend who was looking for a discreet designer to work on a temporary basis. Tyler had done the preliminary design mock-ups, and was now ready for the interview. She took a taxi to the train, and the train into the city. After arriving in Penn Station, she took the subway uptown. She missed the convenience of the city. In Atlanta, the public transportation was horrible, and you had to drive everywhere, but in New York, it was easier and faster to hop on the train. Tyler hadn't been uptown to Washington Heights in years, and was amazed at the transformation of the neighborhood. What were once abandoned buildings and crack-infested neighborhoods were now renovated million-dollar homes and trendy storefront shops.

She fished the address of the building out of her jacket pocket and glanced down at the paper. Tyler made a right on Broadway and walked over to Riverside Drive. Simon had told her once she got there to call the owner, so he could come down and let her in.

Since it wasn't regular business hours, there would be no one at the door. Tyler did as instructed, and waited outside on the stoop. A few minutes later, the door opened.

"Hi there. You must be Tyler Reed?"

"Yes, that would be me." She smiled.

"Come on in." He stepped aside. "I'm Trey Curtis."

Tyler walked into the foyer and was struck by the opulence of the interior. From what she could see, everything seemed to be custom-made, from the brocade wallpaper, to the crystal chandeliers, to plush area rugs. "Wow, this place is amazing!" she marveled.

"Thank you. When I envisioned the Black Door, I envisioned a club where the most well-bred socialite would feel comfortable. I spared no expense in the decorations. As far as I'm concerned, attention to detail is key."

Being an artist, Tyler understood exactly where he was coming from. "I totally agree."

"Come on; let me show you around." Trey gave her the grand tour, starting on the first level and continuing upstairs. Once they reached his office and sat down, he asked to see her portfolio. "Simon told me that you are one of his best artists. He and I go way back. I totally trust his opinion."

"Thanks. Simon said that you're in the market for unique designs for partial face masks," she said as he purused her work.

"Yes, I am. And I'm sure he told you that I'm also looking for someone who has discretion. This is a private club, and I need someone who I can trust."

"Yes, he did. You don't have any worries with me. I'm totally professional, and will not utter a word of this assignment to anyone," she reassured him.

"Good. When the club first opened, I personally designed every single member's mask, but ever since I opened the sister club in the meat-packing district, I just don't have the time to design all the masks myself. Membership is increasing at a rapid pace, and frankly I can't keep up." He flipped another page. "I like your work. The colors you use are so vibrant that the masks seem to jump off the page."

Tyler blushed at the compliment. She was very meticulous about her work, and took pride in every rendering. "Thank you."

"Since you come highly recommended, I'd love for you to assist me in designing masks for the Black Door. I'll start you off with a list of twenty. I'll furnish you with a personality description of the new members. To ensure each member's anonymity, I can't provide you with their names, only a description of what they do for a living, fantasies they may have, and any other pertinent information. I hope that would be enough for you to get an idea of what they're like."

"Yes. I could definitely work with that." Tyler smiled, eager to get going.

"Good. Well, I'd like for you to design the masks based on their individual personalities. Since no two masks are alike, it should be a nice challenge."

"I love challenges."

"Great." He reached across the desk and shook her hand. "Here's my card with my number on it, in case you need to call with any questions. I'll call Simon and hammer out the financials."

"Sounds good." Tyler stood up and put his business card in her jacket pocket. "Thanks, Trey. It was nice meeting you, and I look forward to working with you."

Tyler bounced out of the club on a cloud of excitement. Things were finally starting to look up for her. She had gotten a new assignment, and soon she'd get a paycheck. She didn't want to exhaust her savings. She wanted to add to it, so that she could eventually get a place of her own. Tyler wanted nothing more than to have her own home, and someone in it to love. She thought that she and Liz had the perfect life, but it turned out to be nothing more than a big lie. Tyler wanted another relationship, but she was going to take her time and not rush into anything until the right person came along. Yes, things were finally going her way. Since doing Naomi the babysitting favor, she'd been a bit more hospitable. Not that her sister-in-law was breaking out the Wedgwood and Lalique for a formal dinner service, but on the other hand, she hadn't made any more gay comments, or served Tyler her walking papers either.

By the time she got back to Long Island, her stomach was growling with hunger pains. *I need some fuel. Maybe a turkey sandwich or two will regenerate my brain cells before I start working.* Tyler opened the front door and was making her way to the kitchen when she heard Naomi talking on the phone. She stopped in the hallway and eavesdropped.

"I can't believe you haven't slept with Nigel yet. You guys have been going out for a while now, what are you waiting for? I fucked Jacob on the first date. We even fucked during one of his business flights. Of course that's when he was still a Freak of the Week."

"Ugh." Tyler cringed at the thought of her brother having sex on an airplane. TMI—Too Much Information. Tyler wasn't interested in hearing any more about her brother's love life. She started walking again, but stopped short when Naomi said something that caught her attention.

"Now that you're dating, Ms. Thang, don't forget about the book club. If you drop out, there'd be no one left but me. And as much as I enjoy my own company, it would be difficult to have a book club discussion all by my lonesome. Did you finish reading *A Few Dollars and a Dream?* . . . Good. Have you found any recruits yet? . . . Me neither, but I'm still looking."

Bingo! Here's my chance to befriend Naomi, so that she can see that just because I date women, I'm not a bad person. I may be gay, but I'm as normal as they come, Tyler thought. "I'm joining the book club. I'm joining the book club," she sang silently, clapping her hands quietly. Loaded with this information, Tyler turned around and jetted back out the door. She had no idea where the closest bookstore was located, but chances were good that there was a Barnes and Noble at the local mall. She took their extra car and drove to the mall, and sure enough, the B&N logo was on the directory.

"Excuse me," Tyler said to the information clerk, once inside the store, "do you have a copy of *A Few Dollars and a Dream?*"

"Who's the author?" she asked.

"I don't know. I just know the name of the book." Suddenly her heart began to race. *What if I can't find the book? Then what?*

"No problem, I'll search by title," said the clerk, putting Tyler's unfounded fears to rest. After typing in the title, the clerk scanned the computer screen and said, "We have one copy left. It should be in the back under New Fiction, listed by the author's last name, which is Birkenson. A. B. Birkenson."

"Thank you," Tyler said, dashing to the rear of the store. Scanning the alphabetized row of books, she found *A Few Dollars* on the second shelf. It must have been her lucky day, because just as the clerk said, there was only one copy left. Tyler grabbed the novel and took it to the checkout counter. She thought about going home to plow through the pages, but didn't want to get caught cracking open a new book. If Naomi knew she had rushed out and bought this book, she would no doubt become suspicious and wonder why Tyler was suddenly interested in reading their book club selection. Tyler paid for the book and found a cozy corner seat at the in-house coffee shop. A few hours and a few cappuccinos later, she was two chapters shy of finishing, but ready to discuss the plot nonetheless. Tyler removed the cover and slightly crinkled it, then dog-eared a few pages, giving the novel that well-read look. Getting rid of the incriminating evidence, she tossed the receipt and shopping bag into the trash, tucked the book under her arm, and headed home.

The house was quiet when Tyler returned. *Naomi probably*

went to get Noah from preschool. Tyler looked around the kitchen for an inconspicuous place to leave the book. It would be too obvious if she left it on the counter in clear view. *The solarium. That's it, I'll leave the book in the solarium.* Naomi relaxed in there most nights before going to bed. *Naw.* She changed her mind. *That's still too obvious.* Tyler leaned against the counter trying to think of the perfect place, when the caffeine that she consumed earlier began to stimulate her bladder. She tore off her jacket, threw it on the back of a chair, and rushed into the powder room adjacent to the kitchen, and the idea hit her. *I'll leave the book in here.* She glanced around the small space. *Perfect. Who doesn't read in the bathroom?* No sooner had she put the book on the windowsill and walked back into the kitchen than Naomi and Noah came through the back door.

"Auntie Tyler, Auntie Tyler," Noah cried, running and leaping into her arms.

"Hey, Noah." She kissed him on his chubby cheek. "How's my favorite little nephew?"

"I'm okay." He grinned. "Auntie Tyler, when you gonna let me use those markers and color in your room again?"

"Anytime you want, sweetie. Just let me know."

He scrambled out of her arms and jumped down. "Can we color now? Can we color now," he begged, tugging Tyler by the hand.

"Not now, Noah," Naomi interrupted. "It's snack time. Come on. Let me wash your hands," she said, taking him into the powder room.

Tyler couldn't help but marvel at her timing. Had Naomi come in a few seconds earlier, she would've missed this opportunity. And sure enough, as if on cue, Naomi came out of the bathroom with the book in hand.

"Is this yours?" she asked, holding up the novel.

"Yeah, I've been looking all over the house for it," Tyler said, reaching for the book. "I'm almost finished."

"What a coincidence." Naomi had a surprised look on her face.

"What?" Tyler asked, playing the dumb role.

"I can't believe you're reading this book," Naomi said, turning the novel over and looking at the cover before handing it back.

"Why is it a coincidence?" Tyler asked, egging her on.

"Because my book club is reading the same novel. A. B. Birkenson is a new author and I didn't think this was a popular book. I mean, it hasn't been widely advertised. How did you find out about *A Few Dollars*?" she asked curiously.

"I didn't know you were in a book club," Tyler said, ignoring Naomi's question and getting straight to the point. "I would love to be involved in a book club. Are you guys accepting new members?"

"Mommy, can I have some milk and cookies," Noah begged.

Naomi was grateful for the interruption. It gave her a few minutes to think of an answer as to why Tyler couldn't join their club. "Sure, honey. Sit at the table, and I'll get them for you." She walked over and opened the refrigerator, hoping that Tyler would drop the subject.

"So, are you accepting any new members?" she asked again.

"Uh, uh," Naomi stammered, avoiding eye contact, she still hadn't thought of a viable answer. "I'll have to check with Kennedy," she said, finding the perfect excuse.

What a crock of shit. Naomi just told Kennedy they need new members. What a liar. If she thinks she's getting off that easy, she doesn't know how persistent I can be. Tyler rubbed the cover of the book, then said, "Tell you what, I'll come to your next meeting. I mean, why not? I'm almost finished with the book and would love to discuss the story." Tyler was talking so fast that she was almost panting.

"Uh, okay. I guess Kennedy won't mind."

Tyler couldn't believe Naomi was standing there lying. Suddenly she began having second thoughts about joining their book club and was on the verge of rescinding her offer. But that was just what Naomi wanted. Well, she wasn't about to give Naomi the satisfaction of watching her back down. Besides, Tyler was determined to completely thaw Naomi's icy exterior, and what better way than to sit in on her meeting. She hoped that once Naomi got to know her better, then she would let go of her prejudice and they could become friends. She knew it was a long shot, but miracles did happen. "Great! Let me know when and where and I'll be there." Tyler took her jacket from the back of the chair. "See you later. I've got some work to do," she said, and headed upstairs.

Once she was gone, Naomi went to the cabinet and took out a bag of cookies for Noah's snack. As she was walking back to the table, she noticed there was a shiny black card on the floor. She bent down and picked it up. The front was a picture of a door, and the back read "The Black Door." There was no address, just a name and phone number. *Where the hell did this come from?* Remembering that Tyler had just taken her jacket off the back of the chair, Naomi thought that it must have fallen out of her pocket. *What is Tyler doing with a card from the Black Door?* Naomi was flabbergasted. She had been trying to find information on the club, and now out of the blue, it had fallen into her hands. She started to go directly upstairs and ask Tyler why she had the card, but decided not to. She had to tread lightly. If she started questioning Tyler about the club, Tyler would probably get suspicious and wonder why Naomi was so interested. After all, what housewife was supposed to know about an erotica club? She folded the card and tucked it in her jeans pocket. *I'll casually bring it up at the book club meeting.* Though Naomi was interested in becoming a member, she began to have second thoughts. Her and Jacob's sex life seemed to be back on track, so maybe she didn't need the services of the club. In any event, she definitely couldn't make a move until she knew whether or not Tyler was a member.

21

PELTING HAIL assaulted the plane with such unrelenting force that it felt as if the aircraft were under enemy attack. The sound of hail hitting the metal exterior was loud and piercing, like a round of ammunition being fired from a MAC-10. Glancing out of the porthole at the long stretch of asphalt that seemed to go on for miles, Jacob counted at least ten aircraft lined up nose to tail on the tarmac waiting for the hailstorm to subside. Golf ball–sized pellets were wreaking havoc on the departure schedule. With this delay, they would land at Heathrow forty minutes to an hour behind schedule.

Then, as quickly as the downpour began, it suddenly stopped. "Good," Jacob whispered, breathing a sigh of relief.

"Now that Mother Nature has ceased fire"—it was the captain making a lame attempt at humor—"we can continue taxiing. It looks like we're number eight in line for takeoff."

I should've left yesterday with Mira. She had taken the company's private plane, and invited Jacob to join her. Reluctantly, he had to decline. He wanted nothing more than to join the mile-high club with Mira, but Naomi was in another one of her paranoid moods, accusing him of abandonment, insisting that he preferred work to her. Ever since their night of passion at the Sofitel, Naomi had been extremely clingy and wanted him to make love to her every evening. To quell her ensuing tirade, he shortened the trip a day. Hindsight was indeed twenty-twenty. Had he known that the heavens would open up and disrupt the departure schedule, he would've accepted Mira's offer. *Right now, I could be sharing an after-dinner port with Ms. Rhone, or better yet sharing her bed,* he thought.

Twenty minutes later, they were airborne, soaring above the clouds where the sun was brightly shining. Looking out of the window at the blinding golden orb, he marveled, *Whoever said, "The sun is always shining somewhere," was right.* Mother Nature was amazing. Less than an hour ago, she was unleashing her fury with a fistful of mini-snowballs; now she was smiling a warm dazzling smile, lighting up the horizon.

The flight was seven hours long, and by the time they arrived at the gate, Jacob was sleepy and hungry. The customs agent was taking his sweet time checking passports. Jacob anxiously tapped his foot as he waited impatiently for the clerk to process him. Once he was cleared by the agent, Jacob made a beeline to the taxi stand so that he could go to the hotel and get a few hours of shut-eye before meeting with Mira.

The weather in New York must have been a prelude to the elements in London. As usual, the skies were overcast and cloudy, with light drizzle creating a gentle mist across the ancient city. It wasn't raining hard enough for an umbrella, so he flipped up the collar on his trench coat and ducked inside a waiting taxi outside of the airport. They were staying at the legendary Ritz, located in the heart of London near historic Piccadilly Circus and within walking distance of the fashionable boutiques along Bond Street. The world-renowned auction houses, Christie's and Sotheby's, were also a stone's throw away.

Once he arrived at the hotel, Jacob walked through the ornate lobby and checked in with the registration clerk. With only a garment bag, he didn't need to enlist the help of a bellhop, so he proceeded to his room without assistance.

Walking through the corridor, he was reminded of the time when he and Naomi were dating, and he couldn't wait to get her inside a hotel room and rip off her clothes. They would spend the entire weekend making love and ordering room service. His appetite for her was insatiable. But those days were long over. Throughout the years, he made several, most of them half-hearted, attempts at resurrecting their sex life, but like a loop of a bad B-movie playing over and over, he just couldn't get the visual of her giving birth out of his mind. Even that night at the Sofitel, he had to think about Mira just to get a woody. His insatiable desire for his wife had been permanently quenched, and there was nothing he could do about it.

Jacob dipped the plastic key card into the lock and opened the door. The Junior Suite was exquisitely furnished with the signature colors of the hotel: blue, peach, yellow, and pink. The color combination would have come off as extremely feminine, if it weren't for the handsome Louis XVI chairs that dominated the living area. A welcome basket of fresh fruit sat wrapped in iridescent cellophane on the antique cocktail table. He untied the cord and reached for an apple. Just as he was ready to take a bite out of the forbidden fruit, the phone rang.

"Hello?"

"Hey there, Jacob."

"Mira?"

"Yeah, it's me. When did you get in?"

He was flabbergasted. Mira's tone was casual and light-hearted, which was in stark contrast to her usual stern business demeanor. "My flight was delayed. I just arrived a few minutes ago."

"No problem," she said casually.

No problem? Unforeseen delays were always a problem with Mira. He shook his head at her attitude adjustment, trying to figure out what had brought about this abrupt change in her personality. Maybe it was being in another country, far away from the hectic pressures of work. Well, whatever the nature of her transformation, he wasn't complaining. "What room are you in? I'll come over so we can review the agenda for tomorrow's meeting," he suggested.

"I'm in room four-ten, but there's no rush. I'm sure you're jet-lagged. Why don't you take a nap and we'll meet for dinner, say seven-thirty, downstairs in the restaurant."

She was being so agreeable. He couldn't believe Mira was actually displaying a human trait. A few cocktails before dinner, a bottle of wine with their meal, and she might really loosen up. Loose enough for him to seduce her. "Seven-thirty sounds good. See you then," he said, and hung up.

Jacob called the concierge and requested a wake-up call for six-thirty so that he wouldn't oversleep. He was looking forward to their dinner meeting—in more ways than one—and didn't want to be late.

It seemed as if the minute he laid his head on the down-filled pillow, the phone rang. Through his sleepy haze he reached for the receiver.

"Good evening, Mr. Reed, this is your six-thirty wake-up call."

"Thank you," he mumbled and put the receiver back on the cradle.

Clad only in boxer shorts, he could feel a stiffy poking against the thin cotton fabric of his underwear. Reaching down, he closed his eyes and began massaging his swollen sex. "Mira, tonight all this belongs to you," he said, pulling the shaft of his hefty package. Jacob sat on the side of the bed and jerked off. He pictured Mira kneeling on her knees in between his legs, sucking his cock. At the thought of her, he yanked his dick harder and harder until cum came oozing out of his tiny hole. *I'm going to fuck you so good you're going to be begging me for more.* Masturbating only made Jacob hornier, and he couldn't wait to tap Mira's fine ass. He got up and went into the bathroom to wash the gooey cum off of his body.

After showering, Jacob decided to ditch his suit and tie, in lieu of a more casual outfit, since it was after hours. He dressed in a pair of black gabardine slacks and a tan, silken-wool pullover; he checked his reflection in the mirror. Without sounding vain, he had to admit that for a man of forty-something, he was well preserved, thanks to a regular workout routine and a healthy diet. The sweater hugged his pectorals and biceps just enough to emphasize his toned upper body. Jacob splashed his palms with Dunhill's signature cologne and transferred the scent from his hands to his smooth-shaven face. He felt like a teenager getting ready for the prom. More precisely, he felt like a horny teen getting ready to score after the prom. "Go get 'em, Tiger," he mouthed in the mirror, and headed downstairs to slay his prey.

The hotel restaurant was classy without being overstated. Scanning the room for Mira while he waited for the maître d', Jacob started fidgeting as he began to second-guess his decision. *Maybe I should just forget about these grandiose plans at seduction, concentrate on keeping my dick in my pants, and try to regain the desire for my wife.* But no sooner had the words drifted from his mind than his jimmy twitched, as if to say "Forgitaboutit."

"Looking for me?"

Jacob turned around and nearly passed out from the sheer shock of what stood before him. There in the flesh was Mira, sans the bun and tailored business suit. Her long, wavy hair swung loose, cascading beyond her shoulders and midway down her back. She wore a pair of low-rider jeans that hugged her narrow hips, and a see-through cotton gauze blouse with a plunging neckline. He could see the dark circular areolas that surrounded her perky nipples through the thin tissue-paper fabric of her blouse. To his delight, she was braless and brazen. Nothing turned him on more than an uninhibited woman. And the way Mira was displaying her enticing goods, she was without a doubt a woman who wasn't embarrassed by her sexuality. "Mira Rhone," he said, giving her the obligatory up and down.

"How are you? Were you able to get a nap?"

He smiled slightly, thinking about his naughty after-nap activity. "Yes, I did manage to get in a few winks."

"Well, you sure look rested." She gave him an appraising look of her own. "Jacob, I don't think I've ever seen you without a tie."

Don't worry. Pretty soon, you're going to see me with little or nothing on! "I thought I'd give the noose the night off." He chuckled.

She laughed lightly. "Our table should be ready," she said, looking around the restaurant for the hostess.

While Mira had her back to him, Jacob took a half step back, appreciating the view before him, and said, "I don't mind waiting." Then, out of the corner of his eye, he could see someone approaching the podium.

"How many?" It was the hostess.

Before he could open his mouth, Mira said, "Two. The name is Rhone. Mira Rhone."

The fragile-featured hostess perused her wait list, then said, "Right this way," leading them to a table near the back of the restaurant.

Once seated, Mira took charge, suggesting entrees and ordering appetizers, as well as cocktails. It was obvious that she was more than familiar with the restaurant. "The veal is so succulent that it practically melts in your mouth. And the sea scallops are to die for." She looked up from the menu. "What do you have a taste for, meat or fish?"

Jacob didn't have much of an appetite. Besides, what he craved wasn't on the menu. "Fish will suit me just fine," he answered, the double entendre going right over her pretty head.

"Well, in that case, you have to order the seared tuna. It's served practically rare, but it's extremely flavorful."

Just like your pussy, I bet. "Sounds irresistible." Jacob looked around the restaurant for the waitress. He wanted to hurry up and eat, then go upstairs for "dessert." "Where's our waitress? I'm ready to order."

Mira swung her hair to one side. "Me too."

When the waitress finally arrived, Jacob ordered a round of predinner cocktails and a bottle of vintage wine to drink with their meal. Over dinner, he and Mira chatted effortlessly about topics ranging from politics to religion and everything in between—everything but his schoolboy crush. To his delight, she seemed to become more relaxed with each glass of vino, and he kept pouring, making sure her glass remained full.

"My mother had no interest in running the company. She was more interested in running her social calendar. She's on husband number five now, and he only married her for the money. Her monthly allowance rivals my paycheck." She looked away for a moment. "And I work hard every day. I guess GG knew early on that Mother would be a liability instead of an asset. That's why she left me her legacy to continue."

"And you're doing a stellar job," he complimented her. "Your idea to expand into the children's market is brilliant!" Jacob smiled.

She glanced down into her lap, seemingly embarrassed by the accolades. "Thank you, Jacob." She raised her head. "That means a lot coming from you."

As he wondered what she meant by that, she continued. "I admire your accomplishments as well. You're a partner with one of the nation's top accounting firms, which is a highly coveted position." She reached over and touched his hand. "So, your opinion really matters to me."

Jacob's body heat shot through the stratosphere the moment her skin touched his. He could feel blood rushing through his veins going directly to both of his heads. *Seems like she's digging me,* he thought with delight. This little heart-to-heart was touching, but he was ready to take the conversation upstairs and under the sheets, so that they could talk body language.

"Would you care for dessert?" asked the server, appearing at the side of their table.

Before answering, Jacob looked at Mira for a clue as to whether or not she wanted to linger over Muscat and chocolate mousse, or just get down to *dessert.*

"No thanks." She wiped the corners of her mouth with the linen napkin, folded it, and placed it on the table. She then looked over at Jacob and said, "I'm going up to my room."

"Just the check, please," Jacob responded, trying to mask his disappointment.

Once the bill came, Mira took it and said, "I'll sign this to my room."

"Well, since you're buying, I'm going to stay and have dessert," he said, trying to make a joke, even though he was seething inside. Just when he thought she was feeling him romantically, she was making an exit.

She stood to leave. "Oh, you're not coming up?" She seemed surprised. "In that case, I'll see you in the morning."

Once she was gone, he ordered the special, but halfheartedly picked at the apple crumb cake. The last thing he wanted was a piece of dry cake. He wanted a piece of juicy ass, but now that was nothing more than a pipe dream. He took one last forkful and headed upstairs for a long, lonely night.

Jacob slunk down the hall feeling totally dejected. He was still horny, and wasn't in the mood to masturbate again. He wanted the real thing, but the real thing didn't want him. *Maybe I'll order a porn flick.* No sooner had the thought flashed through his mind than he glanced at room number four-ten, and brightened like a fluorescent bulb. Four-ten was Mira's room and the door was ajar. *She obviously left it open for me. She was probably too shy at dinner to verbalize her desires.* With one giant step, Jacob crossed the hall, and was standing in front of four-ten. He quietly pushed the door farther open, stepped inside, and gently closed it behind him.

His pulse raced, like a thoroughbred at the starting gate in the Kentucky Derby, as he crept down the short hallway that led into the living area and adjacent bedroom. Jacob expected to see her spread-eagled on the bed waiting for "Big Daddy," but she wasn't there. "So she wants to play hide-and-seek," he whispered. The buildup was exciting and he got an immediate erection at the anticipation of finding her. Hearing the sound of the shower, he headed toward the bathroom. *She's probably getting Ms. Kitty all nice and fresh for me.* He unbuckled his belt. *I might as well join her.*

Hot misty steam attacked him the instant he opened the bathroom door. Jacob quickly dropped his pants and underwear on the floor and tore off his sweater. This was the moment he had anticipated for months. He was finally going to bonk long-legged Mira. A broad grin spread across his face as he slid the shower door open. But that grin quickly turned into a grimace.

Standing underneath the pulsating spray wildly caressing and sucking on a pair of overripe sudsy breasts was Mira Rhone. Soap had foamed around her mouth, but obviously she didn't care about the bitter taste. All Mira seemed to care about was devouring her lover's jugs. The redhead on the receiving end had her head thrown back in ecstasy as Mira flicked her tongue, teasing the woman's large erect nipples. Mira let out short moans as the redhead plunged her digits in and out of Mira's smoothly waxed triangle. Finally, the source of Mira's mood swing was crystal clear; it had nothing to do with Jacob, but everything to do with a pair of juicy 38DDs. They must have felt the breeze from the open shower door, because both of their eyes popped open simultaneously, transporting them out of their lust-induced trance.

"Jacob?" Mira blinked, wiping the suds away from her mouth with the back of her hand.

Words escaped him as he scrambled to find his clothes in the fog. Jacob recovered them, but didn't recover his dignity as he fled the scandalous scene.

22

JACOB WAS in London on an important—or so he said—business meeting. Considering the fact that he was going to be across the pond for a few days, Naomi insisted that Jacob handle his "husbandly" duties before he left. He tried to put her off, but she wouldn't relent, so instead of leaving in the evening as planned, he delayed his trip a few hours and took a morning flight the next day. Their sex life had gotten an iota better, but it was nowhere near where it used to be. Naomi longed for those all-nighters, when Jacob would have her ass up on the bed, dick fed. Now the only thing being fed was her sweet tooth. She took a bite of the double-fudge brownie, licked her lips, and put it back on the saucer. Eating calorie-laden carbs would only increase her waistline, and Naomi wanted more than temporary thrills derived from sinking her teeth into a decadent dessert. She wanted lust-induced chills from continuous orgasms.

She reached for her purse sitting on the nightstand, unzipped it, and took out the glossy black card. She turned it over and over in her hands. *Where the hell did Tyler get this from?*

Naomi still hadn't decided how to extract information about the Black Door from her sister-in-law. She just couldn't come right out and ask. The first thing Tyler would probably want to know was where Naomi got the card in the first place. Naomi definitely wasn't going to say that she had swiped it off the floor. Technically, the card belonged to Tyler, and Naomi knew that she should have returned it, but she couldn't bear to part with the card. Naomi had been dying to get information on the club, and now that she had it, she wasn't about to let it slip away.

Naomi put the card next to the phone, picked up the receiver, and called Kennedy. "Hey, girl," she said, once Kennedy answered.

"Hey, there. I haven't talked to you in a while. What's been going on?" Kennedy had been traveling, and missed their regular chat sessions.

Naomi had so much to tell her friend, she didn't know where to start. "Well, let's see. For starters, Jacob and I finally got our groove on!" she said, with excitement in her voice.

"Whaaat??" Kennedy asked, seemingly shocked.

"Yes, it's true. Can you believe he finally made good on his promise?"

"No, I can't. Now give me details."

"Girl, he booked a room at the Sofitel, and when I tell you he rocked my world—believe me! Jacob had me bent over on the vanity table, near the floor-to-ceiling window, he took me from behind and . . ." She paused, as if reliving the moment.

"Okay, okay. I get the picture." Though Kennedy had asked for details, hearing the blow-by-blow account of her friend's love life was a little too much information.

"Since when did you become a prude? I take it you still haven't gotten any?"

"Ha ha, very funny. I see you got jokes. Well, Ms. Thang, if you must know, I'm very close to getting some."

"Do tell."

"Nigel invited me over to his place for dinner, and I was so excited about being with him alone that I masturbated in the elevator on my way up to his apartment," Kennedy confessed. Now that she was actually dating Nigel, and he wasn't just a random passenger on the plane, Kennedy didn't feel ashamed telling Naomi about masturbating with him in mind.

"You did what?!" Naomi asked, surprised. "Why'd you do that, instead of waiting for him to rock your world?"

"Naomi, you of all people should know how it feels to be sexually frustrated, waiting for a man to fulfill your desires."

"Don't remind me."

"Anyway, I wanted to take the edge off and not be tempted to jump his long bone the second he opened the door. I promised myself that I'd wait and get to know Nigel first before sleeping with him. You know how in the past, I've had a bad habit of getting to know the dick before getting to know the man." She chuckled, but was serious.

Naomi picked the card up from the nightstand. She rubbed the smooth surface between her thumb and index finger. "Sounds like you could use a little release."

"That's an understatement, girl. I've burned out one vibrator, and need to make a trek down to the Village and pay the Pleasure Chest a visit to buy another one."

"I don't think that'll be necessary. Guess what I found!" Naomi said, sounding mysterious.

"What?"

Naomi put her hand up to her mouth and covered the receiver. She lowered her voice, just in case Tyler was lurking in the hallway. "Information on the Black Door."

"Are you kidding me? How did you find out about the Black Door?"

"You won't believe this, but a business card for the club fell out of Tyler's jacket pocket. It was lying on the kitchen floor, and I picked it up."

"What does it say? Is there an address? Where are they located?" she asked, full of questions.

Naomi examined the card for the umpteenth time. "There's a picture of a black door on the front, and"—she flipped it over—"on the back there's a name and phone number, but no address."

"Whose name?"

"Trey Curtis. I guess he's the manager."

"Have you called?"

"I've wanted to, but can't. Before I make the call, I need to find out how Tyler knows about the Black Door. I find it hard to believe that she would be a member, since it's not a lesbian club."

"Maybe this Trey guy is a friend of hers," Kennedy offered. "Hey, I have an idea. Why don't I call him, and pretend like I'm interested in joining?"

"That's a great idea. Well, it's not like you'd be pretending. After all, we are thinking about joining," she said, and then gave Kennedy the telephone number.

"I'm going to call now. Hang up. I'll call you back, and do a three-way."

"Okay."

Kennedy released the line and dialed Naomi back. "Hey, girl, hold on." She clicked over, got a dial tone, and called the club. She quickly clicked back to Naomi as the second line started ringing. "Are you there?" she whispered.

"Yes, I'm here," Naomi responded with her heart beating wildly.

"Okay, be quiet." No sooner had Kennedy uttered those words than a male voice answered the line.

"Trey Curtis."

"Hello, Trey," Kennedy said, as if she knew him.

"Hi. Who's calling?" he asked, getting right to the point.

"This is Kendra Brian," she said, using an alias. Kennedy

didn't want to use her real name until they found out more information. For all they knew, this club could be some sort of sleazy sex den, and if that was the case, they didn't want to be associated with it.

"How can I help you, Ms. Brian?"

"A friend of mine gave me your card, and I'm interested in joining."

"Who's your friend?" he asked cautiously. Membership was by referral only. The Black Door was exclusive, and Trey didn't let just anybody join. He only wanted the crème da la crème, and figured that birds of a feather flocked together; that's why he only accepted referrals.

Kennedy hadn't expected him to ask that question. "Tyler Reed," she said, without skipping a beat. She started to say a fictitious name, but the sternness in his voice told her that he was all business and would see through the lie. Trey was probably used to people lying all the time, just to get inside of the club.

"Oh, yes, Tyler. So . . ." his tone softened, "you say you're interested in joining?"

"Yes, that's correct."

"Our initiation process is quite strenuous. First you need to come in for an interview and fill out some paperwork. We'll also need for you to go to our doctor and get a complete checkup, including blood work for STDs," he said, running down the details.

Kennedy didn't want to go through the rigorous process until she saw firsthand what the club had to offer. "I see. Before joining, I'd like to have a tour of the Black Door, if that's possible?" she asked.

"Not a problem. Let's schedule an appointment. How's Friday at six?"

"Sounds good. What's the address?"

Trey gave her the address. "Okay, see you then," he said, and hung up.

Once Kennedy heard the line click off, she said, "Naomi, are you still there?"

"Wow, we're one step closer to getting in. So, he does know Tyler, but the question is how? I'm going with you on Friday. I'll be in the city anyway."

"Really? What are you coming in for?" Kennedy asked, knowing that Naomi rarely came into Manhattan.

"I have a meeting with a company that does business plans. I want to have my business model totally laid out before I ask Jacob for the money. Once he sees that I went to a professional, he'll realize that I'm serious, and that this is not some passing phase."

"That sounds great. I think I'll go with you. Even though I'm nowhere near ready to open my business, it'll be good to see what they have to offer, so when I am ready I'll know exactly where to go."

"Okay, I'll meet you there," Naomi said, and gave Kennedy the address. "Afterward we'll head over to the Black Door. I'm dying to know the connection between Tyler and this Trey person. Maybe I can ask how they know each other, without sounding suspicious."

"Whatever you say, we have to play it cool. Trey sounds like he can see through the BS a mile away."

"True. I got the same impression. We'll tell him that I'm your sister. Since we look alike, it'll ring true. Once we check out the club, and find out how he knows Tyler, we can decide whether or not to join."

"Sounds like a plan. I'll see you Friday."

"Okay. Good night."

Naomi hung up, and began mentally crafting her story. She didn't want any slipups. She couldn't afford to have Jacob find out that she was interested in joining a sex club. Tyler was somehow affiliated with the club, and until Naomi had more information, she'd have to tread lightly.

23

    "DID YOU buzz Nigel's office?" Mira asked her often absentminded secretary. The only reason why she kept the girl on the payroll was as a favor to the Human Resources Director, since she was his niece.

"I buzzed him, Ms. Rhone, but he said, uh"—she hesitated a few seconds as if trying to think of the message she was to relay—"he's on an important call."

"Well, did you remind him that he's supposed to be in my office for a nine-thirty meeting?" Mira didn't wait for an answer. "Buzz him back, and tell him I don't plan to wait all morning."

"Yes, Ms. Rhone."

Nigel's unprofessional behavior was totally unacceptable, and Mira was going to put an end to it posthaste before the situation escalated. Pacing in front of her desk, she impatiently watched the sweeping minute hand on the desk clock. It was now nine-forty. *The nerve of this guy! How dare he not show up for our meeting?* Mira pushed the intercom button, "Buzz Nigel again," she directed her assistant.

"No need to."

Mira turned around to face Nigel standing in the doorway of her office with a smug look plastered on his handsome face. "You're late," she spat out.

"Chill out, Mira." He strutted in nonchalantly, as if *he* owned the company, and planted himself on the sofa in the corner seating area.

Mira swung her head in his direction. She wasn't accustomed to *anyone* speaking to her in that manner. "Excuse me? Nigel, you've worked here long enough to know that when I schedule a meeting, it begins on——"

He quickly cut her off. "Are you going to stand there bitching me out, or are we going to start the meeting?"

His tone was entirely too cocky. "Look, Nigel, let's get one thing straight." Mira zeroed in on him with a penetrating death stare. "*I'm* The BOSS," she said, raising her voice.

"There was a time when you were calling *me* The BOSS." He returned her gaze with a death stare of his own.

Walking within inches of him, Mira squinted her eyes, lowered her tone, and in a tight voice said, "Why can't you leave the past where it belongs? In the past."

"Because it wasn't that long ago when we were signing the gift registry at Tiffany's. Tell me, Mira, did you ever return the wedding presents after you left me at the altar?" he hissed with venom punctuating every word.

"Stop being dramatic, Nigel." Mira turned away from him and walked back to her desk. "I didn't leave you at the altar," she said, retrieving a file from her desk.

"Semantics. At the altar. Three days before. What's the difference? The point is that you left me and for . . . what's her name again?" Nigel tried to sound cavalier, but the pain of being jilted still stung. He had been deeply in love with Mira, and when she called off the wedding, he had been devastated.

"Samantha. And I didn't leave you for——"

"That's right, Samantha. How is good ole Sam? Are you two living happily ever after in your deluxe penthouse in the sky?" he asked sarcastically.

"We're not together anymore. Look, enough of my personal life. Let's get—"

"Does that mean you're into men this season?" he said with another dose of venom.

Mira could tell by his harsh tone that he was still wounded, and she wanted to set the record straight once and for all. "I was up front with you from day one, Nigel. I told you that I was bi, but that didn't seem to bother you. You pursued me anyway," she said, crossing her arms in front of her chest.

He raised one wooly eyebrow. "Aren't you leaving out one little fact?"

"And what might that be?"

"The dreaded four-letter word—L.O.V.E. You said that you loved me." He looked down at the floor, and then looked back up at her. "And wanted to go straight."

"I did love you, Nigel, but not in the way that a wife is supposed to love her husband. The love I had for you was more like love for a good friend. What I didn't realize at the time was that I was trying to change my lifestyle for GG, and now that she's gone, I can be true to myself," she said in a caring tone, trying to soften the blow.

This was the first time that Nigel had heard this explanation. "So you used me to appease your great-grandmother. Is that what you're saying?"

"Not exactly." Mira sat next to him and reached for his hand. "Nigel, I truly cared for you, but I couldn't live a lie. I had to be true to myself."

"Yeah, yeah, you already said that." He snatched his hand away and took a stack of papers out of his briefcase. "Here's the R & D update on the new line," he said, ready to change the subject.

He had heard enough. Besides, reliving the past was a gross waste of his time.

"I'm sorry that I hurt you, Nigel. That was never my intention," Mira said, trying to ease the tension between them. They worked well together and Mira wanted their collaboration to continue. Now that she was embarking on a new project, she couldn't afford to lose her head chemist.

"Who said I was hurt? Let's just drop it and get down to business," he said, handing her the research report.

Mira could tell by the sullen look on his face and the hurt in his voice that their breakup was still a painful memory, a pain Mira wished she could erase. The truth of the matter was that she never meant to get involved with Nigel in the first place, but that was GG's master plan when she hired him.

Her great-grandmother had a sixth sense about Mira's attraction to women, probably because her granddaughter, Mira's mother, was man-hungry, devouring anything with three legs, and Mira was just the opposite, often bringing a "girlfriend" to their beach house in Sag Harbor for the weekend. Occasionally, Mira would invite a platonic male friend to keep suspicions at bay, but GG was no fool.

When the Vice President of Research and Development retired, GG hired Nigel away from BOD E. Ltd., the competition. Though he came with impressive credentials, GG was also impressed with his undeniable good looks and charming personality. She wasted no time scheduling the two of them for one of her infamous twelve-hour "think tanks." With their heads locked together brainstorming over new products, she would comment on what a good team Nigel and Mira made. As usual, GG was right. Not only was Nigel handsome, he was extremely intelligent and on top of his game.

Initially Mira had been attracted to his mind, but over time, she developed a genuine affection for him. Soon their working relationship developed into a personal one—and since she liked a side of dick now and again, it wasn't hard to fall into bed with Nigel, which pleased GG to no end. Mira saw that her great-grandmother took immense pleasure in their dating, so when Nigel proposed, Mira accepted, knowing that their union would send GG over the moon. Mira figured it was a small sacrifice to make for the woman who had been more of a mother to her than her own mother, who was too busy playing socialite to play mommy. And in true GG fashion, she took over planning the wedding and reception, thriving on the minute details. Oftentimes Mira thought it was all of that excitement that caused GG's massive stroke. She lay in a coma for five days before passing away in her sleep. Mira was heartbroken, but content in knowing that GG's last days had truly been happy.

"As you can see on page six, the focus group gave the children's product line a negative rating," Nigel began.

"And why is that? You didn't use those tainted shea pods, did you? This is the first time we've gotten less than stellar ratings from a focus group," she said, staring at the report as if it were erroneous.

"No, I didn't use those pods. That's why I'm going back into the lab to reanalyze the formula," he said defensively.

"Are you telling me we have to start over from square one?"

"Basically," he said matter-of-factly.

"Nigel, I'm sure I don't need to remind you that we don't have the luxury of time in our favor. If we're going to beat BOD E. to market, then we need to ramp up production of the new line, *not* start over."

"What's the use of being first on the shelves if the product isn't any good? But you're the boss," he said sarcastically. "If you want to go ahead with the production schedule as planned, then that's what we'll do." Nigel began stuffing the reports back into his briefcase.

Mira sat there for a moment weighing the odds. He was

right. If they went to market with an inferior product, sales would suffer and BOD E. could blow them out of the water. Mira couldn't risk the company's reputation with substandard products. FACEZ had always led the cosmetics industry in terms of quality, and she wasn't about to jeopardize GG's years of hard work just to be first on the market with a new product. "How long do you think it'll take to correct the problem?"

"I won't know that until I reanalyze the formula. I'll expedite the process, so basically we're looking at another week or two before we're back on track."

"That's not too bad," she sighed. "Thanks, Nigel."

"Not a problem. I'll get the results to you ASAP." Nigel could have quit after Mira ended their relationship, but he deeply cared for and admired GG. Since she hired him personally, he was sure that she would've wanted him to put his feelings aside and stay on board.

After they broke up, Mira had begun to doubt Nigel's loyalty, assuming he would act the role of the scorned lover. But she should have known he was too much of a professional to let personal issues cloud his judgment.

Once Nigel left her office, Mira sat at her desk dreading the next meeting. Speaking of personal issues, she had one of her own to deal with, which was extremely embarrassing.

"Ms. Rhone." It was her assistant speaking through the intercom.

"Yes, Janette?"

"Mr. Reed is here to see you."

Mira exhaled. "Send him in." This meeting had nothing to do with FACEZ business. She had called the meeting to clear up that fiasco in London. During the board meeting the day following the "shower scene," she and Jacob had averted eye contact. Afterward, Jacob scurried to the airport like a dog with his tail between his legs. He checked out of the hotel with such lightning speed that Mira didn't get a chance to offer him a lift back on her private jet. She had called several times since, but he was always unavailable. So she scheduled an appointment with him to resolve their little misunderstanding.

"Hello, Mira," he said, looking down at the floor, again averting his eyes. "How's it going?" he asked, making a lame attempt at small talk.

"Jacob, let's cut to the chase," she said, choosing not to prolong the inevitable. "We need to talk about what happened in London. Have a seat." Mira pointed to the small sofa.

"First of all, I apologize for, uh"—he sat down and nervously fumbled with his hands, putting the right hand over the left, then quickly reversing positions—"intruding on you and your girlfriend."

"She's not my girlfriend," Mira said, taking a seat in the chair across from the sofa. "Anyway"—the image of Jacob standing there in the buff flashed through her mind—"what were you doing in my bathroom in the first place? Didn't your room come with a shower?" Mira couldn't help but joke about the radically kinky scene, both of them being caught with their pants down, per se.

Jacob must have been reminiscing as well, because a wide grin spread across his face and quickly turned into a chuckle, which turned into a hardy roar. The robust laughter broke the tension in the room, putting them both at ease. "Oh, *my* room had a shower? Who knew?" He laughed. Jacob was relieved that Mira found the incident humorous and wasn't pissed at him for barging in.

"Obviously not you, since you came across the hall to my suite. But seriously, Jacob"—Mira stopped laughing—"what were you doing in my room?"

Now that she had switched her tone back to serious, Jacob felt sheepish, and started fumbling with his hands again. He didn't quite know how to answer the question without sounding like he was smitten. So he just said, "I thought you were sending me signals."

"Signals?" Mira looked confused. "What type of signals? Jacob, you're a married man, and I don't flirt or have affairs with married men."

"Yes, I am married and should have kept my feelings to myself, but the way you came dressed for dinner without a power suit on . . ." He hesitated a second, trying to find the right words. "I mean, you were so casual, and sexy. Your hair was loose, and your usual uptight attitude was gone. Well, I just thought we shared the same feelings."

Mira had no clue that Jacob thought of her as anything other than a client, but seeing him blush, she now realized that he was smitten with her. "And what feelings are those?" she asked, even though she knew the answer.

"I think you're extremely attractive, and to be honest, I have, or should I say had, a major crush on you, Mira," he admitted.

"What's the matter, Jacob? You not into gay women?" she teased, trying to lighten the mood.

"No, I'm not, but I'm not homophobic either. As a matter of fact, my sister is gay."

Mira raised an eyebrow in surprise. Jacob was always so professional, she assumed that he came from one of those superstrict uptight families, and didn't expect Jacob to say that he had a lesbian sister. Mira hadn't been on a date since she and Sam broke up. And they had hardly ever ventured out, preferring to spend most of their time in bed. Even though she fucked around at the Black Door, Mira was ready for another relationship, and not just random sex with servers. "Really? Is she seeing anyone?" Mira asked, cutting to the chase.

"No. She recently broke up with her girlfriend. Why?" He leaned forward. "Are you interested in meeting my sister?"

"Well, since I'm not seriously seeing anyone, why not? Besides, she comes with a top-notch recommendation." Mira winked.

"I don't believe this," Jacob said, shaking his head.

"What?" She smiled.

"A few minutes ago, I was slinking in here with my head in my hands, begging your pardon. Now, I'm playing matchmaker, setting you up with my sister. Talk about a dramatic turn of events."

"So when are you going to arrange a meeting? The sooner the better." Mira smiled broadly, warming up to the idea of a blind date.

"I don't know if Tyler is your type," he said point-blank.

"Why do you say that?" she asked, sounding offended.

"Tyler is the artsy, Bohemian type, and you look like you just stepped off the pages of *Vogue*. I can't picture you two together," he said, wriggling his nose and slightly shaking his head.

"I can do artsy. Besides, let me be the judge of who's my type, and who's not my type," she said, with authority.

"Fair enough, but I hope you're not the player type. Tyler just got out of a bad situation, and I would hate for her to get her heart broken twice in the same year," he said, sounding like an overprotective older brother.

Mira could hear the concern in his voice and it was touching. *He must really love his sister,* she thought. "No, I'm not a player." Mira thought about her membership at the Black Door. As far as she was concerned, what went on behind the closed doors of the club was nobody's business.

"What about the redhead in London? You two were having a pretty good time playing in the shower." He pinned her with a questioning look.

Mira chuckled, and felt a little flush. "Oh, she's a 'playmate' from a service I use from time to time when I'm in the UK."

"A service?" He scooted to the edge of the sofa and lowered his voice, as if someone else were in the room who might over-hear their conversation. "You mean an escort service?"

Mira shook her head up and down. "Yep. I was feeling lonely, so I called the service and ordered some company for the evening. They're the best in London with a stable stocked full of thoroughbreds."

Jacob flashed a broad grin. "Yeah, I saw firsthand."

A wave of embarrassment rushed over Mira at the thought of Jacob catching her with that little filly, and she didn't quite know what to say, so she didn't say anything.

Jacob noticed the blood rush to her face. "Don't worry. Your secret is safe with me." He winked. "We'll consider this a highly classified, proprietary meeting just between the two of us."

"You're right. This information is on a need-to-know basis." Mira felt relieved that that issue was resolved, and couldn't wait to meet Jacob's sister. Maybe this would finally be a true love connection and not another horny lust connection.

TYLER'S ROOM was directly above the kitchen, and she could hear Naomi buzzing around like the Queen Bee that she was, getting the hive ready for today's book club meeting. She put her sketch pad aside and decided to go downstairs and offer to help. Naomi didn't hear Tyler approaching, so she stood in the doorway for a moment and watched Naomi arrange a platter of crudités, slicing the raw vegetables like a seasoned chef. Absent from the picture was a chef's toque and apron. Instead, she wore a faded green New York Giants T-shirt and a pair of running shorts. The threadbare cotton of the shirt was so thin, she could see that Naomi was braless, her breasts hanging freely underneath the fabric. She must have been cold, because her headlights were shining brightly. Tyler tried not to stare at the silhouette of her nipples, but they were mesmerizing. Naomi must have felt Tyler staring. She suddenly turned around and looked up from the tray.

"I came down to help," Tyler offered, darting her eyes from Naomi's breasts to the vegetables.

"Thanks, but I have everything under control." Naomi began to julienne a carrot, and then stopped. "On second thought, you can mix up the dip for the crudités. The ingredients are in the refrigerator, on the top shelf."

Tyler went to the fridge and gathered the sour cream and scallions, but something was missing. Turning around to ask Naomi about the other ingredients, she was greeted by the view of her backside. Naomi was bent over picking something off the floor, her round ass high in the air. The running shorts had run all the way up her butt. She was pantiless, allowing Tyler to see more than she should have. Feeling ashamed at peeping at her sister-in-law's goodies, Tyler turned her head and concentrated on mixing the dip. The phone rang, and Tyler swung around. Her natural instinct was to answer the phone, but Naomi picked it up instead.

Tyler watched Naomi's facial expression change from neutral to negative. Whoever was on the other end, she wasn't too happy to hear from.

"I'm fine," she said, emphasizing the word fine. "Yes, she's right here." Naomi held out her arm, and extended the phone in Tyler's direction without saying a word.

Tyler took the receiver gingerly from her hand. "Hello? Oh, hey, Jacob. I'm good. How you doin'?" she asked in a heavy Brooklyn accent. He chuckled at Tyler's *Sopranos* wiseguy impression. She and Jacob had always enjoyed an easygoing relationship.

Naomi mouthed that she was going upstairs to dress, then rolled her eyes and stomped up the back steps. Judging from the anger in Naomi's voice when she spoke to Jacob and the look that she just flashed, Tyler assumed their relationship was anything but easygoing. "What's up with you and the wife?" she asked, once Naomi was out of earshot.

He sighed. "It's a long story. Basically, she's pissed because I travel too much, and I'm not giving her enough—" He stopped short, preferring not to divulge any more of their personal business. "Anyway," he changed the subject, "the reason why

I'm calling is all about you, not me," he said, sounding quite mysterious.

"What's that supposed to mean?"

"It means that your lonely days are over. Are you ready to get back in the game? If you are, I've got the perfect person for you to meet," he announced quickly, nearly running the sentences together into one.

"So now you're Chuck Woolery from *Love Connection*, trying to hook me up?" Tyler joked, though her interest was beginning to pique.

"Yeah, I am." He deepened his voice and said, "I'll be back in two and two," using Chuck Woolery's famous line.

"There'll be no commercial breaks yet, not until you give me the four-one-one on this mystery woman."

"Her name is Mira Rhone. She's one of my clients, and she wants to meet you," he said zealously.

"How does she know about me?" Now Tyler's curiosity was totally piqued.

"Well, that's another story altogether. Anyway——"

"You're full of long stories today."

"Before I was rudely interrupted, I was going to say that she's the CEO of FACEZ, extremely attractive, and single. Are you interested?"

"Are you kidding me? FACEZ is one of the world's leading cosmetics companies, and the CEO wants to meet me? Wow! I didn't know she was gay. The last thing I read in the tabloids was that she had called off her wedding. Now I understand why. Wow! I'm stunned."

"I'll take that long-drawn-out response as a yes."

"Of course I want to meet her, but I don't want to seem like an eager beaver, desperate for a date."

"Well, aren't you?" he teased.

"Yeah, but she doesn't have to know how desperate. I've got to play it cool. Being the head of a major corporation, I'm sure she has women falling at her feet daily." Tyler thought about the situation for a second, and came up with an idea. "We're having a book club meeting here tonight. Why don't you invite her? That way it's not a date date and I can check her out without committing to a formal date first."

"That sounds like a plan. I don't know if she'll be available since this is the last minute, but I'll call her anyway. Talk to you la—"

"Hold on, wait a minute. Now that I'm thinking about it, I don't know if this is such a good idea. Your wife might have a hissing fit if some random woman showed up out of the blue," she said.

"Don't worry, I'll talk to Naomi, and say that Mira is a client of mine who's interested in joining the club. I'm sure she won't have a problem with that since she's been on the hunt for new members."

"Hold on. I'll tell her you're on the line. Thanks, big brother. Good looking out," Tyler said, before calling Naomi to the phone.

AN HOUR LATER, Tyler was standing in front of the mirror tweaking her makeup. Putting the tube of Nearly Nude lipstick back in her cosmetics case, she thought, *I've been using FACEZ products for years, and now I'm going to meet the CEO. How ironic is that?* The mounting anticipation was making her anxious. She felt like a kid on Christmas Eve waiting for Old Saint Nick to come sliding down the chimney with his sack full of goodies. *Was that the doorbell?* Tyler rushed out of the bathroom and tipped to the door. Her heart was beating wildly as she opened the door and stuck her head out. She could hear voices downstairs, and wondered if that was Mira. *What if she's into the prissy, prissy type,* she thought, running her hand through her golden dreads. Tyler wasn't a lipstick lesbian, nor was she a hard-core dyke. She was a hybrid of the two, feminine with a slight edge. Tyler began to rethink the black slacks and black mock turtleneck that she wore. As she contemplated changing outfits, the doorbell rang a second time. *Well, it's too late. If it wasn't her before, I'm sure that's her now.* Tyler slipped on a pair of black mules and headed downstairs. She stopped on the steps when she heard voices and listened for a minute.

"So, who is she?" That was Kennedy, in the kitchen with Naomi, balancing the tray of crudités in her arms. "I answered the front door when you were upstairs, and there she stood."

"Her name is Mira Rhone. She's the CEO of FACEZ and a client of Jacob's."

"FACEZ? What a small world, that's where Nigel works. How did the CEO of FACEZ wind up at our little ole meeting?"

Naomi rolled her eyes to the ceiling, and then explained, "Jacob called out of the clear blue and said a client of his was interested in joining our book club. I guess he was tired of me complaining about looking for new members."

"Well, she doesn't seem like a big-wig muckety-muck. When I opened the door, she was extremely friendly," Kennedy commented, and turned toward Tyler, who had come back in the kitchen from upstairs. "Oh, hey, how's it going?"

Tyler hadn't seen Kennedy since moving back to New York. They had met at Jacob and Naomi's wedding. The ceremony was small and intimate, with Kennedy and Tyler the only two bridesmaids. Unlike Naomi, Kennedy wasn't homophobic. She and Tyler chatted easily throughout the entire weekend, joking about the hideous teal blue chiffon dresses and matching satin slippers they were forced to wear. "It's going, Kennedy. How've you been?"

"No major complaints, just the usual minor ones," Kennedy joked while balancing the appetizers with one arm. "Let me take this tray into the solarium before I drop it on the floor."

"Please don't drop the crudités. It took me too long to cut up those vegetables. Tyler, can you bring in the fruit tray?" Naomi

asked, pointing to a silver platter sitting in the middle of the island.

"Sure." Tyler's heart rate accelerated as she carried the
beautifully arranged melons, berries, and kiwi down the hallway to the solarium, where Mira Rhone was waiting. Tyler was
anxious to meet her blind date. She had let go of the hurt that
Liz had caused her and was ready to move on. Tyler was a one-
woman woman, and desired to be in a relationship. She crossed
her fingers underneath the tray and prayed that Mira Rhone
wanted the same thing.

"Mira, this is my sister-in-law, Tyler. And this is Kennedy,
my best friend, who opened the door when you arrived," Naomi
said, making introductions all around.

"Nice to meet you," Kennedy said, shaking Mira's hand. She
thought about mentioning that she was dating Nigel, but didn't
want to make a big deal out of it. Besides, she didn't know Mira,
and didn't want to disclose too much personal information on a
first meeting.

Tyler was a walking bundle of nerve endings and nearly top-
pled the tray over at the sight of Mira. She was absolutely tie-
your-tongue-up-in-knots gorgeous. And that was exactly what
happened as she stumbled over her words. "Uh, hi, hello, uh,
I'm . . . uh, nice to meet you," Tyler finally said, setting the tray
on the cocktail table.

Mira looked into Tyler's eyes, and without stumbling over
one word said, "Nice meeting you as well." She shook Tyler's
hand, but held it a little longer than normal. Tyler wasn't as
butch as Sam, but she was attractive nonetheless.

"Welcome to the Naughty Book Club. Shall we get started,
ladies?" Naomi asked, motioning for everyone to have a seat.

Over the next hour they munched on the raw veggies, mini
sandwiches, and fruit while discussing the plot line of *A Few
Dollars and a Dream*. The general consensus was that the story
was interesting enough, but predictable. Mira didn't participate

in the discussion. Obviously, she hadn't had enough time to read the book, so she just sat back and observed. From time to time, Tyler caught Mira cutting her eyes in her direction, checking her out on the sly.

"So much for this novel," Naomi said, tossing her copy on the cocktail table. "I've been thinking that maybe we should read a juicier book. Maybe something that's a little more erotic." She wanted to make a segue into talking about the Black Door, and this seemed like a good intro. Naomi looked over at Kennedy, trying to give her a hint as to where this conversation was headed.

"Hmm, that sounds interesting," Kennedy said, immediately catching on.

"You know how they say life imitates art?" She looked around the room, but no one said anything, so she continued. "Well, I've heard of this club that caters to the carnal needs of women. Men work there, but they can't be members." She hesitated. "I think it's called the Black Door." Naomi finished her sentence and looked directly at Tyler, waiting for her to offer up the goods. But Tyler just sat there like she had never heard of the place, so Naomi went on. "Now, I wonder if this club is real, or if it's just a figment of someone's imagination?" Again she zeroed in on Tyler.

"If it's an actual club, sign me up!" Kennedy said, hoping that Tyler would acknowledge knowing about the club, but she didn't.

How the hell does Naomi know about the Black Door? Tyler thought. She didn't dare mention that she was doing some freelance work for the owner, since he had practically sworn her to secrecy. Besides, Naomi had such a bad attitude about her sexuality that she would probably throw Tyler out if she knew about her designing masks for an erotica club.

Oh, shit! Where is this coming from? Mira wondered. She surely wasn't going to say that she was a card-carrying member.

She had just met these women, and as far as she was concerned, admitting that she frequented the Black Door was TMI—too much information. So she sat there like a deaf mute.

Naomi gave Tyler a hard stare, trying to will her to talk, but Tyler ignored her gaze. Realizing that she wasn't going to get any information out of her sister-in-law, Naomi let the subject drop.

There was dead silence in the room until Mira finally spoke. "I have a suggestion for the next book."

"And what might that be?" Naomi asked, slightly annoyed. She hadn't gotten the information that she was seeking, and now the new kid on the block was suggesting titles. That was usually her job.

"Since you guys thought the plot line of this book was too predictable, why don't we read a sci-fi novel for our next meeting?" When no one spoke up, she continued. "Anything by Michael Crichton would be thrilling. His books are so unpredictable and extremely engrossing."

"I think that's an excellent suggestion," Tyler agreed, coming to her defense, trying to make a good impression. "*Andromeda Strain* definitely had me going."

Neither Naomi nor Kennedy seemed thrilled by the suggestion, so Mira made another attempt. "Well, if you guys"—she looked at Naomi and Kennedy—"don't want to read a sci-fi book, what about *The Lovely Bones,* by Alice Sebold? I know it's been out for a long while, but from what I understand, it's an outstanding story."

"Yeah, it was on the *New York Times* Bestseller list forever," Kennedy commented, warming up to the idea and biting down on a carrot. She was tired of the cheesy love stories that Naomi always chose.

"I wanted to read that book when it came out, but at the time, Noah wasn't in preschool, and I didn't have time to think straight, let alone enjoy a good book. If you guys haven't read it,

I think that's an excellent suggestion," Naomi said, pretending as if the book were her choice.

"Sounds good to me," Tyler said.

"Well, then it's settled. We'll read *The Lovely Bones* for our next meeting," Naomi said, taking command once again. "Speaking of the next meeting, who's going to host it?" she asked, looking around the room.

"Since I'm new to the group, why don't I have it at my place?" Mira offered.

Naomi wasn't too thrilled at having the meeting at a stranger's house, but on the other hand, that stranger happened to be a multimillionaire, and she wanted to see the inside of Mira's home, and maybe get some decorating ideas. "Great. How about a month from today?" Naomi asked everyone.

They all nodded in agreement. As Tyler watched Mira write the date in her agenda, she wondered how long it would be until she had a standing appointment with the sexy CEO.

"CAN YOU believe Tyler just sat there like she didn't know what the hell I was talking about?" Naomi hissed. She was still pissed that Tyler had played the dumb role, and not offered up any information.

"Actually, I'm not too surprised. I mean, it's not like admitting that you have a membership in the New York Sports Club. What was she supposed to say? 'By the way, I get my freak on at the Black Door?'" Kennedy mused. She and Naomi were at one of those tacky wig shops along Sixth Avenue near Thirty-seventh Street. Earlier they had met with the consultant that Naomi had hired to put together her business plan, and were now trying on wigs to hide under before going to the Black Door for the grand tour.

"I guess you have a point. Do you like this one?" Naomi asked, adjusting a long platinum wig around her ears.

"Naw." Kennedy shook her head. "It's too phony-looking." She took a short sassy brunette wig off of its foam head. "Here, try her."

Naomi pulled off the blond hair and replaced it with the more natural-looking one. She turned her head in the mirror, checking out her profile from different angles. "This one's hot!" She tugged the bangs farther down on her forehead, so that it covered more of her face. She then took a pair of shades out of her purse and put them on. "Wow, that's what I call incognito. I hardly recognize myself." Until Naomi knew Tyler's affiliation with the club, she wasn't taking any chances. She had thought twice about going in the first place, but was curious to see what the Black Door had to offer. Besides, with her disguise it was highly unlikely that anyone would be able to identify her, on the off chance that she saw someone she knew.

Kennedy finally settled on a shoulder-length auburn number. They paid for their purchases, went outside, and hailed a taxi to the club. "So, what name are you going by this evening?" Kennedy asked. They were both using false identities until they felt comfortable enough to use their real names.

"Sasha Green," she said, running her hand through the fake hair.

Kennedy cracked up laughing. "With a name like Sasha, I don't think she'd be green. On the contrary, she'd be more of a pro. A twirling around the pole pro!" she joked, making a play on words.

"Touché." Naomi clapped in mock response. "Well, I think my new name is cute, and I'm sticking with it."

"Okay, Sasha, whatever you say. Just remember not to call me Kennedy. I'm Kendra Brian."

"Oh, what a stretch, Kennedy Bryant to Kendra Brian. Couldn't you come up with a more creative choice?"

"If you do recall, I was put on the spot, remember?" Kennedy asked defensively, referring to her initial conversation with Trey.

"Don't get all huffy with me. I'm just kidding." She poked Kennedy in the side. "Lighten up."

"I'm sorry. I guess I'm a little on edge about meeting with Trey. Suppose he asks for ID?"

Naomi hadn't thought of that. "Well, if he does, we'll pretend like we left our wallet in another purse. That's not so far-fetched. I've done that on a few occasions. And if he refuses to show us around, we'll just thank him for his time and leave. Anyway, I can't join if Tyler is a member. The last thing I need is for her to go running back to her brother telling him that I belong to a sex club."

"I'm starting to get an uneasy feeling about going to the Black Door. Maybe we shouldn't, and go to dinner instead. There's this new restaurant on Ninety-third and Broadway that I've been dying to try." Kennedy loved to get her freak on, but joining an erotica club was a bit over the top for her. What she did with a vibrator in the privacy of her home was one thing, but fucking a masked server in a room with other people was an entirely different realm of freakiness.

"What's with the cold feet?" Naomi asked, surprised at Kennedy's shift in attitude. "I thought you wanted a distraction from Nigel."

"I do. It's just that I'm not ready to go through a rigorous screening process. Trey mentioned that we'd have to make an appointment with the club's physician. The thought of visiting another gynecologist is a turnoff. I've been going to my doctor for eons, and frankly, I don't want another doctor looking at my cooch. I think I'd rather wait until Nigel and I do the deed."

"Have you even talked to him since dinner at his apartment?"

"Yeah, we went to a late movie the other night. Girl, he's so romantic, we smooched and cuddled throughout the entire movie. Who knows, maybe we'll do the deed, sooner rather than later."

"I hear what you're saying, but don't back out on me now, Kennedy. Let's follow through with the tour. I really need to find out how Tyler knows about the club. I'm going to casually ask Trey how he knows her. It could be that they're just old friends from school, and she's not even a member. If that's the case, then I'm seriously thinking about joining. I need sex more than once a quarter. I swear, the older I get, the more I crave the dick. In my twenties, I could care less about making love, but now I'm perpetually horny, and waiting for Jacob to throw me his bone every blue moon just isn't working for me."

"I know what you mean. I guess that's why older women and younger men are the perfect match in bed. Both are sexually charged. But if you join, aren't you afraid that this Trey guy will tell Tyler you're a member?" Kennedy asked.

"No. Not at all. If he's a true businessman, he'll keep my business to himself. I'm sure the club wouldn't be successful if he was a blabbermouth."

"True. If the members were afraid that their identities would be leaked, this would be the last club they'd join. I'm sure in this line of business, discretion is key. But I think I'm still going to wait for Nigel."

"Why don't you wait until you see the inside of the club before you make that decision? I'm sure there are private areas where you can get your freak on," Naomi said, trying to sway her friend.

Kennedy shrugged her shoulders. "We'll see."

They rode the rest of the way in silence. Naomi was figuring out the right way to approach Trey, and Kennedy was deep in thought trying to decide when would be the perfect time to fuck Nigel, without jeopardizing their relationship.

"That'll be seventeen-twenty," the driver said, parking in front of the club.

"I got it." Naomi took out her wallet, paid the fare, and they got out. She stood at the curb and stared at the building. "This doesn't look like a sex club." She commented on the unassuming-looking brownstone, whose only discerning mark was a humongous shiny black door.

"Sure doesn't."

They each adjusted their false hair, and casually made their way up the walk. Naomi led the way and arrived at the door first. She knocked hard as if she belonged inside. A few seconds later, a small window inside of the front door slid open.

"Password, please?" asked a deep Michael Duncan–type voice.

"We have a meeting scheduled with Trey Curtis," Naomi said into the tiny opening.

"Just a second," the doorman said, and slid the window closed. After a minute or so, he opened the door. "You'll have to put these on before entering." He handed them each a half-mask. Naomi's was black with black fringes on the sides, and Kennedy's was indigo with pink feathers. After their masks were secured, he pointed to a mahogany pocket door. "You can wait inside there. Trey will be right with you."

Once inside the parlor, they sat on an emerald green sofa and glanced around. The room had a Victorian-type feel, with a huge, embroidered tapestry hanging on one wall and a gilded beveled mirror hanging on another. The furniture was antique, with overstuffed sofas, chairs, and beautifully carved mahogany tables. The hardwood floor was covered with imported carpets, and an exquisite chandelier hung from the twelve-foot ceiling.

"This is nothing like I imagined," Naomi said, wrinkling her nose. "Not that I don't like antiques. I adore them. I just thought this place would look like a den of iniquity, with bearskin rugs, leather furniture, and those hideous black velvet plantings." Since they were the only two in the room, she spoke freely.

"I know what you mean. This place seems more suited to the tastes of old-money matrons who sit around and sip sherry," Kennedy added.

As they were giving their unsolicited opinions, the pocket door eased open and in walked Trey. Naomi gasped slightly, and Kennedy's eyes nearly popped out of her head at the sight of him. Trey was over six feet of perfection. He was clean-shaven, and his mocha complexion was flawless. His hair was cut so close that it resembled a five o'clock shadow. He was wearing a black leather mask, so they could see his eyes, which were narrow, sexy slits. If it wasn't for his full kissable lips, he could have easily passed for a black Chinaman—if such a thing existed.

"Good evening, ladies. I'm Trey Curtis." He extended his hand to Naomi. "The doorman told me there were two of you, but I was only expecting Ms. Brian. Which one of you is Ms. Brian?" he asked, without cracking a smile.

Kennedy spoke up. "That would be me. This is my sister Sasha. She's also interested in joining, and I didn't think it would be a problem if she came along for the tour."

Trey gave them each a hard look, taking in their wigs and tightly drawn trench coats. It was obvious they were trying to be incognito. He wasn't surprised. Some women were a bit apprehensive on the first visit, as if they were doing something dirty—actually, they were on the verge of doing the dirty—and felt guilty. "No, it's not a problem. So tell me, how do you know Tyler?" he asked Kennedy.

"We went to school together." She quickly remembered Naomi mentioning that maybe Tyler and Trey went to school together, so she used that lie. Kennedy suddenly started to panic, thinking that if they attended school together then it would cancel out her lie.

"Oh, I see. She's a talented artist. Are you an artist too?"

Thank God, they're not former classmates, Kennedy thought. "Not anymore. I was never as good as Tyler, so I hung up my painter's smock." She chuckled nervously.

"What do you do now?"

"I hate to interrupt, but I'm running short on time. Do you mind if we start the tour?" Naomi interrupted, before the lies continued. She wanted to ask him how he knew Tyler, but now was not the right time. He seemed a little too suspicious, so she decided to wait until the end of the tour.

"Sure, no problem." Trey led the way out of the room. "There are two parlors here on the main level. The one that you were just sitting in is basically for the older members who just want to sip their cocktails and have a conversation with a handsome young man." He crossed the foyer and slid open another pocket door.

They walked in and gawked. This parlor was similar to the previous one, except there was an ornate champagne fountain in the middle of the floor, with several people milling around drinking. Most of the members were topless, wearing nothing more than thongs and heels. Naomi didn't spot a sagging tit in the room. They were all perky and seemed to be surgically enhanced. And the servers were even finer than Trey, with muscles so defined that they looked manufactured by Nautilus. *Now, this is what I'm talking about,* Naomi thought. Looking at all the exposed skin, Kennedy and Naomi felt overdressed in their coats.

"This room serves as the portal to the land of decadence. See those red drapes," Trey whispered, and nodded his head toward the rear of the room. They both nodded. "Behind those drapes is a staircase that leads up to where the various theme rooms are located."

"Theme rooms?" Naomi asked.

"Yes, there's the Voyeurism Room, for those who like to be watched. The Game Room, but the games played are not for kids. The Leopard Lounge, if you want to kick back and have a cocktail while having your clit licked," he said with a straight face, and then continued. "If you're into toys, we have the Tantalizing Toy Room, and . . ."

"I'd love to see what toys you guys have," Kennedy said, wondering if they had the "Rabbit," her favorite vibrator.

"Well, ladies, I'm sorry to say that this is where the tour ends. If you want to see more, you'll need to go through our screening process," Trey told them point-blank.

Naomi and Kennedy looked at each other in sheer disbelief.

Just when they were warming up to the idea of the club, the tour was over. Trey was an astute businessman; he had whetted their appetites just enough, leaving them yearning for more.

"Oh, I see." Naomi nodded her head. She had seen enough to make a decision, and the decision was that without a doubt, she would join the club, but first she had a question.

Trey walked them out of the parlor, into the foyer. "Thank you, ladies, for coming by. I hope you'll call and schedule an appointment for your interview."

"Of course we will, and thanks for your time," Naomi said, and turned toward the door, but then turned back to him. "Trey, how do you know Tyler?" she asked, trying to sound casual.

"She's doing some work for me," he told her without elaborating.

"Oh." Naomi wanted to ask what type of work, but based on his dry tone, she decided against prying further. Besides, now her question was partially answered. At least Tyler wasn't a member. "Good night, Trey. Talk to you soon," Naomi said. She and Kennedy walked out of the foyer into the doorman area.

"I'll need those masks," the beefy doorman said, and reached out his large, meaty hand.

"Sure, no problem." They each removed their masks, handed them over, then removed their wigs and stuffed them into their purses. Since they were leaving the club there was no need to continue with the charade.

"Wow, that was amazing!" Kennedy exclaimed, opening the door and walking out.

"So, have you changed your mind about joining?" Naomi asked, walking down the steps.

"After looking at all those fine men, I'm reconsidering." Kennedy smiled.

"Naomi and Kennedy! What are you guys doing here?"

"Tyler!" Naomi couldn't believe that her sister-in-law was standing right in front of her.

"What are you doing here?" Tyler asked again, this time posing the question directly to Naomi.

"Uh, we, uh . . ." She didn't know what to say. "Come on, Kennedy, let's go."

They rushed past Tyler and down the street without answering her question. Naomi needed time to think of a proper answer, and fleeing seemed to be a better option than saying something stupid. So they left Tyler standing on the steps with her mouth hanging open.

26

   "HEY THERE, Kennedy, it's been a long time," said Valerie, the co-owner of Kaminsky's.

"Too long," Kennedy replied, kissing her on the cheek. She had known Valerie for years. They had met on a flight to Paris. Kennedy was going to do a little light shopping and Valerie was traveling there to work the spring fashion shows. At the time, Valerie was one of the select black models who graced the European circuit, strutting the catwalk like a long-legged gazelle.

"Kaminsky was just asking about you the other day." Val was married to renowned chef Kaminsky Thomas. Their restaurant was on the radar of discerning food critics across the country, with impressive write-ups in *Gourmet* and *Bon Appétit.*

"How is that handsome husband of yours?"

"He's fine. He's in the kitchen now whipping up one of his specialties."

Kennedy inhaled the aroma wafting throughout the restaurant. "Whatever he's cooking sure smells good. What's on the lunch menu today?"

"Lobster BLT, with Nueske's bacon, heirloom tomatoes, sunflower greens, and chive mayonnaise on brioche with sweet potato chips, and that's just for starters." Val chuckled.

"Hmmm"—Kennedy licked her bottom lip—"that sounds delicious. I can't wait to chow down."

"You want to be seated now or are you waiting for someone?"

"I'm having lunch with my new beau." She blushed.

"New beau?" Val put her hand on her slender hip. "Do tell."

"There isn't much to tell. His name is Nigel Charles. We met in-flight and have been dating ever since," she said, giving Val the abbreviated version.

Known for asking pointed questions, Val pinned her with an inquiring-minds-want-to-know look. "What does he do for a living?"

"He's the Vice President of Research and Development for FACEZ."

"Okay," she said, nodding her head up and down in an approving gesture. "He has a good job, but more importantly, does he have good looks?" Valerie teased.

Nigel's face flashed through Kennedy's mind and a broad smile immediately erupted before she could respond.

"I'll take that as a yes." Val chuckled. "Guess I'll see for myself when he gets here. Lunch with a handsome man needs a nice bottle of Riesling, and I have the perfect one. It's an Albert Mann Cuvee, and it's light and crisp." Being a certified sommelier, Val could rattle off at least a dozen vintages before you could say Chardonnay.

She escorted Kennedy to a choice booth and sent over a bottle of wine. As Kennedy sipped her wine, she couldn't help but think about being busted by Tyler. She and Naomi were in such shock that they hardly spoke when they fled the club. She took out her cell and called Naomi.

"Hey, girl," Kennedy said as soon as Naomi picked up the phone. "Have you talked to Tyler?"

"Not yet. She hasn't been in the house all day."

"I knew we shouldn't have gone to the Black Door. I had such a bad feeling, and we should have followed my intuition."

"Well, that's a moot point now," Naomi said, shrugging her shoulders even though Kennedy couldn't see her.

"Well, I know I'm not joining the club now."

"That makes two of us," Naomi said with a hint of disappointment in her voice.

"What are you going to tell her about us being at the Black Door?"

"I've been thinking about that, and I've decided to play the dumb role, and pretend like we were looking for a friend's house, and just so happened to wind up on the steps of the club, by accident of course. I'm so glad we took off the wigs, otherwise we would have really looked suspicious. And then I'm going to turn the tables and ask what she was doing there."

"That's sounds like a good plan. Make her think that *she* was doing something wrong."

"Exactly! Fortunately, Jacob is in London again. As much as I didn't want him to go, I'm actually glad. At least now I don't have to worry about Tyler telling him half-truths."

"Wasn't Jacob just in London?" Kennedy asked.

"Yeah, less than two weeks ago. He said an impromptu meeting came up, and he had no other choice but to attend. By the time he gets back I will have convinced Tyler that we were at the wrong address, and nothing more."

"Let me know what happens. I've got to run. I'm having lunch with Nigel, and he should be here any minute."

"Wish me luck."

"Good luck, girl."

"Okay, talk to you later," Naomi said, and hung up.

The waitress came over and refilled her glass. Kennedy glanced down at her watch. He was twenty minutes late. She dialed his number, but got a ring followed immediately by a short beep indicating that he was on another call. She hung up before his voice mail answered. *That's odd. He usually clicks over when he sees my number.* Before she had a chance to give it a second thought, Nigel was rushing toward the booth with the phone glued to his ear.

"Did you get the report? I had it messengered over to your place this morning." He looked at Kennedy, put up his index finger, and mouthed, "One second."

She mouthed back, "Okay."

"Great. I'll have the final stats to you next week," he said, clicking off the phone. "Hey there, beautiful." He leaned in and lightly kissed her lips. "Sorry I'm late. My plan was to have a laid-back Saturday morning, but I had to go into the office at the last minute and copy some files. There's some work I want to do at home this weekend, and I didn't have the information I need on my personal computer. Sometimes I feel like Kunta Kinte working from sunup to sundown," he mused, sliding into the booth.

"Funny, she doesn't look like a slave driver."

"Who?" he asked with a puzzled expression.

"Mira Rhone," Kennedy said casually, taking another sip of wine. "She's your boss, isn't she?" she added, catching him by surprise.

"Yeah. How did you know that? When did you see her? Do you know Mira?" he asked, quickly running all three questions together.

Taking the mystery a step further, she decided to toy with him. "There's very little that I don't know, my dear." She grinned, arching an eyebrow.

"Seriously, Kennedy"—he looked directly into her eyes— "how do you know Mira?"

"We're in the same club," she answered, giving up very little information.

"Club? What type of club? You mean sorority?" he asked, trying to extract the facts.

"Not a sorority, a private club, for members only." She winked, thinking about the Black Door. *Wouldn't it be ironic if Mira was a member?* Kennedy didn't know what made her think about Mira being a member, since she had only met the woman once. But the thought was interesting nonetheless.

"Come on, Kennedy, stop playing around and tell me how you two know each other."

From the stern look registered on his face and the urgency in his voice, Kennedy could tell he found no humor in her little game of cat and mouse. "We're in the same book club," she finally admitted, ending the charade.

"Book club? I didn't know you were in a book club."

"My friend Naomi started it awhile ago, and we've been trying to replace members that have dropped out. Naomi's husband Jacob . . ."

"Jacob Reed?" he interrupted.

"You know him?" Now Kennedy was the one with the puzzled expression.

"Yeah, I know him. He's the accountant for FACEZ."

"What a small world."

"And getting smaller all the time," he muttered.

"Taking on our drive for fresh blood, Jacob invited Mira to one of our meetings. I've only met her once, but she seems cool."

Nigel looked away for a split second. "Yeah, she's cool all right, among other things," he said with disdain.

Kennedy assumed that Mira, being a young executive, would be a liberal boss, but judging from the contempt in Nigel's voice, it was probably the opposite. "Why'd you say that? Is she a taskmaster?"

He didn't answer immediately, and then said cryptically, "You could say that."

"Is it tough working for a wo—"

"Let's change the subject. I don't feel like talking about Mira or work," he said abruptly. Nigel purposely didn't tell Kennedy that it was Mira who dumped him. He started to but didn't want to deal with a million and two questions. He and Mira were history, so there was really nothing to tell. Besides, Kennedy already knew that he had been engaged before, so it wasn't like he was harboring a huge secret.

The way Nigel cut Kennedy off, she couldn't help but think there was something he was holding back. Not wanting to be pushy, she stopped the inquisition short. She knew how guarded some men could be about their work, and didn't want to overstep her bounds. But on the other hand, women were much more forthcoming with information, so she would just bide her time, wait until the next book club meeting, and get the 411 straight from the horse's mouth.

"So, sexy, what have you been up to?" Nigel asked, changing his tone.

Once again the Black Door entered her mind. Kennedy wanted to say, *Checking out an erotica club to possibly get my freak on.* But of course she didn't. "Nothing too exciting. What about you?"

"I've been thinking about your self-imposed rule." He scooted a little closer to her.

"Exactly what have you been thinking?" She smiled.

"That we've been dating for nearly two months, and I'd like to take our relationship to the next level."

"And what level is that?" Kennedy asked, even though she knew what he was alluding to.

He put his arm around her shoulders and pulled her closer until she was wedged into his side. "The other night at the movies I think we both really enjoyed hugging and kissing in the dark, so much so that we need to take our relationship to another level," he said, tightening his grip around her shoulder.

Kennedy could feel her juices heating up. Being that close to Nigel was making her horny, and she wanted to fuck him right there at the table. She looked around the restaurant, making sure no one was eyeing them. Luckily, they were seated in the back in a booth, outside of clear view. Kennedy put her hand on his thigh. "I truly enjoyed our night at the movies, even though we really didn't see much of the film, since we were busy sucking face."

Nigel didn't object to her hand resting on his leg. "And what a lovely face you have." He lightly kissed the tip of her nose.

His tenderness was really turning her on. Some men were totally barbaric in their approach to kissing, slobbering all over a woman's face, but Nigel's moves were sweet and gentle, like he truly cared for her. Kennedy eased her fingers up his leg, and didn't stop until she landed at his crotch. She began caressing his balls. They were thick and warm. Imagining how they would feel *and* taste in her mouth, Kennedy licked her lips. Transferring her hand from his scrotum to the outline of his penis, she asked, "What are you going to do with this once we're horizontal?"

Nigel was shocked. He couldn't believe that she was feeling him up underneath the table. Kennedy had been so strict about her no-sex rule; now she had done a complete about-face, and was acting like a woman who wanted to get fucked. He could feel himself getting hard at the thought of finally tasting her pussy. "I'm going to take this hard rod"—he pressed her hand farther down on his rising erection—"and ease it into you ever so gently, and then I'm going to take my time and make sweet love to you all night," he whispered in her ear.

"Mmm," she moaned, "that sounds greaaat!"

"Come on." He took her free hand into his. "Let's forget about lunch, go to my place, and take care of some long-overdue business."

Lust was surging through Kennedy's veins at a rapid pace, and she was ready to explode. "Okay, let's go."

"Waitress." He waved the server over to pay for the wine.

As they waited for the waitress to bring back his credit card,

Kennedy began to have second thoughts. She wanted Nigel in the worst way, but she couldn't get the failed relationships out of her mind. She was tired of making the same mistake over and over and over again. Kennedy wanted more than just sex from Nigel. She wanted a lasting relationship, and possibly marriage.

The waitress came back, and he began to sign his name.

"Wait a minute," she blurted out before he finished signing.

"Yes, baby, what is it?" he asked, not looking up.

"You're going to think I'm schizophrenic, but I've changed my mind. I can't make love to you yet." Though she had initiated the intimate contact, she couldn't carry out the mission.

Nigel put the pen down and glared at her. "What? Why are you playing games, Kennedy? You feel me up. Get me all hot and ready, and now you're saying no." His dick was pulsating, and he wanted to release his weapon. He hadn't been laid in months and was beyond horny. "This is crazy. We're both consenting adults, and I don't understand why we're not fucking. I've been more than patient. Most guys that I know would not have waited nearly this long."

Kennedy understood Nigel's shift in attitude. She had turned him on, only to turn him off. She put her hand on top of his. "Please, don't be upset with me, but I think we should wait."

"Wait for what?" He raised his voice slightly.

"To get to know each other a little better," Kennedy said, sounding like a teenager.

Nigel signed the check and tossed the pen on the table. "Yeah, yeah, I've heard it before. Come on, let's go. I'm not hungry anymore."

Kennedy followed him to the door. Once they were outside, Nigel gave her a quick peck on the cheek. "I need to go back to the office. I just remembered something else I forgot." Even though he was pissed, he hailed a taxi for her and opened the door for her to get in, like a true gentleman. "I'll take the next one. Good-bye, Kennedy," he said sternly, and shut the door.

She looked back as the cab pulled off, and Nigel was getting in another taxi. She watched until his cab turned the corner and was out of sight. *I hope this isn't good-bye for good,* she thought, and rested her head on the back of the seat, suddenly regretting her decision.

JACOB SHOULD have been exhausted from taking the red-eye across the pond, but he was running on sheer adrenaline. The excitement of his impending meeting had him wired like a kid waiting on his birthday. And he couldn't wait to unwrap his present. Sitting impatiently in the backseat of a taxi as the driver cruised casually through the London streets on the way to the hotel, Jacob wanted to yell out for him to speed up, or better yet move over and let him drive. The driver was taking his sweet time, putting along well below the speed limit. Ordinarily this wouldn't have bothered Jacob, but the clock was ticking and he planned to make the most of his time. Finally, after about forty minutes, they were easing up to the Ritz. Jacob paid the fare, told the driver to keep the change, and quickly got out. Thankfully, registration was swift, and within minutes, he was upstairs in his standard room. Picking up the phone next to the bed, Jacob punched in Mira's number. After four rings, she answered. "Hello," she said in a groggy voice.

"Mira. Jacob. Listen, I need that number," he blurted into the phone without preamble.

"What number? What are you talking about? What time is it anyway?" she asked, totally clueless.

"You know, the number to that escort service you told me about," he said, answering one question, ignoring the other two.

"Escort service? What escort service?" she asked, obviously still half-asleep. With the time difference, the sun had yet to rise in the States.

"The one with the stable full of thoroughbreds."

"You mean the one in London," she answered, finally catching on.

"Yep, that's the one." He smiled.

"I'll give it to you the next time we're there for a meeting. Right now, I'm going to get in a few more winks before the alarm clock rings," she said, ready to disconnect the line.

"Wait, Mira, don't hang up!" he shouted desperately. "I'm in London now and I need that number. I called you before I left, but you didn't return my call."

"I saw your call, but didn't check the message. What are you doing in London? We're not scheduled to meet with the board again until next quarter."

"Let's just say I'm here to jockey a thoroughbred."

She began to laugh, finally catching on. "Oh, I get it now. Well, since you introduced me to your sister, I guess I can share my little secret. Just so you know, this information is normally under lock and key."

What started off as a calamity—catching Mira in the act— had actually turned into a good thing, taking their business relationship to a personal one. They were now confidantes, safekeepers of secrets. Jacob knew his escapades would be protected with Mira, as she knew hers would be with him. They both had too much to lose to be carelessly indiscreet.

"By the way, your sister is cute, but your wife is an absolute knockout. Why do you need an escort service when you have a thoroughbred of your own? Aren't you getting any at home?" she asked curiously.

If she only knew that their love life was about as exciting as watching a one-legged stripper navigating the pole.

When he didn't answer right away, she said, "Sorry, didn't mean to pry. Anyway, the number is 881-6969. You know the country code. You have to tell them that I referred you, because they're extremely private and operate on a referral basis only."

Jacob desperately scribbled the digits on the writing pad sitting atop the nightstand, hung up, and dialed.

"Let Us Entertain You, Elaine speaking. How may I direct your call?" asked an extremely intelligent-sounding woman.

Though Jacob had never called an escort service or 900 number for that matter, he expected to hear a panting, come-hither voice on the other end of the line. But this woman spoke as if she were answering the switchboard of a Fortune 500 company instead of a hire-by-the-hour escort service. "Mira Rhone referred me," he said, getting right to the point.

"Oh, yes, Ms. Rhone." At the mention of Mira's name, her voice became softer, and more feminine. "How can I help you this evening?"

"Uh, I'd like to . . ." The words suddenly stuck in his throat. He had fucked around before with random women he had met at bars when he was away on business trips, but never with an escort.

"To have a companion for the evening," she said knowingly, completing his sentence.

"Yes, I'd like a companion for the evening," Jacob said, finding his voice.

"Do you have a preference?"

"Uh, I . . ."

Sensing that he was an inexperienced novice, she began to

run down a laundry list of attributes. "Tall, dark, short, silicone-enhanced or au natural, blonde, brunette, or redhead?"

At the mention of redhead, Jacob flashed back to the fiery-headed vixen who was in the shower with Mira. From what he could see, her ripe, voluptuous boobs were au natural; though they appeared to be 38DDs, her tits didn't have that solid-as-a-rock look. "How about the redhead?" he asked, hoping that the escort service didn't have more than one.

"Oh, yes, Cinnamon, she's one of our most popular girls. Let me check her schedule," she said, putting him on hold. After a few minutes, she came back on the line. "You're in luck, she's available tonight. Her minimum is three hours, at two hundred and fifty pounds an hour. Or if you want the overnight rate, it's a flat fifteen hundred," she said casually, as if it were Monopoly money.

Damn, fifteen hundred dollars *for three hours. She must have an arsenal of tricks in her goodie bag,* Jacob thought converting the pounds to dollars. "I'll take the minimum." He didn't want to commit to overnight, just in case she fell short of his expectations.

"Will you be putting that on a major credit card or paying cash?" she asked, sealing the transaction.

He dug his wallet out of his pocket and quickly counted the bills. Jacob didn't have that much cash on him, but he surely wasn't about to create a paper trail and bill it to a credit card. "Cash. I'll pay cash."

"Before I send her over, I'll need some information from you."

His heart began to race. He hadn't expected to divulge name, rank, and serial number. "What type of information?" he asked skeptically.

Sensing his hesitation, she said, "Our records are kept strictly confidential, but I'll need your driver's license number and a major credit card for our files."

"Why do you need a credit card number if I'm paying cash?"

"It's for our records, Mr. . . . uh, what did you say your name was?" she asked, finally realizing that the only name he had given her was that of his referral.

If Mira felt secure leaving her information with them, then Jacob assumed it was safe. He reluctantly gave up the data, because he surely didn't want to give up a much-anticipated night of pleasure.

"Okay, Mr. Reed, you're all set. Cinnamon should be knocking on your door within the hour," she said, after taking the required information.

With the transaction completed, they both hung up. Jacob wanted to shower, but first had to run downstairs and write a check payable to cash. Luckily, the cashier was still on duty, solving his dilemma. Back in his room, he tore off his clothes and hopped into the shower. No sooner had Jacob turned off the pulsating spray than the doorbell buzzed.

She's early, he thought and quickly wrapped a towel around his waist, rushing out of the bathroom. His heart was pounding with excitement as he turned the knob and opened the door. Standing before him was a tall, curvaceous woman dressed conservatively in a black coat with the belt snugly tightened around her waist. Her hair was stuffed underneath a matching fedora with strands of red peeking out.

"You're all wet," she said, looking at the water dripping from his body, "and I will be too in a minute." She brushed past him and sauntered into the bedroom.

Jacob locked the door behind her and watched as she dropped her duffel bag on the floor near the bed. She turned around, crooked her finger at him, and whispered, "Come here. Once we take care of the financials, we can start having some fun.

His feet seemed to be planted into the carpet fibers. As much as he wanted to, he couldn't move. Jacob was paralyzed with excitement. The only body part moving was his growing sex. He could feel it pushing against the terry-cloth towel. He handed over the envelope of cash without saying a word.

She quickly counted the money, came over to him, and whispered seductively in his ear, "Don't you want to unwrap your present now?"

He unbuckled her belt and watched her coat ease open, exposing the best present he'd ever received—a beautiful pair of 38DDs. Her bare breasts swung free as her coat drifted to the floor. Jacob reached out and fondled the soft mounds of flesh, pinching her large nipples until they firmed to his touch. As he expected, there was nothing artificial about her voluptuousness. His mouth began to water for the taste of her, but before he could get a mouthful, she ripped off his towel, dropped to her knees, and covered his waiting sex with her wet tongue. The fedora came tumbling off as he grabbed her red hair and forced himself deeper into her mouth. She didn't flinch, just sucked faster and harder until he was on the verge of coming. Feeling the hot cum rising to the top, he tried to withdraw, but she grabbed his butt, pressing his dick farther into her mouth. "I'm cumming! I'm cumming!" he screamed in ecstasy, shooting his hot load down her deep throat. She got up, wiped her mouth with the back of her hand, and said, "Is that all you got?"

So this is what a pro does, he thought, then smirked and said, "That's just an appetizer. Now get your ass on the bed and I'll show you what I'm working with."

She turned around and strutted butt naked over to the bed. For a white girl, she had the best ass he had ever seen—round and tight. His dick began to swell again at the thought of penetrating that ass. She bent over and unzipped her bag. He came up close behind and began grinding his now rock-hard penis against her, trying to spread apart her cheeks.

"Just a second," she said, standing up. "Let me pop one of these." She held out her hand toward him. "Want one?"

Jacob looked in her palm at the two small pills. "What's that?"

"Ecstasy. It'll make you feel really, really lovely. Try one," she said, popping a pill into her mouth.

He wasn't into drugs, but had read a report on the love drug, as Ecstasy was often referred to. The article said that Ecstasy, which was man-made, heightened the senses, making the user feel euphoric and extremely sexual. "No, thanks." He didn't need a jump-start. His senses were already heightened at the thought of penetrating her where he would never dream of touching his wife.

"Suit yourself," she said, popping the second pill in her mouth. She then spread-eagled on the bed and began fondling her breast with one hand while massaging her clit with the other. "Now where were we?"

Jacob stood at the edge of the bed and watched as she brought herself close to orgasm. When she was on the brink, he said, "Turn over."

Before turning onto her stomach, she reached down into her bag and took out several condoms. "Pick one, big boy."

He chose the ribbed Magnum for extra stimulation, slid it on his erect sex, and said in a demanding tone, "Now spread that ass."

Jacob rode her like a prized thoroughbred in the Kentucky Derby, and did things in the next few hours that were probably illegal in most states. He fucked her in the ass, changed condoms, and fucked her in the pussy. They sixty-nined each other, with his mouth sucking her clit while her mouth feasted on his cock. He made her get on the floor like a dog, and rammed her from behind, pimp-style. Then he flipped her over and came all over her face. Once he came, Jacob made her lick his joystick until it was hard again, and again he fucked her silly. He was a man on a mission. Since they only had three hours together, he wanted to make sure that he got his money's worth, and fucked up until the last second.

Lying there totally satiated after she left, he felt like a new man and slept like a baby until it was time to check out.

Guilt started to creep into his soul the moment the plane

touched down in New York. The last thing he needed was to get caught with his pants down with a call girl. He had too much to lose over an indiscretion of that sort. Jacob had taken infidelity to an entirely new level. He had never hired a professional for sex before, and was starting to feel out of control. *Maybe I need to talk to a therapist,* he thought. He was from the old school of thought, and that was if you paid the cost, you could be the boss. And since he was the sole breadwinner, he felt entitled to screw around on the side, but now he was beginning to have second thoughts. He truly loved his wife, and maybe a psychotherapist could help him rekindle the feelings he once had for Naomi.

On the way home, he stopped by the florist and bought Naomi a dozen white roses, her favorite. She was probably still sulking over his impromptu trip, and flowers were just the thing to bring a smile to her face. When he drove up to the house, it was dark.

"I'm home!" Jacob yelled, walking into the foyer and clicking on the light. But no one answered back. *She's probably asleep,* he thought.

He tiptoed upstairs and eased open their bedroom door to surprise Naomi with the bouquet, but got a surprise himself. He expected to see her curled up under the covers with a book, but she wasn't there. Jacob went down the hall to ask Tyler if she knew where Naomi was, but her room was also empty, as was Noah's. Standing in the middle of the hallway, with the flowers dangling at his side, he scratched his head and wondered, *Where is everyone?*

Naomi had decided to call a truce with Tyler. Being busted .d softened her resolve, and made her take a long look at herself. .ere she was judging Tyler for her sexual preference, while at the ame time Naomi was seriously contemplating fucking another nan. Tyler may have been gay, but at least she wasn't an adulterer. As soon as her sister-in-law came through the door, Naomi invited her out to dinner. At first, Tyler had tried to decline. She was still pissed about being dissed on the front steps of the Black Door, but Naomi wouldn't take "no" for an answer. Jacob wasn't due back from London until later that night, and Noah was at a friend's house for a sleepover. She told Tyler that she didn't want to eat alone. Being the kindhearted person that she was, Tyler relented and they went to the local Italian restaurant.

Once their drinks came, Naomi started right in, before she changed her mind. "First of all, Tyler, I want to apologize to you for being so rude to you over the past few weeks."

Tyler couldn't believe her ears. She never thought that she would hear Naomi utter those words. She was speechless.

Naomi took one look at Tyler's face and knew that she had taken her by surprise, so she went on. "Tyler, I don't tell many people this, only because I'm ashamed. But when I was younger, my favorite cousin moved in with us, and at first we did every-thing together, and then she kicked me to the curb for the girl next door. I had no idea that she was gay, and truly didn't under-stand at the time exactly what it meant. All I knew was that my best friend was spending time with someone else. In my mind I equated gay with negative feelings of abandonment, instead of seeing it as two people enjoying each other's company. I guess I've been harboring resentment all of these years. I took my bit-terness out on you, and for that I'm sorry."

"Naomi, I really appreciate your candor. It takes a big person to admit when they're wrong."

"You're welcome. I just hope that you can forgive me."

"Of course I can, we're family after all." Tyler smiled, but

28

"EARTH TO Naomi, earth to Naomi," chanted Rio Sta-nis, the flamboyant curator of the Museum of Urban Art. Naomi was at her volunteer job. Initially, it had just been something to get her out of the house and around adults, but it turned into a perpetual course in Art History. She could now distinguish the difference between a Renoir and a Degas, and could also inter-pret the surrealism of a convoluted Dali. This knowledge would come in handy once she started her interior design business.

"Sorry, Rio, what were you saying?" Naomi asked, coming out of her self-induced trance.

"I was *saying* that whatever has you preoccupied must be re-ally important, because usually you're a chatterbox, but you've barely said three words to me since this morning."

Rio was right on the money. Normally she would've come right into the office giving him a bimonthly update on her life, detail by detail. She was indeed preoccupied. Her mind was in-undated with thoughts of Tyler and the dinner they shared the night before.

then switched gears. "So, Naomi, you never answered my question."

Naomi took a sip of water and cleared her throat. "And what question is that?" she asked, feigning ignorance. Naomi had hoped that her apology would make Tyler forget about the incident the other night.

"What were you doing at the Black Door? You aren't a member, are you?" she asked skeptically.

"The Black Door? What's the Black Door?"

Tyler cocked her head to one side, and gave Naomi a "come on, don't give me that" look. "It's a club for women," she said, slowly and determinately, so that Naomi could get the drift of what a club for women actually meant.

"Oh, like a spa?" Naomi asked, raising her voice a decibel, so that she sounded like a ditsy Valley Girl.

Tyler shook her head. "No, it's not a spa. It's an erotica club." She put her elbows on the table and leaned in closer to Naomi. "You know, a place where women go to have *sex*," she said, putting emphasis on the word *sex*.

Naomi put her hand to her mouth, as if shocked. "What? You're kidding?"

"No, I'm not kidding. So, you're saying that you had no idea where you were?" she asked, cocking her head again in disbelief.

"God no!" she exclaimed. "Kennedy and I were uptown to visit a friend of ours. Obviously we got the addresses mixed up. You know how all those brownstones look alike," she said with a straight face, thankful that they had taken off their wigs before leaving the club, otherwise she'd have more explaining to do.

"Ump," Tyler grunted, as if she didn't believe Naomi's lame story, but since she hadn't actually seen them inside of the club, she had no proof as to whether they were members or not. "Okay, that explains why you guys were on the front steps of the club, but it doesn't explain why you ran away the moment you saw me," Tyler said, refusing to let Naomi off the hook so easily.

"We didn't mean to leave so suddenly, but we had tickets to a Broadway show, and you know that once the curtain goes up, the ushers won't seat you right away," Naomi lied, and then turned the tables on Tyler before she had a chance to ask any more questions. "Now that I think about it, what were *you* doing there? Are you a member?" Naomi pinned Tyler with a penetrating stare.

"No, I'm not a member. I work there," she said with indignation, as if being a member of a sex club was beneath her.

"What do you do there?" Trey mentioned that Tyler worked for him, but he never mentioned what she did.

Tyler hesitated a moment. She had promised Trey that she would keep her assignment a secret, but now that she had halfway let the cat out of the bag, she was stuck. She didn't want Naomi thinking that she actually worked inside of the club, so she had no choice but to tell her the truth. "This has to remain just between the two of us, and you can't tell Kennedy," she said, giving Naomi a serious look.

"I promise, I won't say a word."

"The owner, Trey, hired me on a freelance basis to design masks for some of the members."

"Oh." It was definitely confirmed. There was no way on God's good earth that she could join now. Since Tyler was designing masks for members, she would eventually see Naomi's name on the roster, and she could never let that happen. Now Naomi's only alternative for constant sex was her husband. He was her first choice, but obviously she wasn't Jacob's. With him constantly denying her sexual pleasures, Naomi was beginning to think that he was having an affair. His early-morning meetings, late nights, and constant business trips were a little too suspicious. *Once Jacob gets back from London, we're going to have a serious talk*, she thought.

By the time they got back from dinner, Jacob was home from

his trip, but Naomi didn't have a chance to confront him because he was snoring louder than a drunken truck driver.

"SO TELL ME, Ms. Thang"—Rio perched himself on the edge of her desk—"what's got you so preoccupied?" he asked, ready for an earful.

Even though they were buds, Naomi wasn't about to tell him about her visit to the Black Door. Knowing Rio, he would want to know more about the club, and if gay men were allowed to join, and she wasn't up to an inquisition. "Nothing serious, just thinking about life in general," she lied.

"Whatever you say, Ms. Thang." He smirked and rolled his eyes. "But if you want to talk, I'll be in my office," he said, pinning her with a knowing look.

Rio was such a queen and his facial expression—mouth twisted to one side and bulging eyes—was more than comical. "If I feel a confession coming on, I'll be sure to knock on your door, Dr. Phil." Naomi chuckled.

"I'm glad you find my concern funny." He snapped his fingers, jumped up, and strutted off in a dramatic huff.

Once he was gone, she got back to cataloging the artwork for the Jacob Lawrence exhibit next month and was up to her eyeballs in slides when Rio came bolting out of his office a few hours later.

"You gonna spend the night here, or are you going home?" he asked sarcastically, with his manicured hand resting comfortably on his slender hip.

Naomi looked at her watch and realized that it was after five o'clock. "I'm almost finished with these"—she held up a slide—"then I'm outta here. These pieces are amazing. I didn't realize what a dynamic force Jacob Lawrence was in the art community."

"This exhibit is going to be a major coup, especially once I secure a few rare pieces from a private collector." Rio leaned over and air-kissed her on both cheeks. "Ciao. See you in two weeks," he said, making a swift exit.

"Ciao." *He probably has a hot date tonight*, she thought as she watched him switch away.

Forty minutes later, Naomi was in her car speeding along the LIE on her way home. When she pulled into the driveway, she was shocked to see Jacob's car. Naomi could count on one hand the number of times in the past year when he had arrived home before eight o'clock. As much as she wanted to know the truth, a confession of adultery wasn't what she wanted to hear from her husband, but since he was home at a decent hour, this would be the perfect time for their much-needed heart-to-heart. Naomi exhaled nervously and unlocked the door.

Soft music greeted her the moment she stepped into the foyer. *That's unusual*, she thought. Whenever Jacob was home either he was locked away in his study or upstairs under the covers. The music seemed to be floating from the dining room, so she walked in that direction. Naomi's jaw dropped the second she reached the entryway. The table was formally set, almost identical to the way she set it, the only difference being a beautiful bouquet of white roses—her favorite—in a leaded crystal vase as the centerpiece instead of the antique candelabrum. Jacob wasn't much of a cook, so she was surprised to see steam wafting through glass-topped Pyrex serving dishes.

"Hey, beautiful," Jacob whispered into her ear from behind, "welcome home." Before Naomi could say a word, he began kissing the back of her neck and nibbling on her earlobes. He wrapped his arms around her waist and pulled her close to him. "I've missed you, Naomi, and I promise I'm going to cut back on my work hours and spend more time at home with you and Noah."

Naomi inched away. "Jacob, I'm glad to hear that you're going to be spending more time at home, but—" she hesitated.

Naomi didn't want to pour water on the evening, especially since Jacob was being so sweet, but his behavior was that of a guilty person, which made her really want to pose the question of him cheating. "We need to talk. I don't know how to say it, so I'm just going to come right out and——"

Before she could ask if he was having an affair, Jacob swung her around and began kissing her passionately. He fed Naomi his tongue with an erotic urgency that she hadn't felt from him since their hedonistic London trips. Her body automatically responded with an urgency of its own, as she wrapped her arms around his neck and returned his hungry kisses. She had also planned to talk to Jacob about the seed money for her business, but he had totally distracted her. At the moment she wasn't thinking about adulterous affairs, or business plans, just making love to her husband.

Jacob swept her up in his arms and carried her upstairs, all the while never taking his lips off of hers. The feel of his soft lips was making her hot, and she wanted more.

When they reached the bedroom, he laid her down on the comforter, took off her clothes, buried his head between her legs, and munched her out. Naomi pushed his head down farther, so that his tongue was directly on her pleasure point. He responded by sucking and licking her clit.

"Oh, baaabby, yes!" she cried out in ecstasy.

After Jacob ate his wife out, he made love to her like never before. His renewed appetite for her was a direct result of the guilt he was feeling from screwing a hooker. In his mind, making love to his wife canceled out his nasty indiscretion, and now he felt vindicated, as if the London affair had never happened.

After their lovefest, Jacob held her close, and Naomi totally forgot about confronting him about cheating.

Good dick could make a woman forget about nearly anything, and that was exactly what Jacob was counting on.

29

JACOB AND Mira were wrapping up their meeting, and it was business as usual, except Mira had a burning question. She had been dying to ask Jacob what had happened in London, but Nina had also been in the meeting. As soon as she left, Mira whispered, "Well, was she all that or what?"

Jacob blushed. "Yeah, she was all that and a firecracker. But I tore up the number," he said, stacking the numerous FACEZ folders.

"Why'd you do that?"

Jacob turned toward the door, making sure it was closed, and said, "Between you and me, I've fucked around occasionally, but never with an escort. Don't get me wrong, it was a night I won't soon forget, but . . ." His words trailed off, as if he were deep in thought.

"But what?" Mira asked, inching closer to him so that she could hear better.

"When does it end? At first, I started messing around with women at bars when I was out of town, but then that got old. Now

I'm flying to another country and hiring drug-addicted prostitutes," he said, thinking about how the redhead needed to pop some X before having sex. "If I don't put a stop to this now, I'm afraid the bar will keep getting raised, and at some point, I'm bound to get busted. My family is too high of a price to pay for my pleasure. Besides, Naomi and I used to have a healthy sex life and I plan to get that back on track." Having the experience with the hooker, and being outside of himself for that moment, made Jacob realize that lust was a dangerous emotion. If he didn't snap back to reality and understand that just because a woman bore a child it didn't mean that her vagina was now sacred and untouchable, then he would lose his wife and the family he cherished. And after the heated sex he and Naomi had the night before, he was convinced that he could erase the picture of her giving birth from his mind once and for all.

"Good for you." She smiled. "Most men would order from the take-out menu, as well as eat at home."

"As appetizing as the take-out menu is, I now prefer a home-cooked meal. Besides, I've scheduled a session with a sex therapist to make sure my libido stays focused on my wife," Jacob said, like a man with a renewed sense of purpose.

The conference phone rang, interrupting their conversation.

"Mr. Reed, Nigel Charles is calling for Ms. Rhone," said Jacob's assistant through the speakers.

"Do you mind? I've been expecting his call for the past week. I'm anxious to hear the outcome of his latest report. Put him through," Mira instructed.

"Hey there, Nigel, tell me something good."

He was silent for a few seconds, and then said solemnly, "In that case I have nothing to say."

"So, you're telling me the lab didn't yield the results from the shea pods that we were looking for?" She leaned back in her chair. "Is that what you're trying to tell me?"

"Basically," he said matter-of-factly. "I thought we could

salvage the formulas that we had already worked on for the new line, but we're going to have to start over from square one."

"That's exactly what we were trying to avoid." She exhaled loudly. "If we start over, the product won't be on the shelves until next year at the earliest and by that time BOD E.'s children's line will be off and running. And I don't plan on playing catch-up. What happened to salvaging the initial formula? At our last meeting, you told me we were looking at a week, two tops. What happened to that time frame?"

"What I told you was that I wouldn't know what we were dealing with until I reanalyzed the formula. And now that I have the lab results back, I can say unequivocally that we have to scrap the old formula and start over."

"Are you kidding me?"

"I wish I were, but the truth of the matter is, in our haste to rush to market, we overlooked one crucial element."

"And what might that be? You said the line tested well in the lab; now please tell me, Nigel, what crucial element did *you* overlook?" she asked, in measured tones.

"The shea pods that we shipped in from Ghana are incompatible with the base formula. Their acidity level is too high for the children's line."

"And why is this fact just coming to light? Those pods should have been analyzed and approved months ago!" she yelled into the speaker sitting on the conference-room table.

"The junior chemist that we hired last quarter mistakenly tested the pods for the adult line, which, when combined with that formula, yielded positive results," he explained.

"Now I'm confused." She shook her head back and forth in frustration. "How could you give an assistant that type of responsibility?"

"I was traveling and as per *your* request, *you* wanted to get a jump-start on the new line, so I delegated."

"Nigel, this is totally unacceptable!" She pounded the desk. "Who is this new chemist anyway? I don't remember approving a new hire," she said, refusing to take any of the blame for the snafu.

"His name is Henry Bishop and you not only interviewed him, you raved over his credentials," he reminded her.

She waved her hand in midair. "That's neither here nor there. From this point on, I want you to personally oversee this project and not delegate, not even the smallest detail to anyone. Is that understood?"

"Understood."

"So what's this blunder going to cost in terms of time?"

"Mira, I know your plan was to beat BOD E. to market, but the most we can hope for at this point is to meet them at market. In other words, our product debut will probably coincide with their new line."

"There's time left on the clock and with any luck we'll still beat them to market," she responded optimistically, refusing to concede to the competition.

"I wouldn't count on it," Nigel said with certainty.

"Why are you being so negative? Don't you want to beat BOD E. to market, or do you still have a sense of loyalty to Rob Sherr?"

"Rob Sherr?"

"Yeah, your old boss at BOD E. I'm sure you remember that asshole." Mira despised Rob. She had suspected him of trying to infiltrate FACEZ with spies to steal their trade secrets, but she never could find concrete proof. "If you're harboring some type of secret devotion to him, you can hit the road and hightail it back to that second-rate company!" she shouted, without mincing words.

"I'm hurt that you could even think that," he said in a low register, barely audible through the speaker. "Have I ever given you any reason to doubt my loyalty?"

"No, but—"

"No buts," he cut her off. "Mira, either you trust me or you don't."

"I'm sorry. Nigel, I didn't mean to offend you," she said, harnessing her anger. "I'm just upset that's all. GG had faith in you and so do I."

"Does that mean I have total autonomy over the new line?" he asked, knowing full well the answer.

"You know the control freak that I am. I could never relinquish total control." She chuckled, lightening the mood. "Take care of this R & D issue and I'll try to be patient and not hound you every day."

"Just every other day," he joked.

"Ha, ha. Very funny," she said without cracking a smile. "Just keep me in the loop and I won't have to bug you."

"Consider it done. I should have an updated report on your desk within the next week."

"Thanks, Nigel," she said, depressing the end call button. "This entire process is taking far too long." She exhaled. "Though he's a gifted chemist, I'm beginning to doubt Nigel's abilities," she said, telling Jacob her true feelings. "We should be in the final phase of development instead of reinventing the wheel. The thought of BOD E. beating us to market, with their inferior line, makes me want to rupture a vessel." She rubbed her temples. "For years, FACEZ has been the forerunner in the cosmetics industry with BOD E. a distant second. Now for the first time in decades, they're in a position to take the lead, and I just can't let that happen. I won't let that happen!"

"Don't worry, I'm sure Nigel will come through for you," Jacob said, trying to comfort her. "Sounds like you could use a drink."

"You're right." She suddenly looked exhausted.

"Why don't you call Tyler? I'm sure she could use a night out as well. Every time I come home, she's up in her room working. That girl never seems to get out."

"That's a good idea," Mira said, pushing the buttons on the speakerphone.

"Hello?" answered a female voice.

"Naomi?"

"Yes."

"This is Mira. How are you?"

"Hey there, Mira, I'm fine, and you?"

"I'm good, thanks."

"Well, I certainly hope you're not calling to cancel the book club meeting. I'm really looking forward to it," she said in a cheery voice.

At the sound of his wife's voice through the speaker, Jacob perked up and listened closely. Judging from her upbeat tone, he surmised that Naomi was still swooning from their heated love-making.

"No, no, the meeting is still on. Actually I was calling to speak to Tyler. Is she in?" Mira asked.

"Hold on. She's right here."

"Hello?"

"Hi, Tyler, this is Mira."

"Oh, hi!" She seemed thrilled to hear from Mira.

"I'm calling to see if you want to meet for a drink?" she asked.

"I would love to, but I can't tonight. I have a deadline looming, and don't want to fall behind."

"Well, I wasn't necessarily talking about tonight," Mira lied. She didn't want to seem desperate. "Maybe one day next week."

"That sounds great." Tyler couldn't wait to meet with Mira one-on-one. They really didn't have a chance to talk at the book club.

"Okay, I'll give you a call then," Mira said, and hung up.

"What did I tell you?" Jacob said. "She's always working."

"Not a problem. I totally understand," Mira said, and rose to leave.

Once she was gone, Jacob gathered the file folders, but couldn't get Naomi's chipper voice out of his mind. He had banked that their lovemaking would make her forget about his impromptu London trip, and after hearing her voice he was certain that it had, or at least he hoped so.

KENNEDY HAD only spoken to Nigel once since their fiasco of a lunch, and during that call, he had rushed her off the phone, saying that he was heading into a meeting, and that he would call her back later that night, which he didn't. She tried not to take it personally, since she knew how busy he was trying to develop the formula for a new skin care line. They hadn't talked about it in detail, but she had overheard enough of his phone calls to surmise that he was up to his neck with deadlines. She wanted to erase her schizophrenic behavior at lunch, so she called and invited him over to her place to make up. Kennedy didn't like that he had walked away that day upset with her, and she wanted desperately to make amends. She didn't want to lose him, and realized that it was time she gave him the prize inside her Cracker Jack box. Nigel accepted, but told her that it would have to be an early evening, since he was still under a strict deadline.

Kennedy spent the better part of the afternoon at the market shopping for dinner. She'd planned to make broiled lamb chops, potatoes au gratin, broccoli rabe, and for dessert a triple-layer German chocolate cake with freshly grated coconut—her grandmother's recipe. She wanted tonight to be perfect, so she took the extra time to bake.

After setting the table, Kennedy went into the bathroom to pamper herself for an evening of decadent indulgence. If she was lucky, dessert wouldn't be the only thing that Nigel would be feasting on. In the shower, she slathered on a foaming body wash and shaved in between hidden crevices, getting rid of all unwanted hairs, so *dessert* would be follicle-free. She grabbed a fluffy terry-cloth towel off the rack, once she stepped out of the shower, and patted herself dry. Her skin felt as smooth as a newborn's as she rubbed on a rich fragrant lotion, and then layered it with the matching perfume, spritzed in all the right places— behind the ears, the back of the calves, and in between the thighs.

What to wear? she thought, standing in the doorway of her closet. She didn't want to wear anything too formal, nor did she want to come to the door looking like a stripper in a G-string and boa. She definitely wanted to indicate to him that tonight was *the* night. She didn't want to give mixed signals, especially after the lunch debacle.

"Ah, this is perfect," Kennedy said aloud, taking a black silk wrap dress off the hanger. Normally, she wore the dress with a one-piece bodysuit, but tonight, for obvious reasons, she decided to go commando—sans underwear—for easy access. Kennedy slipped on the dress, tied it around her waist, and walked over to the full-length mirror. "Perfect," she commented, admiring the sexy imprint of her ripe nipples underneath the thin silk fabric. "They look good enough to eat." She giggled, slipped on a pair of five-inch CFM pumps, and strutted out of the bedroom, ready to bag her man.

The doorbell rang the minute she took the lamb chops out of the oven. Before going to the door, she quickly took an ice cube out of the freezer, reached inside the dress, and rubbed the cold cube across her bare nipples, creating the ultimate tweak. Kennedy threw the ice in the sink and sauntered to the door.

"Hey, sweetie," she said, kissing him full on the lips and then stepping back so that he could get an eyeful.

Nigel gave Kennedy an appraising look. He zeroed right in on her hard nipples. If he didn't know any better, he would've sworn that she was trying to seduce him. But he wasn't going to make that mistake twice. The embarrassment at lunch was enough for him. He wasn't about to get his jimmy excited for a big letdown. So he just said hello.

Kennedy noticed his stiff body language and realized that she'd have to do more work than she thought. She stepped aside and let him in, then in her most seductive voice asked, "Would you care to start with an appetizer or go right to the main course?"

"Look, Kennedy, I'm not in the mood for games. If you're just going to tease me, and send me home with blue balls, then I might as well leave now," he said, still holding onto his briefcase, ready to bolt out the door.

She walked up close to him and said, "Baby, I'm sorry for leading you on."

Hearing her apology softened Nigel's disposition. "And I'm sorry for being short with you over the phone, but I was still upset with you for changing your mind at lunch. Do you forgive me?" he asked, kissing her neck.

Kennedy leaned into his embrace. "Of course I forgive you, and I'm ready now."

"Ready for what?"

"Ready to make love to you. I've fixed a nice dinner, and after we eat, we'll have dessert in bed," she said, suggestively rubbing her breasts against him.

Those were the magic words Nigel had been waiting to hear. He dropped his briefcase, loosened his tie, took off his jacket, and dropped it on the floor along with the briefcase. He then untied her dress, exposing her naked body. He rubbed his massive hands over her pert nipples, fondling them until they grew even harder. Kennedy instantly moistened with his touch. He then continued his exploration down her taut stomach and in between her thighs. Gently spreading her legs apart, he slowly inserted his finger into her clean-shaven vagina.

"Forget dinner. I'm going to start with a taste of this wet pussy," he whispered, dropping to his knees.

Kennedy threw her leg over his broad shoulder as he began feasting on the first course.

"Now that's what I call quality sushi," he remarked with a grin, coming up for air and wiping his mouth with the back of his hand.

"One good appetizer deserves another," she remarked and sauntered over to the sofa. Sitting on the edge of the couch with her legs spread wide apart, she crooked her finger at him and mouthed, "Come here." Once he was standing between her thighs, she unbuckled his belt, unzipped his pants, and watched them fall to the floor. Kennedy looked in amazement at the size of his erect penis bulging out of his underwear. Reaching for the band on his boxers, she ripped them off, releasing his captive manhood. Taking him in her ready mouth, she eagerly consumed the entire length of his shaft while massaging his testicles.

"Oh, yeah, baby, that's it, that's it," he moaned, on the brink of ecstasy.

Then, to her surprise, he switched gears, flipped her back on the couch, and slid in between her legs. He was by far the largest man she had ever been with, and she gasped as he made his grand entry.

He suddenly hesitated. "Am I hurting you?"

"No, please don't stop." She opened up wider to accommodate him, and they quickly found their rhythm, but the sofa was too confining for all the humping and pumping. "Come on. Let's go to the bedroom," she panted, eager for more.

Nigel didn't say a word, just swept her up in his arms and

carried her off to bed. Their desire for one another was animalistic, as they dropped all inhibition and hungrily devoured each other over the next few hours.

"Now that's what I call sufficient dining," he said, resting his head on her chest.

Kennedy laced her hands through his hair. "Hope I was worth the wait."

He reached up and kissed her passionately, looked directly into her eyes, and said with conviction, "You're what I've been waiting for all my life."

Those words were music to her soul. No man had ever uttered such a sentiment to her in her entire life, and suddenly she craved him all over again. Wrapping her legs around his back, Kennedy began to grind into him until she felt his limp cock spring to attention. She didn't think it possible, but this round of lovemaking was better than before. She didn't know if it was his endearing words or the exercising of her pussy that let his dick slide in easier. Their bodies naturally meshed, as if designed to fit perfectly together. As they lay in the aftermath, totally exhausted, she thought, *I could love this man for the rest of my life,* and then she drifted off into a peaceful sleep, nestled comfortably in his arms.

Soft rays from the morning sun peeked through the silhouette blinds, awakening Kennedy from a serene slumber. Blinking her eyes open, she glanced over at Nigel who was snoring lightly. She quietly crept out of bed and into the bathroom. After a quick shower, she decided to make a hearty breakfast, since they hadn't gotten a chance to eat a proper dinner the night before.

Walking into the living room, Kennedy had a flashback the instant she saw Nigel's briefcase and jacket strewn by the front door. Smiling at the thought, she bent over to collect his belongings. The moment she picked up his briefcase by the handle, it popped opened, scattering the contents all over the floor. Kennedy knelt down to gather his papers, and as she was putting the various reports back, a check slipped out of one of his folders. Thinking she still had remnants of sleep in her eyes, she blinked twice at the amount. The bank draft was made out to Nigel Charles in the amount of two hundred and fifty thousand dollars. There was a brief note clipped on the back that read:

ONE MORE TRANSACTION,
THEN OUR BUSINESS WILL BE COMPLETE.
THANKS FOR HOLDING UP YOUR END OF THE DEAL,
        R. S.

One more transaction? she thought. "Who the hell is R. S., and what could be so important that it would be worth a quarter of a million dollars?" she whispered.

TYLER WAS playing "Beat the Clock." It was five hours before tonight's book club meeting, and she still had four more masks to design. The meeting was being held at Mira's apartment, and Tyler wanted to be early. They had yet to have their first date, so she wanted to arrive before the other members, to have a little private time.

Tyler had finished designing masks for the first set of profiles that Trey had given her. He was so pleased with her work that he faxed over a second set of profiles. She read over each description, to get a sense of the person, and then whipped up two different renderings for Trey to choose from. Even though Tyler had a degree in graphic design, drawing came naturally to her, and in no time flat, she was finished with the list.

She went to the antique armoire to choose an outfit for tonight's meeting. Tyler didn't want to wear all black like she did the first time she met Mira. She wanted to look a bit more fashionable. She browsed through the hangers, and decided on an ankle-length Jon Berry camouflage skirt, one of the few designer pieces that she owned, a hunter green blouse, and to add a little punch to the outfit, she selected a thick, red leather belt. Tyler showered, dressed, and applied a touch of makeup—FACEZ, of course. She checked out her reflection in the mirror and hardly recognized herself. The skirt hugged her hips suggestively. The silken-wool top fit like a glove, accentuating her ample breasts, which she rarely displayed, and the belt pulled her waist in at least two inches. She turned from one side to the other, admiring her transformation. Gone was her normal attire of baggy jeans, T-shirt, and artist's smock, and she now resembled an accomplished professional, instead of a college student. She fingered her dreads, and added a pair of hoop earrings. "Perfect," she said into the mirror.

Tyler looked at her watch. She still had two more hours to kill. She was so anxious to get to Mira's place that she had raced through work and dressed in record time. *What the hell am I going to do now?* she thought. Tyler wanted to be early, but not two hours early; she didn't want to appear desperate. She turned on the television, but nothing worth watching was on, so she turned it off. Tyler began to pace with nervous energy. She felt like a caged animal ready to be set free. The adrenaline flowing through her bloodstream was making her edgy. She thought about going downstairs to make a sandwich, but didn't want to eat before the meeting. Besides, the belt was squeezing her stomach, but she didn't want to loosen it any, since it made her shape more defined. There was only one thing that would cool her jets and that was sex. She hadn't been with another woman since she left Liz, but since sex wasn't an option now, she opted for work instead. Tyler went to the nightstand, picked up the phone, and dialed the Black Door.

"Trey Curtis speaking."

"Hey, Trey. It's me, Tyler."

"Hey, Tyler, what's up?"

"Well, I finished the last list you faxed me, and was wondering if you have any more masks for me to design?"

"Damn, girl, you're fast! You're like the Evelyn Wood of designing," he joked.

Tyler laughed, and said thank you.

"As a matter of fact, it'll really help me out if you can finish the last few profiles for me. They're for members who want a different look, and I promised them that I'd have their new masks ready in two weeks. In order to meet that deadline, I have to get the designs to the manufacturing company by tomorrow. Can I fax over the list? It's short, and as fast as you work, I'm sure you'll have 'em done in an hour," he joked. "But seriously, I won't need them until tomorrow morning."

"Sure, no problem. Consider it done."

"Thanks a million," he said, and hung up.

A few minutes later, Tyler heard the hum of the fax machine and went over to retrieve her new assignment. She put her smock back on and sat down at the drafting table. She was grateful for the distraction. She rolled up her sleeves and reached for her sketch pad. Tyler read the first profile, which was for a frumpy housewife whose current fantasy was to be like her husband—a successful stockbroker. She immediately got an idea for the mask. She outlined the design and colored it in. She tore off the paper and held it out. The mask was the exact hue of money, and instead of being angled like cat-eyes like most masks, she chose an oblong shape resembling a dollar bill. Tyler also made a small sketch at the bottom of the page, detailing what the woman should wear—a pinstriped suit jacket, sans pants, and a pair of stack-heeled Mary Janes.

She then turned to the next page and read the profile. *A young CEO of a major cosmetics conglomerate, and her password is Powerbroker Pussy. She enjoys both male and female servers. Her original mask wasn't designed by the club, but was made in Venice. She wants a second mask, but wants it to look completely different so that she can switch between the two. One for when she's fucking women, and one for when she's fucking men.*

Tyler's mouth dropped open. "It can't be," she said aloud. She read the description again. The words described Mira to a tee. Tyler knew she was gay, but not bisexual. Suddenly the image of her ex-girlfriend flashed through her mind, and she didn't know if she wanted to get involved with another switch-hitter. The pain of being jilted for a man still stung, but at least now she knew up front that Mira liked a little dick on the side. Unlike Liz, who hid her desire for the beef, until she got busted.

Tyler put down the profile, took off the smock, gathered her things, and headed out the door. She had the keys to Jacob's spare car, jumped in, and sped off for the city. Forty minutes later, she had parked and was entering Mira's building. Tyler walked through the lavish lobby and admired its old-world charm. The fresco-covered cathedral ceiling was at least thirty feet high, with dimly lit chandeliers throughout.

"I'm here to see Mira Rhone," she said to the doorman, who looked as old as the building.

"Your name?"

"Tyler Reed."

After calling up, he said, "Go right up. She's in PH5."

From the looks of the opulent building, located in the exclusive section of Tudor City—a city within the city—Mira was probably a spoiled-rotten brat who had grown up with a house filled with servants, eating out of silver spoons. *She may be filthy rich, but she's a stone freak,* Tyler thought, and rang the bell. As soon as Mira answered, she said, "Do I need a password?"

Mira looked at her oddly. "What do you mean?"

"Powerbroker Pussy. Does that ring a bell?" Tyler knew that she was taking a chance of getting slapped, but she said it anyway. She thought there was no better way to break the ice.

Hearing the words, Mira instantly started smiling. "How did you know I was a member of the Black Door?"

Tyler stepped into the foyer. Since Mira was already a member, Tyler didn't see the harm in revealing that she was working for Trey. "I'm doing some freelance work designing masks for the owner, and I ran across your profile. There was no name attached," she added, making sure that Mira knew Trey wasn't giving up her identity to strangers, "but I took a wild guess, and guess whose name popped into my head?"

"So, now that you know, what are you going to do about it?" Mira asked, walking up close to her.

"First, I want to know if you have a boyfriend?" she asked point-blank. Tyler wasn't trying to walk into another situation blind.

"A boyfriend?" Mira seemed shocked at the question. "Why do you ask?"

"The profile mentioned that you wanted two masks. One for when your have fish on your plate, and one for when there's beef on the menu." Tyler raised her eyebrow and gave her a look like "don't even try to deny it."

Mira couldn't help but laugh at her analogy. "It's true, I have been known to pony up to the pole. But to answer your question, no, I don't have a boyfriend. And don't want one."

"Good. The last person I dated wanted me *and* a man, and I couldn't deal with that. I'm a one-woman woman, and don't double-dip," Tyler said, making her feelings clear.

"Then I take it that you don't go both ways?"

"No, I'm strictly on a fish and vegetable diet."

Mira put her hand on each side of Tyler's red belt, pulled her in, and gave her a sloppy, wet kiss. "I've been wanting to do that since the first day I met you."

Tyler blushed. "Is that right?"

"Yep. My last relationship ended rather abruptly, and I haven't felt close to anyone since."

"What about the servers at the Black Door? I'm sure they provide some type of closeness?" Tyler asked, with a hint of jealousy in her voice.

"Well, yes, but that's what they're paid to do. I want genuine affection," she said, giving Tyler another kiss.

"Are you saying that you want a relationship?" Tyler asked, getting straight to the point.

"Since we both just got out of situations that didn't end well, why don't we spend more time together before jumping into a committed relationship? In the meantime, do you mind if I sample your goods?" Mira asked without waiting for an answer, and then began unbuttoning Tyler's blouse. She unhooked the front hook of her bra, exposing Tyler's ample boobs. Mira tasted her nipples gently, and then began sucking hard, adding small bites every now and then.

"Oh, that feels so good." Tyler squirmed.

Mira reached around, unzipped Tyler's skirt, and pushed the waistband down. She reached inside Tyler's panties and started sliding her fingers in and out of Tyler. She was finger-fucking her, and sucking her tits so intently that she didn't hear the doorman ring up.

Tyler gasped for air. "Is that the phone?"

"What?" Mira asked, still in a lust-induced fog.

The phone rang again. "That. It's probably the doorman trying to get you," Tyler said.

"Who cares?" Mira went back to sucking Tyler's nipples, one and then the other.

"Mira, we gotta stop. The other members are probably downstairs, waiting to come up."

The last thing Mira wanted to do was stop. She was horny as hell, and was jonesing to taste Tyler's wet pussy. "Okay, I'll stop, but only if you promise to stay after the meeting is over. I'm not done with you yet."

Tyler fixed her clothes. "I promise, but just so you know, I'm not into just fucking around. I'm looking for something real."

"So am I. Tyler, there's no doubt that we have chemistry, but only time will tell if it'll turn into something else, so let's just enjoy the moment," Mira said.

Tyler had never just "enjoyed the moment" without rushing into a relationship. Maybe Mira had a point. If she had dated Liz casually before they moved in together, then she would've probably found out that Liz also liked men. "This is new territory for me, but I'm willing to give it a try," she said, kissing Mira on the lips and then walking into the dining room.

Mira answered the phone and told the doorman to send up her guest. "Welcome," Mira said, opening the door a few minutes later.

Kennedy stepped inside and looked around at the intricate art deco molding throughout the living room. "Your place is amazing."

"Thanks. This was my great-grandmother's duplex and I had it gutted, but kept the charming details intact since that type of craftsmanship no longer exists," Mira said modestly, with no hint that she had just finished finger-fucking Tyler. "Would you care for an alcoholic or nonalcoholic beverage?"

"Alcoholic, please." Kennedy laughed.

"Come on in the dining room. Tyler's already here."

"Hey, Kennedy." Tyler threw up her hand as Mira poured each of them a glass of champagne.

"Hi, Tyler. How's it going?"

Tyler smiled broadly. "It's going fabulously!" She grinned and glanced at Mira.

"That's good to hear. At least somebody's having a great day." She then turned to Mira. "So, I understand you're the CEO of FACEZ," she said, taking a sip of bubbly.

"Yeah, my great-grandmother started the company, and since her passing, I've taken over the reins. Well, actually, I was running the company before she died. I feel extremely blessed that GG trusted me enough to leave her legacy in my hands."

"She must have known that you were up to the task," Tyler said with admiration for her new lover.

Mira looked into her glass, as if thinking about her great-grandmother and how disappointed she'd be if she knew her golden girl liked girls. "You're right, GG knew I could handle the pressure. She'd been grooming me for this position all of my life."

Out of the clear blue, Kennedy switched gears and blurted out, "You know my boyfriend," as if she couldn't wait any longer to divulge that information.

"Oh, really? And who might that be?" Mira asked, baffled.

"He's one of your employees," she answered.

Mira seemed to think for a second, then asked, "Really? Who?"

"Nigel. Nigel Charles." Kennedy smiled.

"Of course I know Nigel. We were engaged once upon a time, but I'm sure you know that," Mira said matter-of-factly.

Kennedy nearly choked on her champagne and turned as white as a snowflake in a midwestern blizzard. "Excuse me." She coughed.

"Are you okay?" Tyler asked, reaching out to pat her back.

"Uh, I'm, I'm fine," Kennedy stuttered, put her flute on the table, and patted her chest.

"As a matter of fact, I was just about to call him before you guys arrived. I tell you, the way he's dragging his feet on our latest project, if I didn't know any better, I'd swear he was selling trade secrets to his old boss Rob Sherr over at BOD E."

Before they had a chance to continue the "getting to know you" session, the buzzer rang again. "Come on in the living room, guys," Mira instructed.

"Nice place," Naomi commented with a keen eye as she entered the foyer, filled with priceless antiques and artwork.

"Thanks. Can I get you a glass of bubbly?" Mira offered Naomi.

"That would be great."

Mira walked into the dining room, and Tyler followed closely behind. She kissed Mira on the back of the neck as she was pouring the champagne. "I can't wait to munch on your rug," she whispered in her ear.

Mira giggled. "Who said I have a rug? I'm a bald kinda girl."

"Well, in that case, I can't wait to visit your Bermuda triangle."

"Excuse me," Naomi interrupted, clearing her throat. She noticed how close Tyler and Mira seemed, and for once she wasn't repulsed by a homosexual exchange. "Who did your decorating? I just love the use of art deco blended with modern touches."

"Thanks. I used Beverly Smith Lashley, she's a talented decorator with exquisite tastes."

"Well, tell her that she's going to have some competition. I'm going to finally start my interior design business, hopefully I should be up and running by next year," Naomi announced.

"Wow, that's great," Mira said.

"I didn't know you had an interest in starting a business," Tyler said.

"Well, I've always wanted to be more than just a housewife, and now that Noah is in school, I have more time on my hands," Naomi told them.

"Good luck. Now I guess we should get this meeting started," Mira said. "Let me get the munchies and I'll be right in."

When Mira returned, she was carrying a tray of hors d'oeuvres and a chilled bottle of vintage champagne. She looked around the room and noticed that Kennedy was sitting silently, with her arms folded so tightly across her chest, it looked as if she were squeezing her diaphragm. "Are you okay, Kennedy?"

"I'm fine," she said with a chillness to her voice.

"Sushi, anyone?" Mira offered.

"Sure, it looks delicious," Naomi said, taking a piece, as did Tyler.

"Kennedy, would you like a piece?"

"No thank you."

"Want beef carpaccio? It's really delicious." She smiled.

"No thank you," Kennedy said again.

"Alrighty then," she said, putting the tray on the cocktail table. Kennedy's mood had quickly changed and Mira didn't know why. She didn't know Kennedy well enough to probe, so she sat down and began the discussion. "So what did you guys think about *The Lovely Bones*?"

"It was touching," Tyler said.

"Yes, it was. I really felt bad for the girl's parents and what they went through after she died," Naomi said, spoken like a true mother.

The three of them chatted about the book while Kennedy just sat there like she was in a trance. Their discussion ended with the general consensus being it was a well-written and moving story.

"So . . ." Mira said, ready to end the meeting so that she and Tyler could get busy. "Any suggestions for our next book? What about *Who Moved My Cheese*? It's gotten rave reviews," she suggested.

"That sounds good to me," Tyler answered, also eager to end the meeting.

"Good. Now the next item on the agenda would be, who's going to host the next meeting?"

"I'll host it," Naomi said.

"No, let me. You hosted the last meeting," Kennedy said, finally adding to the conversation.

"Girl, with your travel schedule, when are you going to have time to plan a meeting? Don't worry about it, I'll host the meeting. Besides, I'm dying to try out this new recipe."

"Okay, if you insist," Kennedy conceded.

Once that was settled, Naomi and Kennedy began to walk out, but Tyler lagged behind.

"Thanks, Mira, this was great," Naomi said.

"You're welcome." Once they were gone, she led Tyler back to her boudoir for a meeting of their own.

KENNEDY PACED the floor half the night, then tossed and turned the other half, unable to sleep. Her dreams were all over the place. She dreamed she was in the movie *Sleeping with the Enemy*, playing the role of Julia Roberts, trying to escape a deranged husband. And that was just for starters. In the second sequence of dreams, she was a private detective trying to solve an intriguing espionage caper. Her body twisted in the sweat-drenched covers as she tried in vain to capture the faceless villain.

By seven o'clock the next morning, she was up and wearing a trench into the carpeting with her constant pacing. Kennedy couldn't wrap her mind around the possibility of Nigel selling trade secrets. She reached for the cordless to call him. She had two important questions. Like who was R. S. and why was this person paying him two hundred and fifty big ones? She quickly punched in his number, but after three rings, got the answering machine. She hit end call and dialed his cell. "Damn it! Where is he?" she yelled after hanging up once his voice mail intercepted the call. She had spoken to him the day he left her apartment. He had called that afternoon, and expressed how much he enjoyed consummating their relationship. That was two days ago, and she hadn't spoken with him since. They didn't talk every day, so it wasn't a big deal. But now she needed to talk to him, but he was nowhere around.

She needed to talk to Naomi; maybe she could make some sense out of this madness. Even in high school, Naomi was always the voice of reason; when Kennedy wanted to cut class, Naomi would give her one hundred and two reasons as to why she shouldn't. If there was one person who could put the pieces of this puzzle together, it was Naomi.

"Hello?" Naomi answered after the third ring.

"Are you asleep?"

"No, I'm up, just about to get Noah ready for school. What's going on? Is everything okay?" she asked, knowing that Kennedy rarely called this early.

"It's Nigel. He . . ." Before she could complete the sentence, a flood of tears came pouring out.

"Has he been in an accident? Is he okay?" she asked, alarmed.

Calming herself enough to answer her questions, Kennedy said, "No, he hasn't been in an accident. He's fine as far as I know."

"Then what's the problem? Why are you so upset? Did you guys break up?" Naomi asked, trying to get to the heart of the problem.

"He's sabotaging FACEZ," Kennedy blurted out in between tears.

"Stop crying, and tell me what you're talking about."

She sniffled, grabbed a piece of tissue out of the dispenser on the nightstand, and blew her nose. "He's selling information to their competitor."

"What? Why would you say something crazy like that?" she asked doubtfully, as if Kennedy was fabricating the story.

"I know it sounds insane, but it's true."

"How do you know he's sabotaging FACEZ?"

"Because I found a check with his name on it." She went on to tell Naomi about the check for $250,000 that slipped out of Nigel's folder and the note attached with the initials R. S. "Talking to Mira yesterday, she mentioned Nigel's former boss Rob Sherr, R. S., get it?" Kennedy asked, making sure that Naomi was keeping up with the story.

"Yeah, I get it. Now go on."

"Anyway, she said if she didn't know any better, she'd swear the reason why Nigel has been dragging his feet on their new project is because he might be selling trade secrets to his old boss. And now I find a check for a quarter of a million dollars, and a note with the initials R. S."

Naomi paused for a moment as if digesting the information. "Now wait a minute, let's not go jumping to any rash conclusions. R. S. could be any number of people."

"I know. I've thought about that, but Nigel has also been hiding the truth from me on another important issue," Kennedy interrupted. "Mira and Nigel were once engaged, but she left him for another woman."

"What? This is like a bad episode of *Peyton Place*. Gay lovers, stolen secrets, and large sums of money, what more can you add?" Naomi mused.

"Tell me about it. The only thing missing is a dead body."

"Girl, don't even kid like that," Naomi said.

"I know it's not funny. It's just that I'm so frustrated, and bad humor is my way of coping. I can't get in touch with Nigel, and don't know if I should tell Mira about the check."

"First, you need to talk to Nigel and ask him point-blank if he's selling company secrets. What if you're mistaken, and go to Mira with false accusations? What will that do to your relationship?"

Kennedy hadn't thought about that. If she was wrong, Nigel

would never forgive her, and she could kiss their future good-bye. He had been betrayed once by a woman, and would proba-bly view her mistrust of him as yet another unforgivable betrayal. "I tried to call him, but he's not at home and is not an-swering his cell."

"Well, I think you should wait and talk to him first before you go to Mira with this."

Naomi was right. "You have a point, but what if he hasn't gotten over Mira jilting him and he's trying to sabotage her company for revenge?"

"Don't you think that's a bit melodramatic? Have you called him at work?"

"No," Kennedy said, suddenly feeling like she had jumped the gun. "He's probably in the lab as we speak. Mira did say they're working on an important project." For the first time in hours, Kennedy began to calm down. "You're right, I'm being a drama queen. Thanks, Naomi."

"For what?"

"For pulling my reins. Girl, you know once I get on a tan-gent, I'm off and running before the race even starts." Kennedy chuckled nervously, trying to make light of her paranoia.

"No problem; now get off the phone with me and call your man, so he can ease your mind."

Kennedy's pacing ceased as she calmly dialed Nigel's work number. *I'm sure he has a reasonable explanation*, she thought as the phone rang.

"Good morning, FACEZ. How may I direct your call?"

"Nigel Charles, please."

"Hold on. I'll transfer you to the lab," said the receptionist.

"FACEZ, Henry Bishop speaking," said a strange voice. Usu-ally when she called Nigel at work, he was alone in the lab.

"Hello, may I speak to Nigel Charles?"

"I'm sorry, but he's out of the lab today."

Kennedy began to pace again. "Do you know when he'll return?"

"I'm sorry, I'm not at liberty to say. Would you like to leave a message?"

"Uh," she thought for a second, "no thank you."

Kennedy slumped down on the bed in despair. Where was he? She held the phone and stared at the number pad. She was tempted to call Mira, but Naomi's words of wisdom kept ringing in her ears. What if he had a reasonable explanation? Then she would look as if she didn't trust him, and what was a relationship if it didn't have trust?

BEING TRUE to his word to Naomi that things would be different, Jacob cut back on the long hours, coming home at a reasonable time, instead of being the workaholic, absentee husband and father that he had been in the past. His tryst in London, though exhilarating beyond belief, was over and done with. The sex therapist he had been seeing was doing wonders in changing Jacob's mindset toward his wife. He was glad that the sessions were working. He now realized that his family was much too precious to jeopardize for a few hours of carnal pleasure.

He was at work, trying to clear his desk of the myriad of papers, so that he could leave the office by five. He picked up the latest spreadsheet for FACEZ and was pleased to see that the quarterly financials were right on track. With any luck, the roll-out for their new children's line should be on schedule. He was up to his eyelids in financial projections for a new client when Charlotte buzzed the intercom.

"Mr. Reed, your wife is on the line."

"Hey, honey, what a pleasant surprise."

"Well, I don't know how pleasant you'll think this conversation will be once you hear what I have to say." She spoke with attitude.

Jacob was caught off guard by her tone. He had been the dutiful husband as of late, and hoped that it had erased his neglectful past, but obviously Naomi wasn't going to let the past stay in the past. "And why is that?" he asked, pretending like he didn't have a clue where this conversation was headed.

"Jacob, you must think I'm a fool."

"Why would I think that, honey?" he asked calmly.

"All of a sudden, you do a one-eighty, acting like you can't keep your hands off of me, when not too long ago, I couldn't get you to touch me. Don't get me wrong, I love the new you, but I want—no—I *need* to know exactly what made you change."

"Naomi, why are you getting yourself all worked up? I've cut back on my hours, and I'm spending more time at home. What more do you want?" Jacob asked, getting agitated. It was just like a woman to never be satisfied. When he was working long hours, she was complaining, and now that he was home, she wasn't satisfied either.

"I want the truth. At first I thought it was work that was keeping you away, but lately my intuition has been telling me you're seeing someone, or should I say you were seeing someone. Since you have all of this free time, I'm guessing that your affair, or whatever it was, is over."

"Naomi, please stop with these irrational accusations. Are you hormonal this week?" he asked, trying to make light of her statement.

"No. I don't have my period, if that's what you mean!" She sounded pissed. "Anyway, I see I'm not going to get a straight answer out of you. I'm going to drop this for now, but like I told you before, I'm not stupid. If your work schedule and out-of-town trips suddenly increase again, then I'll know that your lover is back on the scene," she spat out, and hung up.

Jacob sat there dumbfounded. He knew it was coming, but he didn't think that Naomi's wrath would be this harsh. He was so glad that he had come to his senses before his wife had actual proof of his infidelities. He tried to put their conversation out of his head and went back to work. Twenty minutes later, his secretary buzzed again.

"Excuse me, Mr. Reed, there's a Mr. Davis on line one."

"From?" he inquired.

"I'm sorry, but he wouldn't say."

"He wouldn't say?" Jacob was a bit put off. Charlotte was usually extremely efficient, getting the necessary information from random callers. "Well, tell this Mr. Davis, whoever he is, that I'm in a meeting, and take a message," he instructed and disconnected the line.

Jacob ran out for a quick lunch. Twenty minutes later he was back behind his desk, plowing through a mountain of work, when Charlotte buzzed again.

"Yes, Charlotte?" he asked, annoyed. He was right in the middle of finalizing the annual projections for FACEZ and didn't want to be disturbed.

"I'm sorry to interrupt you," she said timidly, picking up on his tone, "but Mr. Davis is calling again."

"Well, tell him if he can't disclose the nature of his business, then he can stop calling, because I don't have time to entertain random callers," Jacob said, ready to hang up.

"Wait a minute," she raised her voice an octave, "he said to tell you 'Remember Cinnamon.' "

At the mention of the redheaded vixen, Jacob's heart skipped a few beats and his blood pressure shot up. He unloosened the knot in his tie, cleared his throat, and said, "Uh, send his call through."

"Mr. Reed. Davis here," said a gruff voice.

Jacob deepened his pitch and asked, "What can I do for you, Mr. Davis?"

"Remember Cinnamon?"

"Excuse me."

"Cinnamon. London. A romp in the sack," he said in brief, fragmented sentences.

"I'm sorry, I don't know what you're talking about," Jacob lied. As far as he was concerned, that episode was a onetime occurrence that he chose not to revisit, especially with a stranger. "What company did you say you're with?"

"I didn't," was his glib response. "But since you asked, I'm a private investigator, looking into the disappearance of Cinnamon."

"And what makes you think I know the whereabouts of this China person?"

"Cinnamon. Her name is Cinnamon, and you were one of her last clients. She's the most requested girl at Let Us Entertain You, and frankly, without her in rotation, sales have dipped. So you can see why the service is in a hurry to track her down," he said, disclosing more information than Jacob cared to know.

"Look, mister, I don't know what you're talking about. Now if you don't mind, I'm late for an important meeting," Jacob said, trying to end this unpleasant conversation.

"Actually I do mind. If you could just answer a few questions, it would be helpful. Like did she say anything about taking off for a while?" he asked, ignoring Jacob's comment.

"I told you I don't know any Cinnabun. Now I really have to go. Good-bye." Jacob slammed down the receiver before the PI had a chance to ask any more questions.

His heart was racing so fast that he thought he would go into cardiac arrest any second. Jacob leaned back in his chair and wiped the beads of perspiration from his forehead. *How the hell did he find me? After all, I paid her in cash*, he thought.

Thinking that he didn't leave a paper trail, Jacob felt vindicated and breathed a welcome sigh of relief, which was short-lived. Suddenly that same breath caught in his throat, choking him. "Oh, shit!" He nearly flipped out of his chair as he thought about the personal information that he gave the receptionist that had led directly to his door. Not only did he give the escort service his credit card number, he also gave them his driver's license number, which was a surefire tracking device.

"Well, it's not like I had anything to do with her disappearance," Jacob reasoned. "She probably ran off with one of her johns, popping Ecstasy pills."

He really didn't care where she was, what she was doing, or whom she was doing it with; his only concern was steering clear of that nosy investigator. He prayed his dumb role was convincing, and had thrown the detective off the trail. "She's a hooker with a gazillion johns. I'm sure he'll be too busy investigating her many *clients* to come knocking on my door."

Jacob couldn't help but think about the conversation with his wife. *If Naomi ever finds out about this, my ass is toast!*

NAOMI WAS still fuming from her conversation with Jacob. She shouldn't have been so worked up, since the end result—more sex, and him spending time at home—was exactly what she wanted, but she felt like she was getting her husband's attention by default. She may not have found any evidence of him having an affair when she combed through his pockets, but that didn't prove a thing. People who cheated were adept at hiding the evidence. *I'll just have to keep a close eye on him,* she thought.

Though Naomi was at her volunteer job, she took the time to call Kennedy. Rio was in his office on a conference call, so she had used the opportunity to confront Jacob. She had planned to call him and talk about the seed money for her business, but the more she thought about his complete shift in attitude, the more suspicious she became, until she couldn't control her anger any longer. Now that she had calmed down, it was time to find out the status of Kennedy's situation with Nigel.

"Hey, girl, what's up?" she asked the moment Kennedy picked up.

"Hey," she said, sounding depressed.

"Have you talked to your guy yet?"

"No. He still hasn't returned any of my calls."

"Did you call him at work?"

"Yeah, and somebody named Henry something answered the phone in the lab. He said Nigel wasn't available, and he really didn't offer up any other information. I called his cell phone several times after that, but his phone goes directly to voice mail. I don't know if he's out of town or what. This is so unlike Nigel, not to call me," she said sadly.

"Don't sound so sad, Ken, I'm sure he's just busy with work," Naomi said, trying to console her.

"Thanks, girl."

"Kennedy, I hate to cut our conversation short. I've been on the phone all morning, and I need to finish cataloging these slides before the end of the day."

"Okay, no problem. Thanks for lending your ear. I'll talk to you later."

Naomi hung up and delved into work. She played catch-up for the next few hours, and didn't take the time to eat or drink anything. Her stomach began to growl, signaling lunchtime. She put the slides aside, got up, and knocked on Rio's closed door.

"Come in," he yelled from within.

She eased the door open. "You wanna get something to eat? I'm starving." She rubbed her belly for emphasis.

"I've been on the phone all morning, and I'm starving like Marvin too. You want to go down to Kaminz?"

Chef Kaminsky Thomas had recently opened a café on the ground level of the museum that overlooked the elaborate Sculpture Garden. The menu was an abbreviated version of his ultra-swank Tribeca location. "Sounds good to me."

"Let me check my messages before we leave. I'm expecting an important call, and a few came through when I was on the phone." He picked up the receiver and dialed the code to his voice mail. "It won't take long."

Naomi walked back to her desk. Five minutes later, Rio came bouncing out of his office, all smiles.

Standing up and looking into his giddy face, Naomi asked, "What are you so happy about?"

"I just secured the last piece for the Jacob Lawrence exhibit. The collector is out of the country on business, but called and left a message that he's going to sell us his painting. Come on"—he draped his arm through hers—"I'll tell you all about it over lunch."

The elevator was taking forever, so they took the winding white marble staircase instead. Showing no signs of the former dank and dreary Peace Corps armory, the museum had been gutted and renovated into a six-story modern marvel, with airy skylights and glass-block walls. As they made their way across the main gallery, Rio stopped.

"This is where the Lawrence exhibit will be hung," he said, waving his arms toward the blank walls that were being primed with a fresh coat of museum-issue stark white paint.

"It's going to be an awesome show."

"Yes, it is," he said, picking up the pace.

The aroma from the café greeted them long before they graced the threshold. Walking over to the cafeteria-style counter, they salivated at the gourmet entrées. Naomi selected a poached salmon and dill wrap, and Rio chose a blue cheese burger with sweet potato chips. After paying for their meals, they settled at one of the white ceramic tables.

Taking a huge bite out of his burger, Rio patted the edges of his mouth with a napkin and said, "Like I was saying upstairs, after months of negotiation, I will finally purchase the final painting that'll complete the Lawrence exhibit."

Naomi had cataloged the slides for the show a few weeks ago, and didn't notice any missing pieces. "I thought the series was complete," Naomi said, savoring the delicious salmon wrap.

"Nearly complete," he said, munching on an auburn-colored chip. "There were two pieces held by a private collector. He sold the museum the first piece, but was reluctant to let go of the last piece, but after negotiating for months I finally convinced him to sell." Taking a final bite out of his burger, Rio continued. "Once we finish with lunch, I'll need for you to complete the paperwork, so we can have the artwork transported from his apartment to the museum once he gets back in the country."

"No problem."

They devoured their meals like pigs pulling up to the trough, and headed back up to the office. Naomi could hear the phones ringing off the hook as they walked down the hallway. Once inside, she proceeded to check the voice mail, while Rio retreated into his office.

"Hey, babe, just called to say that I love you." That was Jacob sounding like a sappy greeting card. *He's probably feeling guilty from whatever he's done,* she thought.

"Hello, my name is Eleanor Sharpio, and I'm calling to inquire about docent positions at the museum. I can be reached at 212-555-6330. Thank you."

Naomi couldn't count the number of calls she received from lonely trophy wives tired of spending their days in and out of the designer boutiques along Madison Avenue, longing for a more meaningful pastime. She wrote the woman's name and number on a pad, erased the message, and went on to the next.

"Naomi, it's Kennedy. Call me as soon as you get this message." Click.

Before Naomi could call her back, Rio came out of his office with a manila folder tucked under his arm.

"Here's the file on the Lawrence acquisition. When you get a chance, can you go over the paperwork and make sure I've crossed all the I's and dotted all the T's?" He laughed. " 'Cause you know what a scatterbrain I can be sometimes."

Laughing along with him, she took the folder out of his hand and said, "Sure." He was absolutely right; most weeks Rio was a brilliant curator, orchestrating exhibits with his eyes closed. But then there were weeks when he could barely orchestrate his way out of his office. Naomi attributed those days to the breakup with his beau of the week. Rio changed boyfriends like some people changed dry cleaners—often.

She put the folder on her desk unopened and returned Kennedy's call.

"Hello?" Kennedy answered, frantically picking up on the first ring.

"Hey, Ken, what's up? Did you hear from Nigel?"

"No, that's why I've decided to go over to FACEZ and have a little chat with Mira," she blurted into the receiver.

"Why are going to do that? I thought we discussed the implications of falsely accusing Nigel."

"I'm not going to accuse him of anything. I'm just going to feel her out and see if she knows anything."

"Anything, like what?"

"Like his whereabouts. Not knowing where Nigel is, is driving me crazy. Maybe Mira found out about the check, and he skipped town with the money before being thrown in jail."

"Don't be silly, Kennedy. I never met the man, but I'm sure he isn't a criminal. You do realize that what you're accusing him of—espionage—is criminal?" Naomi asked, trying to bring her friend back to reality.

Kennedy hesitated a moment, letting Naomi's words sink in.

Naomi took Kennedy's silence to continue to try to talk some sense into her friend. "Look, you're really being irrational. You don't even know Mira that well, so why do you have a vested interest in her company?" Naomi said, asking the million-dollar question.

"It's not that I care what goes on over at FACEZ, it's just that if Nigel is selling company secrets, I need to know. Because if that is the case, then he's not someone I want to be involved with. If he can lie and cheat to his boss, then there's no telling what kind of lies he'll try to feed me."

"Kennedy, do you honestly think that Nigel would do something like that? I mean, think about it. You've been dating him for a few months, and if he was involved in a slimy deal like spying and selling what he knows, then I think your instincts would have detected a glitch in his personality. Don't you?"

Kennedy thought for a second, and said, "Maybe you're right."

"Okay, then it's settled. You're going to steer clear of FACEZ. Right?" Naomi asked, still trying to convince Kennedy not to make a fool of herself.

"I hear what you're saying, but I have to find out for myself. I'll call you back once I talk to Mira," she said, and hung up before Naomi could plead more of Nigel's case.

"Oh, well," Naomi sighed, and prayed that Kennedy's visit wouldn't backfire in her face.

Naomi hung up the phone and went back to work. The rest of the afternoon was a blur as she cataloged slides for a modular installation scheduled for the mini gallery adjacent to the main gallery. "Oops, I forgot to schedule a pickup for the Lawrence piece," Naomi said, glancing at the file that had gotten buried underneath the slides. She opened the folder, thumbed through the invoices and attached notes; everything seemed to be in order. Just as she was about to close the folder and call down to shipping and receiving, a copy of a brief handwritten note caught her eye. She read it, and gasped.

"Oh, shit!" Naomi said, and quickly dialed Kennedy's number as she reread the note. But there was no answer. "I gotta get to Kennedy before she confronts Mira!"

MIRA AND Tyler had been inseparable since the night of the book club meeting. They had fucked every day since the meeting. True to form, Mira had insisted that Tyler abandon work and spend all her time in bed. Tyler readily agreed, but said that she had to complete one last assignment, and then she would be free. Tyler went back to the house to finish the sketches, and then pack so that she could head back over to Mira's.

Though it was a workday, Mira didn't feel much like working. She had lust on her mind, and wanted to munch and be munched. She rarely took an entire day off, but she felt entitled. After all, she was the boss. Mira called her assistant and instructed her to cancel all meetings, but to forward any important calls to her home phone.

While Mira waited for Tyler to return, she showered and shaved her fuzzy triangle. She normally got Brazilian waxes in the comfort of her home, but her regular technician was on vacation, and she didn't want a stranger in the crack of her ass—unless they were down there eating her out.

Instead of wearing clothes, she wore a layer of lavender-scented body butter. She perched herself on the bed and called Tyler. "Hey there, what's taking you so long? I'm horny, and can hardly wait for you to get back."

"I can't wait to get back either. I'm almost finished with my work, and should be there in a few hours."

"Well, draw faster. I'm lying here in the buff, waiting for you to eat my muff."

Tyler chuckled at her rhyme. "I didn't know you were a poet."

"There are a lot of things you don't know about me," Mira said slyly. "And as soon as you get over here, I'm going to show you a few."

"Okay, okay. Now you've got me all hot and bothered. Let me get off the phone. The faster I get finished, the faster I can be at your front door." And with that, Tyler hung up.

Mira went into the kitchen and popped a bottle of Dom. She wanted to jump-start the party, so that by the time Tyler arrived she'd have a nice buzz.

Mira went back into her bedroom with the champagne. She picked up the remote to the plasma television mounted to the wall, and pressed the on button. She sat on the bed and switched channels. Mira was trying to occupy her time until Tyler arrived but there was nothing interesting on. She was accustomed to hectic workdays filled with meetings and snuffing out fires. Sitting around watching the boob tube was foreign territory to Mira.

She poured another glass of champagne and glanced at the clock on her nightstand. Only fifteen minutes had passed. *If I sit here another second, I'm going to die of boredom*, she thought. With the liquor fueling her desire, and time on her hands, Mira decided to put the television to good use and watch a porn flick. She walked over to the entertainment center, pushed the corner of one of the doors, and it popped open. She took a DVD out of the compartment, slid it into the player, and got back into bed.

The movie was one of her favorites. She poured another glass of bubbly, spread her legs, and got ready to perform along with the actors.

The opening shot was of two pairs of bare feet standing on white shag carpeting. The feet were facing each other, and the smaller pair, with orange-painted toenails, was on tippy-toe. The camera slowly panned up the legs, to the thighs, to the two erect dicks. One cock belonged to a hairy man, and the other one belonged to a double D-cup "tranny." The transsexual had a serious rack, and an equally big dick. Obviously she was still waiting to get "downsized." The pair was engaged in a heated kiss, with their tongues battling for power. The tranny lost the fight, and was forced down on her knees by her lover. She then began to lick his balls, and suck the head on his cock. He grabbed her hair, forcing his jimmy farther down her throat, until it disappeared, and all you could see was his scrotum slapping against her chin as she feasted on his sausage.

"Suck that dick, girl," Mira said as she slipped her fingers in and out of her hot box. Though she was into eating pussy, she still loved dick—especially a big one—and enjoyed riding the sole pole from time to time. Unlike Tyler, Mira was a true-blue bisexual. Now that she was seeing Tyler, she promised herself she wouldn't double-dip. But that didn't include watching a little dick action, so she kept her eyes glued to the screen.

While the b.j. was taking place, in walked a set of identical twins, both with bad weaves, but with killer bodies. The women stood on each side of the man, and began kissing his neck, cheeks, and mouth. He responded in turn by backing up and lying on the bed, all the while pulling the tranny by the hair so that her grip on his dick didn't slip. The moment he lay on his back, one of the twins squatted on his face, and he started eating her out.

Watching the quarto-trios, Mira salivated as his tongue flicked in and out of the woman's twat. She wanted a little action herself, so she opened the nightstand drawer and took out her trusty vibrator. But before she could pleasure herself, the phone rang.

Mira started to let the machine take the call, but she thought it might be Tyler, so she pressed pause on the remote and picked up.

"Hello?"

"Ms. Rhone, this is Henry Bishop calling from the lab."

"Hi, Henry, what can I do for you?" Mira hoped that he had a quick question, so that she could get back to her movie.

"Your assistant told me that you were taking a personal day, and I'm sorry to bother you, but I need for you to come down to the lab."

"Why? Where's Nigel? Can't he handle whatever's going on?"

"I can't get in touch with him, and I need for you to sign off on the new formula. I know there are time restraints on getting the product to market, and the sooner this is approved, the sooner we can go to the next phase," he said, speaking in a rushed tone.

"Sure, Henry. I'll be right there."

Mira disconnected the call and then phoned Tyler. "Hey, I need to rush down to the office. I'll leave the key with the doorman, so you won't have to wait in the lobby in case I'm not back when you get here."

"Okay, no problem. See you later."

The moment Mira hung up, she put the vibrator back in the drawer, took the DVD out of the player, and made the transformation from freak momma to CEO. Mira dressed in a black tailored Armani pants suit with a white silk blouse, brushed her hair into a bun, grabbed her briefcase, and headed out the door. On her way to the office, all she could think was, *Where the hell is Nigel?*

THE CARS along Lexington Avenue were lined bumper to bumper, parking lot–style, in a complete standstill. Waiting impatiently in the traffic, Kennedy nervously fidgeted from side to side in the backseat of the taxi. She craned her neck out of the passenger window to see what the holdup was, but all she saw was a sea of yellow cabs, with a smattering of town cars.

Kennedy dug in her handbag for her cell phone to try Nigel one more time before storming Mira's office. His cell rang once, before going directly into voice mail. She tried his home number but again no answer. *Where the hell is he?* Out of frustration, she pressed the power button, turned the phone off and threw it back in her purse.

Just as the traffic was working on her one good nerve, it began to move at a snail's pace. She could have run faster than the slow-moving vehicles and was tempted to jump out of the taxi and sprint down the street, but she stayed put. *Patience is a virtue*, she thought as the traffic revved up a few minutes later.

Once the cab pulled up in front of FACEZ's sleek granite

building, it occurred to Kennedy that she hadn't formulated a script in her mind. She didn't want to come right out and accuse Nigel of treason, nor did she want to play cat and mouse. Mira seemed much too smart for that game. Kennedy paid the driver, got out, and played Soul Train Scramble Broad with the jumbled words in her mind, tossing them around until the puzzle was solved. With the dialogue solidified, she exhaled a breath of confidence and went through the revolving door.

Kennedy's heels clicked loudly as she crossed the marble lobby toward the directory panel to her left. She scanned the alphabetical list and found Mira's name, rank, and suite number. Armed with the exact location, Kennedy took the elevator to the twenty-first floor.

"Can you please direct me to Ms. Rhone's office?" she asked the receptionist.

"Your name, please."

"Kennedy Bryant."

The receptionist called Mira's secretary and then said, "It's the last office at the end of the hall," pointing the way.

Kennedy's armpits were moist with perspiration from the nervous energy coursing through her body as she neared Mira's office. "I'm here to see Ms. Rhone," she announced to the secretary.

"Do you have an appointment?" asked the assistant, giving Kennedy a scrutinizing look.

Kennedy hadn't thought of calling ahead to schedule a meeting with Mira. What if she isn't available? "Uh, no," she responded, feeling like an imbecile for not anticipating the obvious.

"I'm sorry, but she doesn't see *anyone* without an appointment," the woman said in a condescending tone.

"Can you just tell her Kennedy Bryant is here?"

She raised an eyebrow and asked, "From?"

"I'm a personal friend," Kennedy said, stretching the truth, and smiled, trying to disarm her. "I was in the neighborhood and thought I'd stop by to say hello," she said, lying again.

The overprotective assistant looked skeptical, and then slowly dialed Mira's extension on the intercom. "Ms. Rhone, I know you just walked in a little while ago, but a Ms. Kennedy Bryant is here to see you." She nodded, hung up, and said reluctantly, "You can go in."

When Kennedy entered Mira's office, she was on the phone and motioned for her to have a seat. Kennedy couldn't believe the opulence of the furnishings. Mira's desk, a five-foot Biedermeier, must have cost a small fortune. A crimson ultra-suede sofa in the same hue as FACEZ's signature red lipstick sat in the far corner in a living room–type environment. She took a seat in one of the matching chairs and waited for Mira to complete her call.

"Henry, I'll be right down. I'm just finishing up another call." She released one line, clicked over to another, and instantly jumped back into the conversation. "Oliver, I'm looking at the report as we speak," Mira said, holding a spreadsheet in one hand and the receiver in the other. "I see the numbers for the DNA 4U beauty cream are up from last quarter." She leaned back in her chair smiling.

While Mira engaged in her business call, Kennedy decided to turn her phone back on and check messages. Sixty seconds after she clicked the phone on, it beeped three consecutive times, indicating that she had messages. *Maybe it's from Nigel,* she thought, dialing into the voice-mail system.

"Kennedy, this is Monica, calling to see if you can switch off days with me? Hit me back when you get this message. Bye." Kennedy made a mental note to call her back and erased the call.

"Ken, call me, it's extremely important!" It was Naomi, sounding frantic.

She began to immediately dial the number. Normally Naomi

was calm and reserved, but there was an urgency in her voice that was alarming.

"What a surprise!" Mira spoke from across the room once she finished her call. The last time she saw Kennedy was at the book club meeting, and Kennedy seemed to be in a bad mood. Mira started to mention the incident, but decided not to. Being a busy executive, she didn't have many friends, and was actually enjoying the camaraderie of the book club.

Kennedy stopped in mid-dial, stood up, walked over to Mira's desk, and took a seat in one of the chairs facing her. "Hey there, I was in the neighborhood and thought I'd drop by to check out the haunts of a mogul." She smiled. Kennedy knew that she had acted ugly at the book club meeting, and hoped that Mira wouldn't mention it.

"What mogul? Where?" Mira laughed, turning from side to side, peering over her shoulder.

The prepared script suddenly vanished from Kennedy's mind, and she smiled nervously, not knowing how to broach the subject of Nigel and her suspicions. It wasn't like they were best friends, so she had to tread lightly. "Don't be modest. Your company has been on the Fortune 500 list for years, and it wouldn't be there if it wasn't for good leadership," Kennedy said, stroking Mira's ego, trying to extend the idle chitchat until her pre-rehearsed speech reappeared.

"So . . . what really brings you by?" Mira asked, curious to know the real reason for Kennedy's visit.

Realizing that the direct approach was the best approach, Kennedy said, "It's about Nigel."

Mira furrowed her brow, causing lines to form across her smooth forehead, "Nigel? What about him?"

"I think he's . . ." Kennedy stopped midsentence, looked down, and began to wring her hands. She didn't want to admit that the man she had envisioned a future with was possibly sabotaging FACEZ.

Mira brought her chair closer, put her elbows on the desk, and asked, puzzled, "What is it, Kennedy? You think he's what?"

"He's . . ." Before the words could escape Kennedy's lips, her cell phone rang. The phone was still in her hand from earlier. She looked down at the caller ID. It was Naomi. Kennedy started to let the call go to voice mail, but remembered the urgency in Naomi's voice and decided to answer the phone.

"Excuse me," she mouthed. "Hello?"

"Ken, it's me. Are you with Mira?" Naomi panted, as if out of breath.

"Yeah, what's up?" Kennedy asked, trying to sound casual.

"Have you told her about the check?"

"No, not yet."

Naomi exhaled heavily. "Good. Don't say a word. I can explain everything. Just get the heck out of there and meet me at your apartment."

"Are you sure?"

"Positive. See you in a few," Naomi said, hanging up.

Mira had Kennedy in a death stare, waiting for her to continue. "As you were saying?"

"Uh, uh," Kennedy stammered, trying to devise a clever lie. "I think he's a great guy, and uh, I'm sorry it didn't work out with you two," she said lamely. So much for being clever.

Mira looked at Kennedy as if she were a few fries short of a Happy Meal. "What? You came all the way up here to tell me *that?*"

"Yep." Kennedy stood up. "See you tomorrow at the book club meeting. Gotta run," she said in a huff, and tore out of Mira's office, leaving her sitting there baffled and bewildered.

THE MOMENT THE elevator opened, Naomi rushed up to Kennedy. "Have I got Holiday News for you," she said, using the term they adopted for tantalizing information.

"What? What?" Kennedy asked, anxious to hear what Naomi had to say. Kennedy fumbled with the key, until she unlocked the door. "Tell me what's so important!" she said, once inside the apartment.

Naomi shoved a piece of paper in Kennedy's face without saying a word.

Kennedy took the note out of her hand and read it:

ONE MORE TRANSACTION,
THEN OUR BUSINESS WILL BE COMPLETE.
THANKS FOR HOLDING UP YOUR END OF THE DEAL,
    R. S.

"Where'd you get this?" Kennedy waved the paper in front of Naomi's face. "It's a copy of the same note I found with the check that fell out of Nigel's briefcase," she said, shocked.

"Yeah, I know."

Kennedy shook her head. "What do you mean, you know?" She still didn't have a clue what Naomi was trying to say. "You said you had Holiday News." Kennedy handed the note back to her. "Well, I'm waiting."

"Don't you get it?" Naomi asked as if the obvious was staring Kennedy right in the face, threatening to smack her upside the head. "R. S.?" she asked, as if the initials held the hidden secret.

"I know, R. S., Rob Sherr, Nigel's former boss, so what?" Kennedy asked, totally irritated. "Naomi, pulezzze," she said, emphasizing the word *please*, "tell me something that I don't already know."

"R. S., as in Rio Stanis, not Rob Sherr."

Kennedy stood in the middle of the living room with a blank look. "Who the hell is Rio Stanis?"

"The curator at the Museum of Urban Art."

"Oh, yeah, I remember, your boss. But what does he have to do with this?" Kennedy asked, before Naomi could finish her sentence.

Naomi walked over to the sofa and sat down. "Are you ready for this?"

"I've been ready since we walked into the apartment. Now please tell me what's going on," Kennedy said, joining her on the couch.

"I was at MUA earlier today doing my bimonthly volunteer gig and Rio asked me to schedule a pickup from a private collector. And guess who that collector happened to be?" she asked, continuing with the twenty questions.

"Naomi, enough with the riddles and guessing games; just tell me straight, no chaser."

"Okay, okay." She scooted toward Kennedy. "I was going through the paperwork and guess whose name magically appeared in front of me?"

When Kennedy pinned Naomi with a no-nonsense-don't-toy-with-me stare, she continued without waiting for an answer. "Nigel." She jumped off the sofa. "Girl, he's selling his artwork to the museum. That's what the note was all about. Rio wrote it when Nigel sold him the first Jacob Lawrence piece, and you found it, thinking that he was selling information to Rob Sherr, his old boss. Now do you get it?"

Kennedy let Naomi's words sink in and marinate before answering, and thought back to the magnificent artwork hanging in Nigel's apartment. "You mean to tell me, he's selling his paintings and that's why he had a check for a quarter of a million dollars?"

"Yep." She nodded. "And get this, he's going to receive another check for the same amount for the second painting."

Kennedy slumped back on the sofa feeling like a complete idiot. She thought that Nigel was selling proprietary information, and all along he was selling *his* artwork. Having trust issues with so many men over the years had Kennedy paranoid to the point that she was ready to accuse Nigel, who'd been nothing but honest, of a felony. "Oh," was all she could manage to say.

Naomi looked at Kennedy. "Are you feeling okay?"

"I'm fine. It's just hard to believe, that's all."

"But you believed the espionage theory. I don't get it."

Kennedy held her head down in shame. "Girl, it's all the losers I've dated before Nigel that's got me so paranoid. I should've known that he wouldn't do anything as dubious as selling trade secrets to FACEZ's competitor." She thought for a minute. "Now the question is, why is he selling those paintings? But more importantly, why wouldn't he tell me?"

"You're asking the wrong person, because I don't have a clue. You need to ask Nigel that."

Naomi was right, and as soon as he resurfaced, Kennedy would be armed and loaded with a barrelful of questions.

37

"so where's your sidekick?" Naomi asked Tyler as she walked into the kitchen. She hadn't seen much of Tyler since she'd been spending the majority of her time at Mira's.

"Ha, ha. Mira had a meeting, but she'll be here soon. And by the way, I'll be moving into Mira's place after our book club meeting today. She officially asked me to move in the other day," Tyler said, with a huge grin on her face.

"I'm not surprised. You practically live there anyway." Naomi's attitude toward Tyler had totally changed. After living with her sister-in-law over the past few months, she came to realize that Tyler was no different from any other woman, except for her sexual preference. And just because she liked women didn't make her a monster. Naomi had imposed her prejudgments on Tyler before she really got a chance to know her, and even though they didn't hang out on a regular basis, Tyler was a decent human being. At the end of the day, that was all that really mattered.

"Well, I am. It happened so fast, but I really like Mira. She's a bit of a control freak, but I don't mind. I'm basically a homebody anyway, and when she's at work, I can get my assignments done. I love being in a relationship, so this situation works for me. Besides, you and Jacob need this house to yourselves."

"What do you mean by that?"

"Well . . ." She blushed again. "I heard you guys getting busy the other night. I wasn't trying to pry, but when I came in the house to pick up a few of my things, you guys were *snacking* rather loudly in the solarium."

Naomi started blushing, reminiscing about that night. Jacob had come home from work and nearly attacked her as she sat reading the business plan that she had recently gotten from the consultant. But before Jacob could really get his groove on, Naomi confronted him again about cheating, and once again he denied it. Naomi realized that continuing to accuse him without proof was useless, so she dropped the subject, but broached another one. She told him about her plans for starting an interior design business, and asked him for the seed money. Jacob had a few pointed questions, and when she presented him with the plans, he was impressed and agreed to give her the money. Naomi was so happy that she let Jacob eat her out on the love seat in the solarium. "Well, he agreed to fund my business. I was so happy that I agreed to—let's just say, accommodate him," she said with a giggle.

"I'm glad. There's nothing like running your own business. I may not be getting a paycheck every two weeks, but I love the flexibility of not having a regular nine to five."

"Well, I'm really looking forward to it, since it'll give me something else to do with my time," Naomi said. Now that she wasn't going to be joining the Black Door, she needed an outlet, but of course she wasn't about to tell Tyler this.

"Well, it looks as if we both have good news," Tyler said, grabbing a bottle of water out of the refrigerator and holding it up in a toasting position.

"We need to toast your new love and my business with a real drink instead of water," Naomi said, turning her attention back to making lemon drop shots. After cutting the lemons in wedges, she placed them in a bowl and drenched the entire lot with vodka, then sprinkled them with powdered sugar. Naomi took a wedge out, and handed one to Tyler. "Here's to the future!" They each took a plug out of the lemons.

"Whew," Tyler said, twisting her face at the sweet and sour taste. "That's good. Tart, but good."

Over the next hour, they polished off half of the lemon drop shots and made finger sandwiches for the meeting. Just as Naomi was making another batch of shots, the doorbell rang. She teetered to the door feeling quite lovely, with a mild buzz.

"I need some of whatever you've been drinking," Kennedy said, taking one look at Naomi's slightly inebriated state.

"Girl, get in here." Naomi pulled her by the arm. "And give me the scoop. Have you talked to Nigel?"

Kennedy stepped into the foyer. "Yeah, I've talked to him."

"Well? Don't keep me in suspense. Where has he been and what did he have to say?" she asked, bombarding Kennedy with questions.

"He's been in Uganda setting up a production plant, that's why I hadn't been able to get in touch with him. He's going to——"

Naomi cut her off, "A projection plant?"

"No, a production plant. He's opening his own cosmetics company. That's why he sold his paintings, to generate seed money."

"That's great news!"

"Yeah, I guess," Kennedy said, obviously unimpressed.

"Why do you sound so glum?"

"Don't get me wrong, I'm happy for him. I just wish he'd let me in on his plans, then I wouldn't have gotten all hopped up on this sabotage scheme. I mean, we're supposed to be a couple."

"Not to defend him, but you guys have only been dating for a few months, and maybe he's just not used to sharing his life plans with someone else."

Kennedy thought about it for a moment. "I guess you're right. Besides, he said that because the cosmetics industry is so competitive, he was advised to keep the plans under wraps until everything was finalized. So don't mention anything in the meeting, because Mira doesn't know yet."

"My lips are sealed. That sounds like a valid reason. Anyway, you can't blame the guy for protecting his interest."

Kennedy shrugged her shoulders. "True."

Looking at her friend's defeatist disposition, Naomi put her arm around Kennedy's shoulder and said, "Come on. You need a drink." She then led the way into the kitchen.

"Hey, Kennedy!" Tyler shouted, a bit too loud.

"I see you've been dipping in the sauce too," Kennedy cracked.

"Gurrlll, these lemon drop shots are the bomb!" Tyler thrust the bowl of lemon wedges in Kennedy's face. "Here, have a couple."

"Don't mind if I do." Kennedy reached in and took two wedges.

"Wait, let's toast," Naomi said. "Tyler and Mira are moving in together. And Jacob has agreed to fund my business."

"To new beginnings," Kennedy said, biting into a wedge. "Whew!" she exclaimed, making the same face that Tyler had made earlier.

They were giggling, sucking the vodka out of lemon wedges and giggling some more when the bell rang again. "It must be Mira," Naomi said, and trotted to the door.

"Heeeyyy," Mira sang as she swept into the foyer.

"Looks like somebody's already got the party started," Naomi said, referring to Mira's tipsy state.

"Yep, that would be me." She pointed her index finger into her chest. "I received the best news today!"

"And what might that be?"

"The rollout for Baby FACEZ, our new children's line, is back on schedule. As a matter of fact, it's *ahead* of schedule. After a few R & D mishaps, it seems we're going to beat BOD E. to market," she said, using industry terminology. "So I broke out the champagne." Mira was usually reserved when it came to business, but she was so elated that she told Naomi her good news. Besides, Jacob would probably tell her anyway.

"Well, in that case, let's continue the celebration." On the way to the kitchen Naomi congratulated Mira on her relationship with Tyler.

"To life," Naomi said as they all held up lemon wedges.

"To life," the group agreed in unison.

An hour later, they were as giddy as schoolgirls, laughing uncontrollably at the silliest things. They were gabbing about everything except the book.

"I had the biggest crush on Rodge from *What's Happening,*" Kennedy laughed.

"You've got to be kidding me," Naomi said, bending over with a serious case of the giggles.

"I don't know why you're laughing so hard, Naomi; you know you had it bad for J. J. from *Good Times,*" Kennedy shot back.

"DYNOMITE!" Naomi laughed.

"Thelma rocked my world," Tyler chimed in.

"Mine too, especially when she wore those Afro puffs." That was Mira, enjoying her fourth lemon drop shot.

As they sucked down those potent shots and tripped down memory lane, the doorbell rang.

Naomi wrinkled her face. "Who's that?"

"Maybe it's a new recruit who's heard about how much fun we have and decided to invite herself to our meeting," Kennedy said, making a lame attempt at guessing.

"I haven't invited anybody to join, have you guys?" Naomi asked, looking around the room.

"Naw, not me." That was Tyler.

"Me neither," Mira said.

"I'll be back in a few," Naomi said, and headed to the door, humming the theme song to *Good Times.*

She swung the door wide open, with a vodka-induced grin plastered on her face, "Hel—" she started to greet her guest, but stopped short.

"Is this the home of Jacob Reed?" asked one of New York's finest.

At the sight of the uniformed police officer at her door, her buzz began to fade, along with her cheerful grin. "Yes," was all she could manage to say.

"I'm Officer Mulligan," he said, flashing his silver badge. "Is he in?"

"Uh, no, he hasn't gotten home from work yet."

He took a step toward her. "Do you mind if I wait?" he asked, but Naomi could tell from his body language that he planned to wait whether she invited him in or not.

"Sure, no problem." Naomi stepped aside. "What is this about?" she asked once he was inside the foyer.

"This is a matter for your husband," he said curtly. "If you don't mind, I'll have a seat and wait for him." He looked in the direction of the kitchen, obviously hearing the cackling coming from down the hall. "You can return to your guests. I'll be fine right here," he said, making his way into the solarium.

Naomi wasn't about to leave a strange man alone in her home. She didn't care if he was with the FBI and CIA rolled into one, so she joined him and waited to hear what Jacob had to say.

JACOB'S PALMS were sweating so much that it was hard for him to get a grip on the key fob. Self-consciously glancing back at the squad car parked in the driveway, he thought back to the conversation with that meddling private investigator, putting his nose where it didn't belong. *I bet he called in the police,* Jacob thought. But that didn't make sense. Why would the NYPD investigate the disappearance of a hooker from London? They were probably canvassing the neighborhood for donations for the Fraternal Order of Police, a nonprofit advocacy agency. *Yeah, that's it,* he assured himself.

Jacob could hear laughter coming from the kitchen the moment he stepped inside, which was a good sign. He breathed a sigh of relief and headed up the stairs to get his checkbook, so he could write a check to the officer.

Naomi's voice stopped him on the steps. "Oh, Jacob, can you come into the solarium?"

"Sure," he said, bouncing back down the stairs. A huge grin spread across his face, thinking about their heated romp in the solarium. The sex therapist he had been secretly seeing was doing an excellent job of curing him of the negative feelings that he once harbored toward Naomi. Through hypnosis, the desire for his wife had returned with a vengeance. "You're gonna have to wait until your book club meeting's over before we can have one of our private meetings," Jacob spoke, walking toward the solarium. When Naomi didn't respond, he asked, "Did you hear what I said?"

He appeared in the doorway and Naomi was sitting on the sofa with her hands folded neatly in her lap and a solemn expression on her face. "Hey, babe, did you hear what I said?" he repeated.

"Mr. Reed? Officer Mulligan," said the uniformed officer, flashing his official badge.

Jacob nearly jumped right out of his skin when the policeman appeared from behind the double French doors. Seeing the squad car parked in the driveway, he knew the officer was in the house, but didn't think he would be lurking about. "Yes, what can I do for you?"

The cop looked over at Naomi and said, "Can we talk in private?"

Before Jacob could answer Naomi spoke out, raising her voice: "I'm not going anywhere." She then crossed her arms in front of her chest and sat back hard on the cushions, planting herself firmly on the couch.

From her disposition, Jacob could tell that she wasn't going to budge. "If this is about a donation, let me get my checkbook," he said, turning to leave.

"Wait a minute, Mr. Reed." He looked over at Naomi again. "This isn't about a donation. It's about . . ." he stalled.

"Well?" Jacob asked.

"Do you recall talking to a Mr. Davis?"

At the mention of that nosy PI, Jacob's palms began to sweat again, and he rubbed them up and down on the side of his pants, trying to dry them. "Uh, uh, Naomi, I'll take care of this. Why don't you go entertain your club members?" Jacob said, trying to get her out of the room, realizing that this was one conversation she didn't need to hear.

"I told you, I'm not going anywhere," she spat out, then turned her attention to the police officer. "Who is Mr. Davis? And what does he have to do with my husband."

"He's a good friend of mine and a private investigator who's working on the case of a missing person. He's run into a dead end and asked me as a favor to do some legwork on his behalf."

"What does my husband have to do with some missing persons case?" Naomi looked perplexed.

"Look, miss, you need to ask your husband," he said, seemingly annoyed at her interruptions. Tired of trying to sugarcoat his questioning, he lasered in on Jacob with an intimidating stare. "When you were with Cinnamon, did she mention anything about taking time off?"

"No, she didn't," Jacob answered quickly, ready to end the inquisition before it started. "Now if you don't mind," he said, leading the officer to the front door, "I'd like to get back to my family."

"Okay," he relented, realizing that without a warrant, there was nothing else he could do, "but if you remember anything, give Mr. Davis a call."

"Yeah, okay." Jacob rushed him out and closed the door. He couldn't believe that that Davis person had called his friend the cop to muscle him. How was he going to explain this to Naomi? Their relationship was finally back on track, and now this major snafu could completely derail their marriage. He stood at the door, trying to think of a reasonable explanation, when he heard her storming up from behind.

"Who the hell is Cinnamon?" she screamed at the top of her lungs.

Jacob took a deep breath and tried to explain. "Naomi, I love you." He dropped to his knees and hugged her legs, begging for mercy.

"Just tell me the truth," she said in a measured tone, lowering her voice almost to a whisper.

Jacob didn't know where to begin. How was he going to tell his wife that he had been with a hooker? Tears started to roll down his face as he held his head down in shame. There was no escaping the truth. If he lied, it could come back in the form of Mr. Davis to haunt him. His only hope was to tell Naomi the entire story and pray that she would find it in her heart to forgive him. "Cinnamon is a . . ." he started, but the words stuck in his throat.

"A what, Jacob?"

He gripped her legs tighter, squeezed his eyes shut, and said, "She's a high-priced call girl."

"So when did you solicit her services?" Naomi asked, her voice removed and as cold as steel.

"When I was in London a few months ago."

"So, was that the reason for your spur-of-the-moment *business* trip?"

"Yes." Jacob couldn't lie any longer. He told her the entire story, including the reason behind his adulterous affair. "But I'm in therapy now, Naomi," he said, looking up at her for mercy, but she was looking straight ahead. He continued. "And . . . and I know you can tell the difference. Our love life is better than it's been in years. So you can see the therapy's working. And I swear to you that I'll never cheat again." He slowly stood up, and gently gripped her by the shoulders. "Can you ever forgive me?"

"Turnabout is fair play, Jacob," she said coldly, and walked off.

Running after her, he said, "Naomi, wait." He grabbed her by the arm before she reached the kitchen. "Please tell me that you forgive me," he begged.

"I forgive you," she said with a blank expression. "Now, please let me go. I have guests, remember?" she said, and strutted off without even a backward glance in his direction.

The words came from her mouth but not from her heart and he knew in that instant that he had possibly lost his wife forever.

Epilogue

"WHERE ARE you going?" Nigel asked, pulling Kennedy back into bed.

"I'm getting in the shower. If I don't start getting ready now, we're going to be late for the party."

"Stop stressing. We got time. Now come here." After finally forgiving Nigel for keeping a lid on his plans to start his own company, Kennedy couldn't get enough of him, especially once he told her that he could no longer work for his former lover. He admitted that he had been deeply in love with Mira, and getting over her had taken longer than he expected, but now that Kennedy was in his life the feelings that he once had for Mira were gone. And now that he had gotten FACEZ's new product off the ground, it was time to move on professionally as well.

Nigel pulled Kennedy on top of him.

"You're so naughty," she said, sucking on his bottom lip.

"And you love every second of it." He wrapped his arms around her waist and began sucking her top lip.

Their lip locking was getting Kennedy wet all over again,

and she spread her legs so that her knees were on each side of his legs. "I want you inside of me," she whispered in his ear.

Nigel got a charge from her words, and a surge of blood rushed to his penis until he was as hard as a piece of wood. He positioned the tip of his dick so that it teased her vulva. "Is this what you want?" he asked, poking against her.

"Yes," she moaned. Kennedy was so glad that she hadn't jumped the gun and slept with Nigel too soon. At last she not only had the sex that she desired, but the relationship to go along with it. This was the happiest that Kennedy had been in her entire life, and a tear eased down her cheek as she held onto her man. For the next hour, they actually made love, instead of just fucking around, like she'd done so many times in the past.

THE MUSEUM OF Urban Art was abuzz with activity. Months after the opening of the Jacob Lawrence exhibit, which garnered press coverage from around the country, Mira reserved the Museum for the launch party for Baby FACEZ. Reporters littered the sidewalk along with paparazzi trying to get shots of New York's Who's Who as they entered the party. There was a frenzy of flickering flashbulbs as the company's spokesmodel—a famous child actress—and her parents entered the party.

Mira indeed had reason to celebrate. The company had overcome major R & D obstacles and beat BOD E. to market with FACEZ's new children's line. Before his untimely departure, Nigel made good on his promise by removing the proverbial fly from the ointment. He pinpointed the problem with the initial formula, which was high acidity levels (even with the second set of shea pods), and found another source for the pods in a completely different region. Once that mystery was solved, he worked day and night until the formula for the children's skin care line was blemish free.

As Jacob and Naomi made their way up the crimson-covered steps, a few flashes popped in their direction.

"I guess we're celebrities now," Jacob gushed.

Through the clenched teeth of a smile, Naomi said, "I'm sure they're taking everyone's picture." She still harbored resentment toward Jacob for his scandalous affair, but decided against an ugly drawn-out divorce since she had Noah to think about, and growing up in two separate households wouldn't be healthy for her little boy. Besides, Jacob was being extremely generous with his money. Not only had he given Naomi the initial seed money, he had also hired a real estate agent to find her a commercial space, so that she wouldn't have to work out of the house. Naomi knew it was nothing but Jacob's guilt making him open up his checkbook, so she decided to milk it for all that it was worth.

Mira greeted them with hugs and smooches as they entered the museum. "Thanks for coming. Kennedy and Nigel aren't here yet, but Tyler is in there, looking beautiful, I might add," she gushed. Normally, Mira would have been irritated by their tardiness, but living with Tyler—who was laid-back—had taught her to calm down, and not be so tight about things that were out of her control.

"We wouldn't have missed this for the world." Naomi kissed her on the cheek. "Congratulations."

Jacob echoed Naomi's sentiment, and then said, "I can't wait to see the numbers on Baby FACEZ. I'm sure they're going to be off the charts."

"Always the accountant," Mira mused, jabbing him in the side with her elbow. Since she was living with his sister, she now treated Jacob like a brother-in-law. For all practical purposes they were now family. And since she had grown up an only child, Mira treasured her newfound family.

"This place looks fabulous," Naomi said, taking in the decor.

The entryway was swathed in precious pink and cerulean blue chiffon ribbons streaming from ceiling to floor. "Once my company is up and running you're going to have to let me design the theme for your next party."

"Thank you, but I can't take all the credit. Our Promotions Department took care of the details. I'll give you the phone number of our Promotions Director, so when you're ready all you'll have to do is call, and tell him I recommended you. They work with consultants all the time."

"Thanks, Mira, that's generous of you." Though Naomi had only known Mira for a few months, she genuinely liked her.

"No problem. Come on. Let's find Tyler and get a drink," Mira said, leading the group toward the bar area.

An hour later, Kennedy and Nigel finally made their way through the throng of people, and met up with Mira, Tyler, Naomi, and Jacob.

"There you guys are. What took you so long?" Naomi asked.

Kennedy and Nigel looked at each other and started grinning. He grabbed her hand and said, "We had some last-minute business to take care of." He smiled.

Naomi took one look at the glow on their faces, and knew exactly what he meant. "Oh, I see."

"I understand congratulations are in order," Jacob said to Nigel, shaking his hand. He had learned from Mira that her former chemist was opening his own shop.

Nigel cut his eyes at Mira, who had a nasty scowl plastered on her face. Though he had served out the terms of his contract, she still felt betrayed. Now his company would be one of the opposing teams along with BOD E., trying to dethrone her as the Princess of the Cosmetics Industry. "Thanks, man," Nigel replied.

"So, have you decided on a company name yet?"

"Not yet. The advertising firm I hired has come up with a few good ones. It's just a matter of making up my mind."

"Which accounting firm are you using?" Jacob asked. He would have loved to represent Nigel's company, but it would have been a conflict of interest, since FACEZ was one of Kirschner Gross's major clients.

"I'm using——" Before he could get out his answer Mira butted in.

"Excuse me, gentlemen," she interrupted, "but this night is all about me, I mean Baby FACEZ." She directed the comment at Nigel. Though she had relaxed her ways, she was still a control freak at heart.

"Enjoy it while you can," was his flip response, "because there's a new sheriff in town."

"I'm ready to duel anytime you are," Mira hissed. He may have been a gifted chemist, but there was no way Mira was going to let his company, or any other, weasel in on her territory.

"Is that a challenge?" Nigel asked, egging her on.

She put her hand on her hip. "Call it what you want."

"Well, in that case, let the games begin," Nigel declared, raising his champagne flute.